Hate Story

Thank you for your hospitality, Heather!

Jeff Cottrill

Copyright

First published by Dragonfly Publishing, March 2022

Content warning: This book is largely a work of satire and contains naughty words, violence, suicide, bullying, child abuse, homophobic and other slurs, allusions to sexual assault, assassination trivialization, characters who aren't always "likeable", and general political incorrectness. Many of the characters, events and incidents are drawn in broad strokes, sometimes exaggerated, even cartoonish.

ISBN (sc): 978-0-6453505-4-8

ISBN (e): 978-0-6453505-5-5

Cover art by Brett Bakker

Author photograph by Brian Tao, Luxography.ca

For Mrs. Thomas, Mrs. Cain and Ms. Svatos

Three teachers with the sense to encourage creativity

"The evil that men do lives after them;
The good is oft interred with their bones."

– @nagging_conscience_42, quoting Shakespeare or something

"On the Internet, nobody knows you're a dog."

– Peter Steiner, from an old *New Yorker* cartoon

Hate Story

Jeff Cottrill

ZERO

It was the wildest funeral anybody had ever heard of.

That was what the news websites said. So did the gossip sites and blogs. Many jazzed up the story with the best clickbait headlines of which they could conceive. ***YOU WON'T BELIEVE THE MESS OF CRAZY THIS FUNERAL SERVICE BECAME,*** shrieked one. ***CHAOS ERUPTS AT FUNERAL HOME, ONE INJURED,*** a more respectable outlet offered. The hashtag #PeaceHouseRiot trended on social media sites, especially Spitter, for more than a day. #FuckPaulShoreditch, though not as popular, reached its peak during that period.

The *Toronto Post and Chronicle* reported the incident on its October 23, 2019, front page, accompanied by a photo of the wreckage. The story begins:

> A small funeral home in east Toronto has closed down after a mob of over 100 people stormed a service on Monday afternoon, leaving the service room torn apart and a Greater Toronto Area minister unconscious.

> Peace House Funeral Centre Ltd., located in the Danforth and Coxwell area, suffered damages of an undisclosed sum from the incident during the memorial service for the late Paul Shoreditch, who was 46 when he passed away last Tuesday.
>
> "I've never seen anything like this," Peace House owner and manager Debra Borkowski told the *Post and Chronicle*. "What a mess. I don't know how the business is gonna survive now."
>
> Rev. Gary Casteras, 76, based at the St. Drogo Presbyterian Church in Mississauga, is recovering in hospital with several injuries, including head trauma.
>
> "He deserved it," said one witness, who declined to give her name. "Anybody who'd host a funeral for that motherf----r deserves that and worse." [...]

After specific details about the damage to the building and a few more quotations from Peace House staff, the story goes on:

> [...] The service itself began 21 minutes late because Rev. Casteras and Peace House personnel were waiting to see if others would show up, according to Borkowski. In total, the funeral had only four attendees. All four escaped the incident unharmed.
>
> "What a weird service," said Morty Bozzer, 56, one of the attendees, who identified himself as an aspiring chef. "No one seemed all that sad for [Paul Shoreditch]. More like bored. Real weird."
>
> Another attendee, a "childhood friend of Paul's" who declined to give his name, expressed a similar sentiment. "The feeling in the room was more like duty than mourning. Like, mandatory attendance."
>
> Harvey Shoreditch, 81, and Lydia Shoreditch, 78, the parents of the

> deceased and the remaining two attendees, both declined to comment.
>
> Bozzer described the service delay as "a 20-minute stretch of tacky recorded New Age music" before Rev. Casteras finally mounted the podium in front of Shoreditch's closed wooden coffin. After a pause, the minister began reading passages from the Sermon on the Mount in a "near-monotone" then asked the attendees if they had any words to say about Paul. No one responded, according to Bozzer.
>
> "The room was dead," he added. "As dead as the guy we were supposed to be grieving."
>
> "I heard the parents just hired that minister at the last minute," the childhood friend said. "Paul had no religious bent, so they just picked somebody who used to know Paul when he was a kid." [...]

The *Post and Chronicle* story describes how Reverend Casteras stepped off the podium and stood beside it, gesturing with his hand to encourage somebody, anybody, to come up and say some kind words. The four attendees stared at the empty podium, and a weighty silence ensued.

A crash interrupted the silence. It sounded like a window being smashed.

Reverend Casteras and the attendees stared at each other in bewilderment.

Peace House was a small and *very* inexpensive funeral home. The main floor had a small reception area and a service room, with offices upstairs. The crash seemed to have come from the glass front of the building. Reverend Casteras marched to the back. When he reached the doors, he hesitated. The others watched him.

A gibbering noise came from the crowd outside. It sounded like a noisy schoolyard.

Reverend Casteras opened the doors.

He saw a huge hole in the glass front of the centre, with glass shards sprayed over the carpeted floor. The receptionist cowered in a corner.

"What's going on?" Reverend Casteras shouted.

He received a quick answer. He received it right in the middle of the forehead.

As the reverend lay on the floor, barely conscious and surrounded by broken glass, laughter swept in from outside. The screaming and shouting became louder, and it was now clear to everyone that the voices belonged to grownups, not children.

A young, suited Peace House staff member went to check on the reverend, then took out a cell phone and called for an ambulance. Another one, a forty-something woman also in a suit, picked up the object that had struck the reverend. It was a small, round sphere wrapped in a piece of notepaper, held on by a rubber band. The attendees and Peace House staff watched as she pulled the notepaper off.

A softball.

An old, old softball, the whiteness gone from years of dust and dirt and decay. The letters "PS" were carved into it.

The staff member unfolded the notepaper. In the centre, in big, bold capital letters in black marker, somebody had written:

FUCK. PAUL. SHOREDITCH.

Underneath, in small handwriting, was scribbled in pencil:

HAHA NOT THAT ANYBODY WOULD WANT TO!!!!

The younger staff member looked out of the broken window, wary of falling window shards.

He gasped.

"What is it?" the suited woman asked.

"I have no idea," the other replied, his voice shaky. "Wow. It... it looks like those bigot freaks from the Westboro Baptist Church have taken a field trip here."

Protesters on the sidewalk, on the street, some even blocking traffic. Dozens. Most looked to be in their twenties. Some carried sticks or clubs or baseball bats. Some had homemade signs with statements like **PAUL SHOREDITCH WAS A LOSER** or **NO ONE**

MOURNS A PIECE OF SHIT. *paul shorditch wut a whore bitch!!* read a messy one, held by a pizza-faced teenage boy in a backwards baseball cap. Some were typing on their cell phones.

"It was, in its own way, an ideal portrait of intersectional equality," Dr. Raymond Q. Withers, a University of Toronto humanities professor who lived in the area and witnessed the event, would later tell the *Post and Chronicle*. "A fair mix of races and genders–Caucasians, African Canadians, East Asians, men, women, a few disabled, maybe even a transgender or two–all working together, all united in their loathing of one dead man."

As other staff and attendees gathered near the broken front window watching the melee, the crowd turned its attention to one woman behind them–a tall, mildly overweight woman with a scowling elfin face. Underneath her open fall jacket, one could see a pink T-shirt with a cute cartoon cat on the front. She led the crowd in a group chant.

"Who's the biggest asshole who ever lived?" she screeched.

"*Paul Shoreditch!*" the group yelled back.

"Who's the second-worst?"

"*Anyone who mourns him!*"

This chant was repeated several times until another voice cried, "Let's go in!"

"Are we ready to go in now?" called the screechy woman.

Inside the reception area, the employees trembled.

"Oh... crap," mumbled the female staffer.

"Should we call the police, too?" said the other.

Nobody had a chance to answer as the front doors of Peace House burst open. In flowed a sea of angry voices and rushing footsteps. Guests and staff members dashed out of the way as the crowd stormed into the building, some trampling Reverend Casteras' near-inert body.

They upturned the seats and threw other furniture on the ground. They smashed vases and stomped on the flowers. They ripped apart a wreath. They tore apart the hastily assembled display of old photographs of the deceased. They defaced the walls, a few with spray paint, a few with magic marker, and one by urinating. When Reverend Casteras got on his knees, struggling to get back on his feet, a rioter saved him the trouble by kicking him between the eyes and knocking him out.

Some filmed the chaos with their smartphones. Videos popped

up all over Spitter, joined by the hashtags #PeaceHouseRiot or #FuckPaulShoreditch. A few of them made it onto online news stories later that day, and those stories were later linked on those same Spitter accounts, with gloating and bitter statements by the users.

A handful of giggling college kids stood over the coffin on the front platform, one holding a gasoline can, another a lighter. None of the group, apparently, had thought through the possible consequences of setting a coffin ablaze in a wooden building full of people. They were spared a bleak lesson by a sudden screech:

"Leave the fucker! He's *mine*."

The group made way for the elfin woman in the cat shirt.

She opened the coffin and looked down at the face of the ex-person who had inspired the chaos. Peace House morticians had done a good job on a corpse that had fallen twenty-three storeys. Some of those nearby took a break in their orgy of property damage and watched in silence.

Finally, the woman spoke.

"This is for Fiona, you sack of shit."

And she spat into the corpse's face.

She looked up at the surrounding college kids and said, "Your turn."

The *Post and Chronicle* story continues:

> [...] Witnesses report that several rioters pulled Shoreditch's body out of the coffin and beat and kicked it for several minutes while other rioters stood by and laughed.
>
> "That thing was totally unrecognizable by the time they were done with it," one told the *Post and Chronicle*.
>
> "They totally beat him to a second death."
>
> Details were scant on the reasons for the mob's extreme animosity towards Shoreditch, whose recent falling death in Etobicoke was ruled an accident. Asked why she was taking part in the riot, one young woman simply said, "Because of all the awful things Paul's done." When pressed further, the rioter did not provide

any specific examples.

Another anonymous witness, when asked why he hated Shoreditch so much, responded, "Because he's a scumbag! That's what everybody says."

A third rioter was less sure of her reasons for participating. "I don't know what Paul Shoreditch did," she admitted, "but it must have been terrible to get this kind of response from so many people. I believe them."

Kathy McDougal, editor of the popular Toronto-based news and celebrity-gossip website *Kat's Korner*, was a key player in the incident. Borkowski said that she recognized McDougal as the latter helped lead the first wave of the mob inside the Peace House building.

Asked afterwards why she had taken such a dominant role, McDougal said, "To pay Paul Shoreditch back for all of the ways he has destroyed me. And many others."

When asked for clarification, McDougal responded, "Seriously? Read the website! Avenger's website has everything you need to know," and declined to comment further.

The mangled remains were cremated and given a quick city burial at St. John's Norway Cemetery & Crematorium, with a flat, inconspicuous headstone that read SHOREDITCH. Within days, vandalism began marking the spot. First, someone spray-painted **FUCK PAUL SHOREDITCH** on the stone. After that was cleaned up, someone smashed the stone with a sledgehammer, making the lettering illegible. Later, dog excrement was found on the marker. No perpetrators were caught. The grave was eventually moved to an undisclosed location.

A week later, Peace House Funeral Centre filed a lawsuit against Katherine Elizabeth McDougal for an undisclosed sum of damages. The following day, the Spitter account known as @avenger_of_the_weak_81 stated that the user had "undeniable evidence" the funeral home regularly discriminated against Indian clients. Before Peace House had a chance to respond, the post was forwarded several thousand times, sometimes with additional accusations of racism, misogyny, homophobia, transphobia, anti-disability, and more. No evidence of these accusations ever came to light—no specific incidents were even detailed—but Peace House soon dropped the lawsuit.

And then all the fuss ended, and the world moved on.

There were two facts that the media, including the *Post and Chronicle*, left out of their stories, simply because the reporters were not aware of them. Few were.

One was that the softball that had injured Reverend Casteras had belonged to the deceased.

The second was that Paul Shoreditch's death—that twenty-three-storey fall officially filed as an accident—had been a suicide.

None of the mob who tore apart Peace House Funeral Centre would have cared if they *had* known the latter. But they could have easily figured it out. Paul Shoreditch had a Spitter account, one with zero followers, but many past replies and forwards. And if anybody had bothered to check his profile page, they would have seen one last entry, with a date and time not long before his bloody, squashed remains were peeled from the asphalt.

Don't pretend you feel bad about this, the final Spitter post read. ***This is what you all wanted, and you know it.***

Paul Shoreditch need not have worried. Nobody was pretending anything.

Almost nobody.

ONE

Your stupid, the anonymous comment reads below the blog essay. ***you dont know shit abt movies. why tf should i listen 2 some retard fucken white chick tell me abt racism and movies. you dumb priveliged white hore stick to what you now***

Jackie snorts and smiles. She loves getting these. Sometimes she wonders if that is her favourite reason for keeping this blog.

She posted the essay online yesterday–a lengthy homage to Spike Lee's *Do the Right Thing*. The movie turned thirty years old several months ago, and Jackie likes to use anniversaries divisible by five as an excuse to write critical essays on her favourite films from years past. Previous entries have included a fiftieth birthday homage to *2001: A Space Odyssey* and a seventy-fifth anniversary rant about the studio butchering of *The Magnificent Ambersons*. The *Scarborough Indie Voice*, the online mag for which she reviews, has no interest in the classics, so she writes these lengthy blog posts on her own time for fun. She models these articles on Roger Ebert's "Great Movies" essay series, although she does not fancy herself anywhere near as talented a critic.

Jackie clicks in the Reply box under the anonymous comment, then stares at the cursor for a few seconds.

Then she types, ***My stupid what?*** She chuckles but deletes it. Too subtle for this moron. She thinks for a moment, then types again.

I know more than you think, O Nameless One. I've been watching movies and reading film criticism since before you were the smallest, wimpiest sperm in your daddy's tiny dick. And surely, I don't have to be a visible minority to understand that racism is still a big problem in society?

She reads it over, thinks, and adds: ***I may be white and privileged, but I'll value that over being a worthless troll like you any day.*** The comment is posted with a quick click.

Another lazy Saturday morning of sitting around, surfing the web and trolling the trolls. Jackie might go to a movie by herself at one of the city's second-run theatres tonight; she has not decided yet. She might stay in and watch a DVD or stream a movie online instead. Either way, she likes to spend Saturdays on her own, relaxing in her small East York bachelor pad. The flat is cluttered and cramped but a perfect refuge for her. Classic-movie posters watch over her from the walls and doors. The bookshelves above her bed include titles by Ebert, Elmore Leonard, Pauline Kael, Andrew Sarris, Patricia Highsmith, Timothy Findley and Bill Watterson. The far wall is lined with years of DVD purchases, in a bookcase and on more shelves. Everything from Criterion editions of foreign classics and sets of 1970s TV shows to a few Marvel Cinematic Universe hits decorate the wall.

The fridge and cupboards are near bare, but if she decides to stay in all weekend, there is enough sustenance and entertainment around to keep her going.

She opens another browser tab and logs into Spitter. "Spit Your Thoughts at the World!" the slogan reads at the top of the home page. Jackie wonders who will pick a fight with her this morning or if she will be in the mood to pick one herself.

She does not wait long. One of the first posts she spots is a forward from an account in Alabama. ***Charming social commentary from a distinguished gentleman,*** the forwarder has written above the post, which reads: ***Libtards and there movies. Just saw the shape of Water wat a piece a crap. Only Holly-weird fagit think its ok to show woman having relations with a fish creature. Pervs.***

Jackie licks her lips. She clicks Reply and types directly to the original poster, who goes by the username @TrumpLover1776 and displays a low-res photo of an American flag as the profile pic.

"The Shape of Water" is a beautiful movie full of love, she types. ***You are an ugly person full of hate.*** She posts the reply, then types a second: ***And besides, what's wrong with "relations" between a woman and a fish? You clearly had no problem about your mom and her brother.***

Jackie laughs out loud. For a second or two, she wonders if the response is too cheap, if it is beneath her. She decides she does not care and posts it anyway. Out of curiosity, she flips back to JackieRoberts.com to see if there is any follow-up to her reply to Anonymous.

fuck you cunt, Anonymous has written.

Now there's *a well-thought-out response*, she thinks. She is about to continue that conversation when she hears a tinny rendition of the *Midnight Cowboy* theme playing from her ten-year-old wooden IKEA coffee table.

She picks up her cell phone. "Rick Pevere" and his number are flashing on it. *On a Saturday?* she thinks. Jackie considers letting it go to voicemail or texting him back. Before she can stop herself, she answers the ring and taps the speakerphone on.

"You busy today?" Rick says.

For fuck's sake. Should I lie?

"Nnnnnnot really," she answers.

"You sure? You sound hesitant."

Too late. "Yes. I mean–yes, I'm not busy."

"Good. I'm in the office today. Wanna come down for a few minutes? Something I wanna talk to you about."

Huh? "Sure. Now?"

"If you're free."

"What's it about?"

"Tell you when you get here."

Crap. Rick has never asked her to come see him on a weekend before. Something she has done or said? Is she about to be fired from the *Indie Voice*, or whatever the equivalent is for such a small publication? Is the site going to shut down, or drop the film section? Or is she worrying about nothing? *Probably nothing.*

Jackie closes the web browser on her computer and grabs an elastic band to put her dark brown hair into her usual ponytail. Humphrey Bogart, hatted and suited as Sam Spade, looks at her from the screen wallpaper pic. He does not look optimistic.

She is about to shut down the computer but feels compelled to check Spitter again.

One new notification. Somebody under the user ID @nagging_conscience_42 has replied to her last post to @TrumpLover1776. *That's not fair, Jackie*, the former has written. ***Not everybody shares your life experience or cultural education. Not everybody can relate to "Shape" the way you do. Think about that before you condescend to others, OK?***

The profile pic for @nagging_conscience_42 is a fuzzy photo of a pert beagle puppy.

Jackie reads the comment again and shrugs. "I got nothing," she says out loud.

"The office", as Rick Pevere put it, is the basement of his parents' beachfront house in a quiet, dull Scarborough neighbourhood. This is where he runs and edits ScarboroughIndieVoice.ca. Books, CDs, newspapers, and printed-out e-mail press releases lie haphazardly all over some tables and chairs. Thick piles of dust cover the corners and tiny cloth bits and dirt specks dot the dull grey carpet. The little room "where the magic happens," as Rick self-deprecatingly describes it, has a distinct smell of Popeye's chicken because Rick munches on a breaded wing as he talks.

"Sure you don't want a piece?" he says, indicating the cardboard box of chicken. "There's a couple of breasts in there."

"No thanks. Trying to cut down on the junk food."

Rick keeps talking with his mouth full. "I should take a page from your book," he says. "This stuff is gonna give me a heart attack before I'm forty. Maybe a stroke too." He swallows. "Maybe it'll be worth it. So yummy."

Jackie nods. "Junk is yummy. That's why we're addicted to it."

Rick drops some bones in the garbage bin under his desk. A short, awkward silence.

"Right," he says. "So what'd you want to see me about, again?"

Jackie squints.

"You called *me*," she says.

Rick blinks, then slaps his forehead.

"I'm an idiot," he says. He takes three sheets of paper from the other side of his desk and hands them to her. "Just wondering if you saw this the other day?"

A printout of the *Post and Chronicle* online news story about the Peace House fiasco.

"Yeah," says Jackie. "Think I saw it in the *Star*."

"What d'you think?"

She does not know what she thinks.

"Uh, yeah," she says with a shrug. "Pretty messed up."

"Pretty messed up indeed." He sips from a can of Diet Pepsi.

"Sort of like the wildest Coen Brothers movie. And not one of their good ones."

"I thought it was funny how the media–even the mainstream stuff–said so little about Paul Shoreditch himself. Some stuff I saw just went on and on about what a shame it was that the *property* was trashed." He sniggers.

"Why wouldn't they say more about the guy?"

Rick shrugs. "Your faith in the integrity of contemporary journalism is touching." Shaking his head with a grin, he adds, "Man. At least he went out with a blast."

He stares at Jackie as if waiting for an answer.

"Um," she says. "Yeah. To amass all this hatred... what exactly did this guy *do*?"

"*That,*" says Rick, "is what I want to get from *you*."

"Excuse me?"

"I was thinking of doing it as a Rick Roll," he goes on, referring to his own sporadic editorial column on the website, "but I didn't know what angle to take on it. And it seems a little big for that." He takes a leg from the Popeye's box and starts gnawing on it. "Jackie, what if we did some kind of, like, feature story on this? You know. Do some research. Interview some peeps. Find out what the deal was with this freak. Right?"

Jackie stares at Rick. After she's taken it in, she laughs.

"You're asking *me*," she says, "to do a news feature? Seriously?"

"Sure. It'll be fun."

"But... that's not what I *do*." Pause. "That's not what *we* do."

Rick blinks. "Why can't we?"

"Rick, the *Indie Voice* isn't even a news website. We do reviews of albums and concerts and movies and plays and stuff. Doesn't this feel out of our scope?"

"Maybe it's time to expand our scope a bit."

"I'm not an investigative journalist. I never even studied journalism–my degree's in English lit. This isn't my line."

"Let's call it a free journalism school, then. For both of us."

"I'd be paid for this too, right?" The only reason Rick can afford to pay his writers a measly twenty bucks per review is because his father, the vice president of some local hardware manufacturer, owns and funds the mag. "How much?"

"We can talk about that another time."

"Well..."

Jackie scours her brain for more excuses. Even to herself, she hesitates to admit the *real* reason she does not want this assignment: her unabashed laziness. Watching movies for free and praising or trashing each one in five hundred words is good enough for her. Her weekday afternoon and evening job at the Hogtown Philharmonic Orchestra's call centre is easy and pays her rent, if barely. But actual grunge work? Not her sack of happy.

"Is this just another one of your whims, Rick?" Jackie asks. "Like that Halloween when you asked Alana to sneak into Old City Hall and stay overnight to try to get a picture of the ghosts? You remember how that turned out."

Rick ignores the memory jog. "Look. I've always thought of the *Indie Voice* as a culture mag. Culture doesn't always mean film and music, though. It can mean, like, society and that type of thing."

"Society... and that type of thing?"

"You know what I mean."

"Actually, no."

"Have a look at this." He types something on his keyboard and turns the computer monitor to face Jackie.

The screen shows a web page with a stark black background. At the top of the browser reads the title:

FUCK PAUL SHOREDITCH

in large, bold, white Comic Sans font. Underneath is a fuzzy, unflattering black-and-white photo of a teenage boy with a flat nose, big ears, and 1980s-style dark feathered hair. The boy has a shy expression, almost smiling yet not quite getting there, with side snaggleteeth sticking out horribly atop a ludicrous overbite with front buck teeth, all of which make his face look like that of a stupid, sexless giant mouse. Under the photo in smaller Times New Roman blue type, reads:

Click on this little fucker's ugly face to enter the site.

"Holy shit," says Jackie.

Her first thought is also *Holy shit.* Her second is *Huh. Paul* was *a bit ugly.*

"It's a website devoted to Paul Shoreditch," says Rick. "A hate website."

"I can see that." Pause. "Is–is this even *legal*?"

"Probably not. But its content goes back a few years, and nobody's ever shut it down."

"Jesus."

"It's basically a collection of anecdotes and stories about the guy. Anybody can just submit something and have it posted, unedited, on the site." He takes a breath and continues. "So what I'm thinking is: what does it say about our society? About our culture? That some ordinary dude–not a celebrity, not a powerful man in any way–can generate *this* much hatred and bitterness among so many people, even strangers? And what does it say that everybody's already forgotten about this after only a few days?" He shrugs. "Even if he *deserved* it, what is that saying?"

Jackie stares at the grainy photo on the screen. The more she looks at young Paul Shoreditch's dopey, immature face, the more revulsion she feels, even while aware she has no logical reason to feel that way. How can you hate someone you know nothing about?

"One more question," she says. "Why me?"

"Why you?"

"Why are you asking *me*? Why not Alana, or Neil?"

Rick grins and looks away from Jackie. "Well, I hate to sound like a suck-up, but because you're *awesome*, Jackie."

She rolls her eyes. "I know. You tell me after every review I send you."

"You really are the best writer on this site. Way better than Gemma was, and she's had a book review published in the *Star*. Your passion, your snark, your intelligence–you're the only one I could see doing this."

Jackie clears her throat and hopes she is not blushing. "Thanks." Part of her wants to hear more praise. Part of her wants to tell him to shut the hell up. But she says nothing more.

"And you have so much *potential*. Not that there's anything wrong with doing reviews, but I wanna see you stretch yourself a bit."

She nods, unsure. The only stretching she wants to do right now is out on her couch with Netflix as her date.

Rick turns the screen back to face him. "All right. Now get the hell outta here. I've got work to do and chicken to eat." He grins at her as he takes a drumstick out of the box.

This is bullshit, Jackie thinks as she walks home from the subway, her sneakers crunching on the fallen leaves on the sidewalk. She was looking forward to doing nothing for the rest of the day, and she ended up with a thing. Not that she has to start right away–Rick didn't give her a deadline or even a word count–but this project seems too big and strange to put off. *How do I begin this? What does a real reporter even do? What the hell is Rick thinking?*

She enters her first-floor apartment and throws off her fall jacket and shoes. The clock on her stove says 1:12, so she plays a couple of Season 3 *Simpsons* episodes on her computer while she makes and eats a half-assed lunch for herself: two pieces of toast, an apple and a glass of milk. Then it is close to two o'clock, and she plays an old 1960s *Spider-Man* cartoon on YouTube as she washes the few dishes, humming along with the groovy Ray Ellis score.

Fresh out of procrastination, she sits and stares at Sam Spade on the computer screen.

"What should I do, Bogie?" she says out loud. "How do I start this thing?"

Bogie just stares back with those sad eyes.

"Some help you are, you gumshoe twit."

She sits for another ten minutes. *I could check Spitter. No, I'd be on it forever.* Then, *I wonder if he's still in the office.*

Jackie reaches for her cell and taps Rick's number.

"What's the deadline for this Shoreditch thing?"

A brief pause, during which she imagines him shrugging nonchalantly. "I dunno. Can you do it in a month? November... 19th sound good?"

"Okay. And how long?"

Another pause. "I dunno. How long are these things usually?"

"I thought *you'd* know." *Dumbass.*

"Three thousand words? It's the Internet, so exact length doesn't matter."

"And how much is this paying?"

"We can discuss that another time."

Jackie rolls her eyes.

"Anything else?"

"Yeah. Rick... where should I start on this?"

He laughs. "Check your e-mail. I just sent you a few links."

"All right."

"*Definitely* get in touch with Kathy McDougal. She's a name some readers will recognize."

"I don't recognize it."

"Really?" An edge of disbelief in his tone. "You've heard of *Kat's Korner*, right?"

"Heard of it."

"It's sort of the Canadian *Jezebel* but *way* meaner. *Way* nastier."

"Okay."

"Trust me–you'll *love* her."

The first link in Rick's e-mail is F**kPaulShoreditch.com. The second is KatsKorner.ca, and also a few news stories about the Peace House incident. She clicks on the first link and sees the same website homepage Rick showed her. As directed, she clicks on the fucker's ugly face.

An introductory letter to visitors, in plain Times New Roman:

> **welcome to f**kpaulshoreditch.com**
>
> welcome! =D this website is a tribute of sorts, but not that kind of a tribute. ;) it is a safe web space where people can share their stories, their rants, their curses, their vents, their Pain, whatever they want to share, all about that malodorous tit paul shoreditch.

> do you know paul? did he annoy you alot? did he crepe you out? did he hurt you in any way? did he make your life a living hell? =(if so, then you're at the right place. this is where we gather to bask in our dislike for this horrid, pathetic little man and all that he stands for.
>
> so please post on our message board, my friends. e-mail us your story, even write up a poem or paint something to express your rage and hurt. we're not picky. =) anything you can Contribute to this shrine, this homage, this honest and full tribute to a man who has ruined so many lives
>
> lots of love,
>
> Avenger_of_the_Weak
>
> website founder and editor
>
> Spitter: @avenger_of_the_weak_81

On a left sidebar are links to subsections "Stories", "Essays", "Reports", "Forum" and "Miscellaneous". Jackie clicks on "Stories", scrolls down a list that seems to go on forever and then randomly chooses a piece titled, **"Paul and his Stupid Sweater"**, dated August 22, 2014, and authored by site user Tony_Day:

> So I went to high school in Mississauga, Ontario with Paul Shoreditch. He wore a lot of goofy clothes and some of us liked to call him Furley, like Mr. Furley from the old show Threes Company who used to wear all the bad clothes. Well there was this one sweater Paul wore a lot, it was awful even by 80's standards, it was all green with these blue stripes [...]

Really? A sweater? That's a hell of a long way from "ruined so many lives."

Jackie wonders if this is a random guy who stumbled on the website and recognized Paul's name. Bored with Tony, Jackie backtracks to the previous page. She scans the list, which includes such headings as **"The way he slurped when he drank something"** and **"that f*ckin singing!"** and **"What a looser"** and **"Couldn't play soft ball for shit"**. Then she backtracks to the "Reports" section. At the top of the list, dated October 17, 2019, is the heading, **"THE FUCKER IS DEAD! NOW WE ARE FREE"** written by Avenger_of_the_Weak:

> at last, at last! the fucker is dead. =D forever will he remain so. it turns out that paul shoreditch had a little Accident. what kind of an idiot just falls from a building? XD how hard can it be to keep a window closed? well, it doesn't matter. we are free. [...]
>
> i just found out that his funeral is happening on monday. it's at peace house funeral centre, in what used to be east york, toronto. i can't imagine who would want to go to this thing. family? i can't imagine that he had any friends. unless they were masochistic sociopaths! ;) you know what would be a fun thing to do? if alot of us showed up for the funeral and made a mess of it in some way. =) show anyone who was fucked up enough to show up what everybody REALLY thinks of paul. we can make a real statement. what do you say? [...]

Avenger's write-up has more than one hundred and thirty replies. Many of them have headings like ***Lets do it!! =D*** and ***Great idea*** and ***Paul was a Scumbag. Everyone needs 2 know.*** One even reads ***You are a national hero Avenger***.

Jackie cannot find a single reply that suggests the protest is not such a good idea.

She stares at the screen. Her jaw hangs open. Her eyes are wide.

Jesus, Paul. What in the name of God's balls did you DO to all these people?

TWO

Monday morning. Jackie spent much of yesterday scouring through posts on F**kPaulShoreditch.com, and she is back at it. There are hundreds, varying widely in length and literary merit. Some are written by the same people. The more she reads these posts, the more confused she gets and the less insight she has into who Paul was or what he did to rile up this pitchfork mob.

Almost all the submissions to this site fall into two categories. Many are superficial whines and complaints like Tony_Day's, tearing apart Paul Shoreditch's looks or his lack of redeeming social graces like cliquey, gossipy teenagers.

What a mooch, reads a post by AliAndreas32.

> If they had free food out at the store backroom, Paul Shore-Bitch would always make a beeline for it before anybody else. No manners, no consideration, no life. Fucking mooch.

Another example comes from betsy_gall, who has written:

> did you ever see anybody so creepy?? i think its in his eyes. paul has those child molester eyes, like the woody allan. he doesnt have to do anything its just the way he looks at you, you want to run. also i hate those ugly teeth of his

The second category consists of contributors who do not specify what it is about Paul that makes them so furious but make up for the vagueness with the baffling intensity of their anger. Avenger_of_the_Weak has authored a few of these posts.

> i've seen paul shoreditch do some really shady stuff,

Avenger says in one message.

> it burns me up with rage when i think of it. =(i wish he were in jail or that he'd just disappear. that would be a better world. =)

The post Jackie reads now, from the user I_Will_SUrvive_I_Have, is one short sentence:

> Why does this troglodyte even exist?

Jackie registers the username Hildy_Johnson on the site then clicks on "Forum". She types the heading **"Looking for information"** as a new forum topic.

> Hello, she types.

> I'm a reporter for a Toronto websi

She deletes the last unfinished word.

> newspaper and I'm working on a story on Paul Shoreditch. Looking for any useful information. What was he like? Why did he make you all so angry? If you want to chat sometime over the next few weeks, please call

Stupid idea. She does not want the loonier-sounding ones to have her cell number.

> please reply to this post with contact info.

Jackie posts the message, then has another thought. She navigates to Avenger_of_the_Weak's final post about Paul Shoreditch's passing and types a new reply:

> Hey. Are you in Toronto? I was wondering if you'd be available for an interview about Paul Shoreditch. I'm a reporter for a local newspaper, and I'm working on a story on him. Wondering if you have any useful info.

After posting the message, Jackie leans back in her seat and lets out a long, tired sigh. Reading all this blatant animosity is not the healthiest way to spend a weekday morning.

One thing she likes about working in the afternoons and evenings is that she can get up anytime and does not have to rush. She can take her sweet old time about breakfast, she does not have to shower right away, and she can spend what is left of the morning working on her latest *Indie Voice* review or JackieRoberts.com essay. Rick schedules her for press film screenings mostly in the mornings, although if there is a big one she is interested in on a weekday afternoon, she phones Sam at the HPO call centre with an excuse, either illness or an appointment. This week, there are no screenings, and she is putting off new essays for a while.

Now, sick of wallowing in the dregs of the Paul Shoreditch website, Jackie decides to wallow in some different dregs. She calls up Spitter.

"Got Somethin' to Say? Spit It Out!" reads the new slogan at the top. She has received eighteen likes and two replies for her last post–itself a reply to a stranger's glowing endorsement for the Canadian Conservative leader, Andrew Scheer. ***Need some band-aids for your knuckles, my friend?*** Jackie wrote last night. ***Homophobic religious wackos often wind up with cut-up knuckles after years of dragging them on the floor.***

The first reply, from the stranger, reads ***go fuck you're self you Trudeau loving snow flake.***

That is not the reply that makes Jackie uncomfortable. The other one does, accompanied by a familiar image of a pert beagle puppy.

Come on, Jackie, says @nagging_conscience_42. ***I'm no Scheer fan either, but it's not fair to assume every supporter is a homophobe or religious zealot. Or even a conservative, for that matter. When you make these generalizations, you're no better than the bigots you're always mocking.***

Jackie shakes her head in bafflement. *Who is this person?* And… "always"?

I see you're trying really hard to live up to your name, she writes to @nagging_conscience_42, ***but you're just coming off as a self-righteous ass. Excuse the cliché, good sir, but you must be TONS of fun at parties.***

Jackie posts the reply, then thinks. She adds, ***Have we met?***

She does not wait for a response. She has to get ready to go to work. But first, she checks her e-mail. Nothing new unless junk mail counts. A message from GhettoSlut45@freemail.ca has arrived in the junk folder with the subject heading, "FW: Must Read This

Shocking Account Of What Happened To The Ed", with the rest cut off. Jackie empties the folder with barely a glance, imagining yet another ad for Viagra or something. She checks her cell phone—a text from her mother in Ottawa. *HOW ARE YOU JACKIE? WHEN ARE YOU GOING TO COME VISIT US AGAIN?*

She makes a mental note to call her mother later.

The fucking TTC. There's always something with Toronto transit. Jackie sits in a packed subway car that has not moved for five minutes due to alleged "signal problems." The only good thing about the situation is that she managed to nab a seat when she got on. Normally she would be reading, but she can never concentrate during a transit delay. It does not help that the teenage boy sitting at the other side of the car is stealing quick glances at her breasts when he thinks she is not looking. *I barely have breasts—why do they even care?* All she can do is sit with a pretence of patience and suppress the desire to let out a primal scream that would get her dragged away to the mental institution downtown. There are already too many mentally ill people riding Toronto's transit system. She wonders if they got that way from sitting through pointless delays.

One of these days, something very bad is going to happen as a result of these delays and shutdowns. Maybe some freak will set off a bomb. Maybe there'll be a nuclear war and the trapped subway riders will be the only survivors, creating a new underground society of mutants. Jackie laughs inwardly at these mental images. At least the subway line is operational; sometimes they shut it down for maintenance or upgrade work, and then Jackie is stuck with a shuttle bus that takes twice as long.

She arrives at the call centre five minutes late with a water bottle and half-eaten cheese-and-onion sandwich in her hands. Passing Sam in her tiny office and spotting her supervisor's disapproving expression, Jackie mouths the letters "TTC" to her. Sam closes her eyes and nods as if she has heard the excuse ten thousand times before from ten thousand employees. Jackie goes to her cubicle to set up, surrounded by the voices of her co-workers. "So I'll put you down for two for the Mozart package," she hears Julia say into her headset mic on the other side, her fake smile oozing the required corporate customer friendliness. "One ticket left for the *Star Wars* concert! Sound good?" Chris, the handsome, blond twenty-one-year-old guy sitting to her right, chirps to another customer.

This is nobody's dream job, but not as bad as past call centre jobs Jackie has held. Here, she calls past ticket buyers, the vast majority of whom are genuinely interested in classical music–and people who care about culture, in her experience, are friendlier and easier to deal with. Not like the place where she was trying to sell credit card "upgrades" to bank customers–meaning they could pay an extra seventy bucks a year for Air Miles and other vague benefits–or the place where they were calling random households in the States to sell credit card "insurance". She did not last long at that one. Her first suspicion that the operation was not entirely legit came on the first day, when her supervisor instructed her to tell the leads she was calling from Scottsdale, Arizona. Her second came when she realized the same supervisor spent most of every workday in his office practising his golf swing.

The Hogtown Philharmonic Orchestra's call centre is better, but every phone rep has the occasional problem lead–and Jackie gets two in her first hour today. The first is a grumpy guy in Brampton who claims he has never been to an HPO concert. Jackie assures the guy he attended a performance of Stravinsky's "The Firebird" two years ago, or at least that is what her computer screen reads, but he goes into full denial.

"Classical music is so boring," he scoffs. "Why would anybody wanna sit through that stuff? And pay so much money when I could be upgrading my car?"

"A lot of people are happy to spend good money to hear great music in a concert hall with great acoustics," she assures him.

"Yeah. Boring people," he says and hangs up.

"Fucking idiot," Jackie mutters to herself as the computer system calls up the next lead.

The second idiot comes on a few calls later. It is a frail-sounding lady in Willowdale who rambles about her dog, her son, and other irrelevancies for three minutes then sounds enthusiastic about a package of five Tchaikovsky concerts. She has read about it in the seasonal brochure the HPO mailed her but needs a refresher on the specific content.

"The first show, in a few weeks," Jackie describes, reading her information, "is the famous Sixth Symphony in B minor–the *Pathétique*. Along with the *Romeo and Juliet* theme."

"Oh," the lady says, her raspy voice betraying years of cigarettes. "Oh dear. I don't really like that symphony much. Not that one."

"Well, then there's the Christmas show with selections from *The Nutcracker*."

"Oh," says the woman. "Dear, oh dear. I've never liked *The Nutcracker* much either."

Jackie stifles a sigh. "Perhaps I could sell you the other three as a custom package? The next one in January is the first Piano Concerto, along with the *1812 Overture*."

A lengthy pause. "Oh dear," the lady replies. "I can't listen to that *1812 Overture* anymore. Those cannon shots are too much for my high blood pressure."

They don't use real cannons, you silly woman. "What about the one in March–the Violin Concerto in D?"

Another long silence. Jackie imagines the lady shaking her head in senile confusion. "Oh dear," she finally says. "I'm dreadfully sorry, but I don't think I like Tchaikovsky music very much after all. Now that I remember it. My husband used to listen to Tchaikovsky records back when we were young, back when he was working for Mayor Phillips–we liked to call him Nate, of course, he was such a fine man–and I always told him–"

Jackie senses that a long, long story has begun, so she ends the conversation as politely as she can. "Jesus fucking Christ!" she says out loud after disconnecting. "What the fuck? Why the shit do I get stuck with the morons?"

Nobody answers. Which is fine. She does not come here for the conversation.

The next couple of hours go smoothly, with a handful of sales. Jackie is looking forward to her first break, five minutes away, when she senses Sam standing behind her.

"Jackie, can I speak to you in my office for a few minutes?" she says with a polite smile, hands clasped in front of her.

She follows Sam into the tiny side office, where Patty, one of the company's human resources people, sits in a chair holding a clipboard and pen. Sam shuts the door.

"Right," says Sam as she and Jackie sit down. "So we've received a few complaints."

"About what?" Jackie asks innocently as Patty begins jotting down notes.

"About your language. From your neighbours." Sam still has that fake smile, and Jackie knows she is in for another one of those patronizing lectures disguised by a thin streak of manufactured empathy. "Now, I understand that work can be stressful and frustrating at times, and yes, it can be therapeutic to blow off steam. Believe me, Jackie, I've been there. But we have to watch our behaviour when we're in a professional environment. And some people are not going to be offended by vulgarities, but we have to recognize that some are. Agree?"

Jackie nods as Sam carries on and Patty writes mechanically. Sam recommends Jackie go out for a walk for five minutes whenever she gets the urge to swear and warns about the dangers of a customer on somebody else's line overhearing her, and notes that her co-workers need to feel safe and relaxed around her so they can do their jobs without distraction or tension, and so on. Jackie feels bitter only when Sam suggests Jackie might want to enrol in a corporate workshop on how to deal with anger constructively–as if she had the time for that crap, or anybody did.

She listens to Sam yammer on, nodding when it seems appropriate and wishing she had more guts. She wishes she had the guts to tell Sam she has overheard Julia swearing like a deranged homeless person on several occasions, and nobody has had the urge to tattle-tale on Julia like this. She wishes she had the guts to defend herself. She wishes she had the guts to tell Sam and her little HR minion to go fuck themselves. But she needs the job.

I wish I had a keyboard in front of me. Courage is easier that way.

After the lecture, Jackie gets up to leave, then says, "Oh–I need to book Wednesday off."

Sam looks at Jackie. "Excuse me?" she says with a half-amused, half-disbelieving expression as Patty starts writing on the clipboard again.

"Sorry–guess it's not the most appropriate moment. But I have a doctor's appointment. An important one." She is actually taking a Greyhound to Cambridge to do an interview with Paul Shoreditch's mother, but Sam does not need to know that.

Sam blinks, then offers a laboured nod. "Fine."

Jackie returns to her cubicle wearing an armour of suspicion and mistrust. She knows she is surrounded by snitches and cannot trust anyone. Certainly not respect them. Who knows what the next slip will be and which of these jerks will go running to Patty or Sam like a second-grader crying to a teacher? *Teacher, teacher, Bobby said a naughty word! Punish him, teacher!* She looks at her nearest co-workers and wonders who the tattletale could be. *Chris, you little brown-nose? Amanda? If it's Julia, she's the biggest hypocrite in the universe.*

She sits down, puts the headset back on, lays on the fake smile, and goes back to work.

Still angry after what should have been another forgettable workday–and after *another* pointless subway delay–Jackie does not go online when she gets home. She does not want to interact with the outside world. The only concession she makes is to reply to a text from Natalie, her ex, asking if they are still on for brunch at the Greasy Knoll on Thursday. They have been meeting at the Knoll for brunch every few months for years now, though neither remembers why. Jackie usually looks forward more to the meal than to the conversation.

She looks at her mother's text from this morning asking about visiting Ottawa again and sighs. *Fine. I'll answer her tomorrow.*

Yawning, not even changing out of her clothes, Jackie flops into bed.

THREE

The following night, Jackie is dreaming.

It starts as another floating dream. Jackie has those now and then. She enjoys them but wonders what it says about her psychology, if she subconsciously wants to escape from something and float away free. She dreams she is floating above her bed, then up through the ceiling like a ghost into her upstairs neighbours' living room, and through the wall into the quiet, dark street. The street fades. Apropos of nothing, she is sitting at a dinner table in a room in a military headquarters. She recognizes the table and the office. Movie scenes tend to make random cameos in her dreams, and there is no mistaking that she is now Captain Willard in *Apocalypse Now*. But there is no General Corman or Corporal Lucas in the room. It is just Rick Pevere sitting across from her, wearing a stained white T-shirt and a dumb smile, offering her a chicken breast from a Popeye's box. She turns it down, and then Rick says *Here's your mission, Willard,* and hands her an old, faded Polaroid photo of an awkward, mousy teen boy with a flat nose, big ears, dark feathered hair, overbite and snaggleteeth. *No need to terminate his command,* Rick says with a strange laugh. *That job's done. Just find him.*

But whatever you do, and he laughs harder, *do it with extreme prejudice.*

And Jackie is staring into the face of a beagle puppy. The puppy seems neither happy nor angry nor afraid. No expression. It and Jackie stare at each other for a long time. She does not know how long because time does not exist in dreams. It could be an hour, and it could be a thousand years–endless stretches of staring, staring, staring...

Stop it, says the puppy.

"Gah!" Jackie yelps as she jerks awake.

She sits up and takes a minute to catch her breath. *Home. Wednesday. Dog not real.*

After she calms down and wakes up more, she looks at her old digital clock radio on the side table beside her bed. 9:17, it reads.

Fuck. Fuck fuck fuck fuck FUCK.

She grabs her phone from the same table and flicks it on, then goes to the living room to turn on her computer and uses the bathroom while both machines boot up. Then she runs back to the computer and calls up the e-mail with the phone number for Lydia Shoreditch.

"Yeah?" croaks a senior woman's voice on the speakerphone after Jackie dials the number.

"Mrs. Shoreditch? This is Jackie Roberts. Is it okay if we do the interview later this afternoon? I'm gonna miss the Greyhound to Cambridge–have to take the next one."

A moment of uncomfortable silence. The voice barks, "You're gonna miss the bus? How the hell can you miss a *bus*?"

"I slept in. Won't make it to the terminal on time." She does not want to reschedule for another day as booking today off work was awkward enough, and she loses a full day's pay each time.

Jackie thinks she hears a bitter sigh on the other end.

"Sounds unprofessional to me," Mrs. Shoreditch says. "Don't you writers know how to set an alarm clock?"

"I did. It didn't go off."

"I heard that one before, young lady." *Young? I'm thirty-six.* "Seems like you people need to learn to take some personal responsibility."

You people? Huh? Jackie clenches her teeth. Then she takes a breath and counts to five in her head. "Sorry. I'll be there when I can."

Mrs. Shoreditch hangs up without saying goodbye.

Jackie does not bother to shower. She grabs a pair of jeans and a T-shirt from the floor and dresses quickly, then takes stock of what she needs to bring with her. Notebook–check. Pen–check. Folder of printouts–check. Phone–check. Most important, she cannot forget the $69 Olympus recorder she bought the other day. She had e-mailed Sylvie, a former *Indie Voice* contributor currently writing for *NOW* magazine, for interview advice. "Get a recorder," was all Sylvie had replied.

"Here we go," she sighs before she leaves. "God, I hate buses."

Has there ever been a lawn like this? Jackie thinks as she approaches the Shoreditch house in Cambridge. The front lawn–it cannot be real. Even in October, every blade of grass is too perfect. Every one the same colour, the same height, the same space apart from each other. No bald patches anywhere. The lawn is so perfect it has a threatening aura, as if commanding to her in a low, authoritarian voice: *Step on me and your head will be on a pike.*

Inside the house, the aura is of cigarettes and coffee. This would be a problem for some people but not for Jackie, who was addicted to Gauloises in her late teens and Second Cup lattes during a brief period in her twenties when she had a nine-to-five job at a computer-rental place. She kicked both habits years ago. Sometimes, she feels mildly suffocated by the smells, but not enough to gripe.

What suffocates her more is the oppressive neatness of this living room. Jackie wonders how the Shoreditches find the time and the will to keep the place–inside and outside–looking so clean and tidy. *A clean house is a sign of a wasted life,* she remembers her high-school friend, Jessica Lee, telling her. There is not an atom of dust on any furniture, not a speck of dirt on the smooth grey carpet. Only Mrs. Shoreditch's well-used black ashtray on the glass-topped coffee table betrays any sign of grime. The walls are as white as if they are cleaned professionally every day, and even the flower figures on the fireplace mantle look brand new. In the few minutes she spent in the bathroom, Jackie noticed that the towels and washcloth were folded perfectly upon the rack like those in a hotel suite.

A large flat-screen TV set sits atop an entertainment centre airing FOX News with the volume muted, and the bookshelf next to it appears to have the entire Danielle Steel oeuvre, along with titles like *The Quotable Ronald Reagan* and Bill O'Reilly's *Culture Warrior*. On the top shelf is a model of an army tank. A well-read copy of *The National Enquirer* lies on the coffee table next to the ashtray. No paintings or family photos hang anywhere; the only arguable concession to art is a large, framed photo that Jackie saw in the bathroom: five nude babies sitting on a yellow beach towel, their backs to the camera and their bare rear ends conspicuous. The photo, which the couple probably bought at a second-hand store or yard sale, is clearly intended to be cute. Jackie found it creepy.

"Interesting choice of bathroom décor," she tells Lydia Shoreditch to break the silence.

"Huh?" croaks Mrs. Shoreditch.

"The baby picture."

"Oh."

More silence, and Jackie adds, "I used to know a guy who photographed babies for a living. He did lots of other photography on his own, too. Is there much of an arts scene in Cambridge?"

"I haven't the foggiest idea."

Jackie nods politely. "We've got a lot of talented people in Toronto."

Mrs. Shoreditch coughs with a note of disdain. "Yeah. Toe-Ron-Toe," she says. "The goddamn centre of the world, huh?"

Jackie shrugs.

Lydia Shoreditch makes Jackie think of an elderly, loud and malevolent Marge Simpson. She wonders how tall Mrs. Shoreditch's beehive hairdo would make her if she stood up straight, but she has been plopped on her wooden rocking chair the whole time, glaring at Jackie with suspicion. Even the beehive seems to be laying judgement on Jackie, and on everything around it.

Her husband has not sat down once since he let Jackie in. Harvey Shoreditch is a skinny, goofy-looking, meek little old man with a shy smile and an absurd comb-over. He has barely said a word to anybody since he answered the front door, mostly just "Yes, m'love," when his wife has ordered him to shut the door, or fetch her cigarettes, or make coffee, or clean the cat's litter box. He has been running back and forth between the living room and the kitchen without cease. Jackie sees him as a mutt-like cross between an old-school British butler and Dobby the elf from *Harry Potter*.

"Well," says Jackie, reaching to the coffee table to flick on her Olympus recorder, "let me start by offering my sincere condolences. I'm so sorry. I'm sure this recent loss has been extremely hard on you and Mr. Shoreditch."

Mrs. Shoreditch squints.

"What're you talking about?" she asks.

"Paul. Your loss of Paul."

"Oh. Yeah."

"How have you two been managing since... the incident?"

"Lousy."

"I'm sorry."

"I mean, our credit debt was already high *enough*, since old Spendy McGarnagle can't hold onto a dollar from our pension cheques to save his goddamn *life*," Mrs. Shoreditch says, pointing to the kitchen where her husband is making coffee. "But the coffin, the funeral, the tombstone, the minister–all that stuff's expensive, young lady. You wouldn't know."

I wouldn't? Jackie just nods.

"And for what?" Mrs. Shoreditch goes on. "What was it all for? The young people all trashed the place and destroyed the goddamn coffin, and some punks ruined the tombstone. We thought we were getting a deal on everything, too, but we got nothing back from it."

"I see."

Mr. Shoreditch enters the room carrying a mug of steaming coffee, setting it down on the side table for his wife. He stands awkwardly and expectantly as she takes a sip.

"Too much sugar," she gripes. "You always put in too much sugar."

"Sorry, m'love," he replies, his head drooping.

"And look at that shirt!" Mrs. Shoreditch points to a small brown blotch on her husband's teal cotton shirt. "Were you stirring it with a blender? And with company over, too. Go put on a clean shirt. You're disgusting."

"Yes, m'love." He turns to exit the room, pausing to ask Jackie, "Sure you don't want coffee?"

"I'm fine, thanks," Jackie says with a smile.

"She doesn't want any, Harvey!" Mrs. Shoreditch slaps her forehead. "What the hell is wrong with you? You just don't listen. Go change."

"Yes, m'love."

After he leaves, Jackie glances at her notebook questions. "Now," she says, "it seems that your son was–how to put this delicately? –not well-liked among a lot of people."

No reply.

"I mean–there must have been a reason."

Mrs. Shoreditch takes a moment to think.

"Well," she says, "he was one *hell* of a wimp."

"A... wimp?"

"A wimp. A sissy. A wuss. A wishy-washy little cream puff."

Jackie gets the idea. "Right. But I've been doing some online research on him over the past few days, and I see a lot of nasty comments, anger and bitterness from a lot of people, but what I can't figure out exactly is–what did he *do*?"

"Do?"

"To make everybody hate him so much."

Mrs. Shoreditch gives her a look of profound pity and confusion, as if to say, *Isn't being a wimp more than enough?*

"I mean, *specifically*. Some specific act. He must have done *something*."

Mrs. Shoreditch thinks again.

"Well," she says, "it could be he went and kissed another man."

"Excuse me?"

"You know what I mean." She grins and winks, a gesture that makes Jackie cringe inside.

She conjures up a vivid fantasy of running up to Mrs. Shoreditch and kicking her in the head like a football player.

"Now," Mrs. Shoreditch continues, raising one eyebrow with a half-smile, "I got nothing against those people. At least not in principle. I'm not stopping them from doing what they do, no matter how sick and degrading it is. And besides, he always told us he wasn't one of them. Always. But you don't think we believed a word of it, do you?" She laughs. "Not with that scrawny little body. Not with the way he ran from fights like a silly coward, and the way he was so lousy at sports. And definitely not with that goddamn *singing* of his." Another laugh.

"Singing?" says Jackie, as she catches herself gritting her teeth. "What about the singing?"

"The kid kept telling us he wanted to be a *singer*." Mrs. Shoreditch sounds as if she is talking about some other boy, a virtual stranger who lives in another town. "He sang in the bathtub all the time, and in his bedroom. And he was *horrible*. Our cat sounds better when she's wailing in the middle of the night. He said he was gonna practise and train real hard and get good, and I told him, for his own good, 'No. First, you're the worst damn singer I ever heard in my life. Second, even if you *were* any good, look at you. You're no Elvis, boy. Nobody ever made it as a star with a weird face.'"

Jackie cannot resist. "Except maybe Freddie Mercury."

"Who?" Mrs. Shoreditch looks genuinely unfamiliar with the name.

"Never mind."

Jackie looks down at her notebook and sighs inwardly. *These questions won't work. Let's try a different route.*

"Mrs. Shoreditch, could you just... tell me about Paul? I mean, in general."

"What about him?"

"Like... what was he like as a kid? Just go from there."

And from there, Jackie gets an earful.

Paul Nixon Shoreditch, Jackie learns from his mother, was born in Mississauga, Ontario, on February 14, 1973, the first and only son of Harvey and Lydia Shoreditch. His first name came from his great grandfather. His middle name came from one of his mother's heroes at the time, the current United States president.

"I know it sounds strange to pay tribute to an American leader," Mrs. Shoreditch tells her, "but there was no way in hell I was gonna go with that goddamn Pee-err Troo-doh. Especially with those Frenchee names."

Jackie nods, fantasizing about whacking Mrs. Shoreditch with a cartoon anvil. "Go on."

Even before Paul was born, Lydia had decided exactly how she and her husband would raise him. Their son would not coast through life like one of those goddamn hippies she had been reading so much about in the papers and seeing on the TV news. Not on her watch. The young people had it too easy, but Paul Shoreditch was going to set a better example. So, every day, she took it upon herself to do the boy right by drilling into him the true golden rule of life.

"Kid," she would tell him, "I want you to be a man. And not like your father–I mean, a *real* man. Things would be different if you was a girl like me, but you're not. As a man, there's one thing you got to remember every day you're on this earth, and that is to Earn Your Salt. The world doesn't owe you a goddamn thing. The world expects you to take personal responsibility. If you can't take responsibility, the world'll murder you with the coldness of a starving tiger. Crush you and chew you and swallow you and shit you out before you get a chance to ask why. And you will feel every inch of that pain. The only way to get out of it is to go out and Earn Your Salt like a real man."

Lydia found it challenging to get that message through to her son. It turned out that infants are usually too busy crying and burping and playing and messing themselves to pay attention to well-meaning life advice. Even when they grow a little, learn to walk and talk, become toddlers, and so forth, they still have trouble understanding a message like that. But Lydia was not one to give up, nor to shirk her parental duties. And as it became more evident that Paul was going to be Harvey's and Lydia's only child– "no help from old Mister Droopy Stick over here," she quips to Jackie, pointing her thumb at her husband, who smiles and nods out of good sportsmanship–Lydia upped her drilling to the maximum. If Paul was going to be it, he would not get away with being a disappointment.

Small even for his age, skinny, and strangely quiet, Paul Shoreditch was an odd preschool child. All he ever wanted to do was watch *Sesame Street* and *Mister Rogers' Neighbourhood* on the TV or play with his LEGOs and Fisher Price sets by himself or lie down or walk around as if deep in thought. Once he started learning how to read, one of Harvey's sisters gave Paul a few books for Christmas, and he showed a suspicious interest in reading, more than what made his mother comfortable, especially when she learned about all the sick, subversive, anti-conformist messages that abounded in such titles as *The Cat in the Hat* and *Mr. Pine's Purple House.* Most of all, Paul seemed like a dreamy little character, and dreamy little characters are not known for their Salt-Earning skills.

Lydia thought of herself as a tolerant and open-minded woman, but she reached the final threshold of that tolerance on the afternoon when she first heard the singing. She was sitting in the kitchen, smoking and reading *Passion's Promise,* when she heard what might have been an announcer on a TV or radio blaring upstairs, but there must have been a lot of static to make it sound so screechy and dissonant, even from up there. She wondered if the clock radio in her bedroom was on, and she walked up the stairs. As she came closer to the noise, she realized it was coming from Paul's bedroom, that it was not from a radio–it was a singing voice.

The voice was belting out a shaky, off-key rendition of the *Sesame Street* song "Somebody Come and Play". It was barely even making a tune.

Lydia opened Paul's bedroom door. There he was, sitting on the floor, moving his Hot Wheels cars around the floor, warbling absent-mindedly as he pushed a blue car into the wall. Then he looked up.

"What the hell are you doing, young man?" Lydia asked.

Paul trembled a little. "Playing cars," he said in a small voice, almost a whisper.

"That's not all you're doing. You trying to *sing*, too?"

Paul looked down at the floor and nodded shyly.

"It's a song I heard on the TV," he said. "On *Sesame Street*."

Lydia glared at him. Then she sighed, shook her head, and went back downstairs.

It would be fine if the boy had a voice, she thought as she sat in the kitchen again. With lessons and practice, a boy with a good voice could have made a fortune for the Shoreditches and given them a better reason to stand out among the neighbours–more than just a perfect lawn and garden. But there was no doing anything with that rusty squeal machine. And that *face*. These days, a man needed a face to get anywhere in the world.

A minute later, the noise started again. She could hear that dental-drill-on-a-glass-bottle wail again, and it was too much for her. It was clear the boy loved singing. And that would not do.

"We have to put the boy to work. For his own damn good," Lydia told her husband, who nodded and replied with the standard "Yes, m'love."

There appeared to be no businesses around that would hire inexperienced five-year-olds for full-time positions. Things might have worked out differently if the Shoreditch family had lived in eastern Asia years later, but under the circumstances, Lydia had no choice but to give her son proper life preparation in the comfort of their own home.

Away went the books. Away went the LEGOs and the other toys. And the TV set, while remaining on almost all day every day, would never show *Sesame Street* or any cartoons again. Paul never again got to hear Mister Rogers say how Paul was all right just the way he was, which was just fine with Lydia. "I always thought that man was a Jumbo Fag anyway," she told her husband. "Probably diddles little kids too."

When Paul asked his mother where his toys and books were, she replied that he had been such a bad boy that morning that a man had come and taken them all away. When Paul asked what he had done, she replied, "You *know*." And when Paul began crying, Lydia groaned and fixed the racket with a sharp smack across the boy's face.

"God damn you," she said, "you know how I feel about that noise. A real man doesn't make that noise. We're gonna make a real man of you if we have to stomp it out of you."

Paul fought to stop the tears from coming, but they came anyway. "Mommy..." he gasped between sobs, "you're so... mean."

"Get used to it, young man," Lydia shot back, arms crossed. "It's all to help you. Sometimes, a mother's got to be cruel to be kind."

From that day on, Lydia and Harvey put their son to work. He was too small to do a lot of things–hold a broom or vacuum cleaner, for example–but with the help of a chair, he could easily reach the kitchen sink to wash and dry dishes or dust items on high shelves. He could also scrub floors and dust table legs and shake the dirt off small rugs. In the spring, he could plant in the garden in the backyard and water Lydia's flowers, and even run around the corner to buy small things from the IGA grocery store. It was a pity that the store clerks would not sell him cigarettes, a rule that prompted a few loud, vicious arguments between Lydia and the store manager. But for the most part, the Shoreditches had worked out a good system.

In months, Lydia had trained Paul to such a degree that she and Harvey barely had to do any housework or errands at all. Lydia could spend most of the day watching TV, reading romance novels or yakking on the phone if she wanted, and when Harvey came home from his job at the printing press, he could relax in front of the tube too. On the rare occasions when the Shoreditches had company, visitors gushed over how clean the house was and how quiet and well-behaved Paul was.

Lydia looked forward to the day when Paul was old and big enough to cook their meals and, most of all, mow the lawn. "One day, when you grow up and get married, you might have a lawn like ours," Lydia would tell her son. "A lawn is something to be proud of, young man. You have to take real good care of it–more than anything else in the world. A lawn gives you high status in a neighbourhood. People judge everything about you by the state of your lawn. It *defines* you." And little Paul nodded dutifully, as if he had any idea what she was talking about.

Complications came when Paul began school. That did not happen until he was six years old, as Lydia had already decided against kindergarten. "What the hell do they even *teach* in kindergarten?" she would say to Harvey, who would respond with a shrug. "I think all the kids do is play with their silly toys all morning and listen to stories and take naps. They don't learn anything useful. We might as well keep the boy at home, so he can keep on learning how to Earn His Salt."

Lydia Shoreditch evidently did not consider basic social skills or personal interaction to be "anything useful," so Paul began the first grade without any extensive background in these areas. And while his academic performance was very good, his teacher had expressed concern about his difficulty in making friends.

"That stupid young woman," Mrs. Shoreditch tells Jackie, shaking her head. "Calls me in for a meeting and says the boy has no playmates. I told her, 'So? That's not *my* problem.' She looks at me like I just talked to her in Russian. So I said, 'He's not here to make friends anyway. He's here to learn the three Rs. If he won't make friends, put him to work. Make him clean the classroom floor or lick stamps or pull out weeds or something. Get some goddamn *use* out of him.' And I just left. Wondering why they just didn't hire *me* to teach these brats instead."

Jackie has a mental picture of a black-and-white montage of screaming newspaper headlines right out of a 1930s Frank Capra movie: **THREE DEAD IN KINDERGARTEN RIOT!** one shrieks. **SALT NOT EARNED, CLAIMS TEACHER SENTENCED TO LIFE!** says another.

Lydia never found out if the school ever put Paul to work, but she found something else out on the day when he came home with a black eye, a bunch of cuts on his face, a split lip, and bruises all over his torso, arms, and legs. Lydia learned that this was not the first time a kid had punched or hit him, although it *was* the first time that a whole mob of them had beaten him up.

And she was furious. With Paul.

"What the hell is wrong with you?" she snapped, smacking him on the top of his head. "What kind of boy runs away from fights? That's why they're all ganging up on you now, 'cause they know you're easy pickings. You got to fight back. I don't want my only kid to be a goddamn wimp who can't fight!" She grabbed his bruised right arm and balled his hand into a fist. "See? That's how you make a fist. That's what hands are *for*."

Paul took this valuable lesson to school with him. He fought back. He also started picking fights with other children at recess, even when they had done nothing to provoke it. But every time, he ended up even more cut and bruised than he had been that first time, and once, was even suspended from school for a week.

"What the hell do you mean, it goes on his permanent record?" Lydia bellowed at the school principal. "All the boy was trying to do was defend himself."

"Mrs. Shoreditch," said Mr. Bascomb, the principal, tapping his fingers nervously on Paul's school record folder, "he climbed up to the top of the jungle gym and deliberately pushed a five-year-old girl off. She broke her arm and broke off two teeth on the gravel. She's lucky she isn't far worse. I fail to see how that constitutes 'defending himself.'"

Lydia thought for a moment.

"So?" she said. "All you're saying is, he *won*."

"Excuse me?"

"The fight. He came out the winner."

"That's–that's all you see here?"

"What I see, mister, is that the boy learned something. Something more valuable to the real world than any of that pansy stuff you've been teaching the kids in your music and art classes, which soften the crap out of them. He's learned how to win a fight. And that's a skill he's gonna need when he gets out there in the world and has to stake his claim among all the wolves and tigers and vultures." Lydia stood up and smiled at Mr. Bascomb with an expression of triumph. "Instead of suspending him," she added, "you should give him an A-plus. In life."

But the lesson did not last. Paul soon found that picking fights had the unfortunate side effect of provoking the other children even more to beat him up. Throughout Grades 1 and 2, Lydia eventually found out he not only stopped picking the fights, he began running away from them again. He would even arrive home from school, exhausted from running, with a few bruises and, worst of all, making "that noise."

In private, Lydia blamed herself. "Guess I'm not a good teacher," she told Harvey. "Or a good motivator. But I hear the community centre down the street has Judo lessons. If the boy's not gonna go out and stake his claims, the least he can do is learn self-defence."

Even Mr. Bascomb and Paul's teacher agreed this was a good idea. So the next Saturday morning, while most of his classmates were at home watching TV cartoons, Harvey drove Paul to his first judo lesson. It was also his last. Every time he was expected to tangle with one of the other boys–whether learning a basic move with a partner or playing British Bulldog with the group–Paul would get scared, burst into tears, and run to the corner of the room. This served only to delight the rest of the class, who pointed and laughed and called him a wimp, a baby, and worse.

Even the Judo teacher could not restrain himself. "Your kid's kind of a sissy," he told Harvey when the latter came to pick Paul up. "It's a miracle he's lived eight full years."

By the time Paul reached the fourth grade, to his mother's despair, he had become skinnier and wimpier. His overbite, snaggleteeth, and big ears had become more prominent. Paul still showed fine prowess in school as far as his grades went, especially in math and science, but he rarely spoke unless asked a question directly, had no friends and, most disappointing to Lydia, showed almost no interest in sports or any other physical activities. Gym class was his only academic weakness.

Lydia knew that the boy was going to hit puberty in a few years, and so would the other kids. She reeled at the prospect of her son remaining weak, effeminate, dreamy, and alone during the years when he was supposed to be getting on with girls. "We got to get him into a sport," she said to Harvey. "A sport will teach him about teamwork and friendly competition. It'll build up his muscles. It'll teach him how to Earn His Salt. If we don't, everybody'll see we've got a little prissy fag on our hands, and they'll blame us for bringing him up wrong. And they'll be right."

It was spring, so she dragged Paul down to the same neighbourhood community centre and signed the boy up for a little-league softball team. It was the only summer sport Paul was not afraid to try. Even soccer made him scared that the other boys would kick him, while he did not know what tennis and badminton were, and football and rugby were just too terrifying to contemplate. Baseball paralyzed him with the fear he would get hit by the ball or even by a bat. But when the exhausted Lydia brought up softball as a last resort, Paul perked up a little.

"It's like baseball," she said, palm rubbing forehead, "but with a softer ball. And the pitcher throws it underhand. And the field's smaller. That's all it is, a wimpy kind of baseball."

Paul relented.

But the softballs they used in the practices and games were still harder than Paul had expected, and the other boys whipped them at each other quickly. In practices, he did not even try to catch balls but ran out of the way. When he was at-bat, he ducked or jumped back at every pitch, scared that the ball would hit his head or hands.

"When they started doing the games," Mrs. Shoreditch tells Jackie, "the stupid coach would sit the boy on the bench most of the time. When he *did* send Paul out to the field, it was always deep left field. And he always put him at bat last. This crap went on until I gave him a piece of my mind. 'You know how much I paid for this?' I told the idiot. 'Get him on the goddamn field, you loser.' I told him right there, at a game, in front of everyone. I'd seen the guy stand up to screaming umpires before, but boy, did he crumble when I gave him what for."

KIDS' COACH IN HOSPITAL AFTER BEING GIVEN WHAT FOR! reads another flying black-and-white movie headline in Jackie's head. **BASEBALL BAT LODGED IN RECTUM!**

So Paul did get better shots at softball glory. But Lydia Shoreditch never got the results she wanted. Paul had missed balls thrown at him because he ducked out of the way, afraid to swing the bat. Worst of all, whenever the coach and other boys castigated him for losing games for them, or whenever attending parents would scream at him from the stands, he would break down and make "that noise," and that was not going to make him a hit with the girls anytime soon.

"We all told him that he had to get on base," Mrs. Shoreditch says. "Any other kid would at least try *swinging* the goddamn bat for once, but not him." She laughs, in a deep, throaty mixture of amusement and hopeless shame. "Know what he did instead? Every time he went up to bat, the boy crouched down to make the strike zone small and *walked*! That was his goddamn strategy!"

Jackie laughs too, in spite of herself. "Did it work?"

Mrs. Shoreditch nods with a frown. "Of course it worked. And the coach even *encouraged* him to do it after a while, if only because it got him on base. 'Creative batting,' the moron called it. But you think anybody respected the boy for it? You bet your ass they didn't. He was a fool. The parents from his team only laughed, and the other team's parents only yelled 'Cheat!'"

Lydia did not give up. The next spring, Paul did not want to go back to softball, but she told him to shut the hell up and signed him up anyway. And she did the same the next year, and again the next. For four years, Paul Shoreditch played softball in Mississauga but never became the "real man" that Lydia wanted, earning only laughs, the occasional pounding, and a nickname: The Croucher. He never impressed a single girl, built his muscles, or learned how to Earn His Salt.

By the end of high school, Paul Shoreditch had achieved stellar grades in every subject except physical education, but he had no friends and had never brought a single girl home for a date. He was a beanpole with a rag of feathered hair drooping over his big ears and a mousy face that was a braille essay of acne. Worst of all, he smelled, and not just of the cigarette smoke from his parents' habit. He showered every day, he changed his clothes most of the time, he even wore deodorant most of the time, but he still reeked of body odour for some reason. The Shoreditch family doctor was baffled; his only explanation for Paul's smell was that it was a possible genetic anomaly.

Lydia Shoreditch was crushed and ashamed. She felt she had shirked her parental responsibility somehow. There was still one idea left in her vault, though.

One evening, not long before Paul was supposed to finish high school, Lydia and Harvey sat with him in the kitchen for a talk. As usual, Lydia did most of the talking.

"Young man," she said, "you're nineteen years old. You're about to finish school, not that it ever did you any good. You're gonna become a man, though I can't see that you have anything man-like about you. Have you ever asked yourself: what are you gonna do with your life?"

Paul did not answer.

"Don't go thinking that you're gonna be living with us for the rest of your life," she went on. "You know I want to help you, but I'm not gonna bend over backwards for any freeloader. Not when it's not my duty as a mother anymore. I don't care how much work you do around this house; I'm not letting you stay here. You got to go out in the world and make something of yourself. Earn Your Salt like a real man."

Again, no answer.

"We talked about this before. In school, you do real good in math and science. You could make some real money with those skills. Why don't you go to business school? Your father and I will pay for it. Won't we, Harvey?"

"Yes, m'love," said Harvey.

There was a short silence, and then Paul shook his head.

"Not interested in that," he said. His speaking voice at this point was a soft, shaky, reedy, effeminate whine, which his mother despised as much as anything else about him.

"What about computers? I hear computers are big these days. Why don't you get into that and make some money?"

He frowned and shook his head again. "Not interested."

"IBM in Markham has a job fair next week. Jobs that start at seventy grand a year! Why don't you go and get a job there?"

"I wouldn't qualify. They want computer science graduates."

"But you know computers. You do your homework in the school computer lab sometimes."

Paul Shoreditch never laughed, but he looked as if he were stifling laughter now. "I know word processing. That's all."

"But that's computers!"

He just shook his head.

"Well–go to college and learn more about them."

"But I'm not interested in them."

Lydia sighed and puffed on her cigarette. "Well, you got to get out of here and do something. Aren't you interested in *anything*?"

Paul cleared his throat. He looked up at his mother.

"I... still like singing," he said softly.

"Oh, for the love of Christ."

"Do you remember," said Paul, his tone becoming stronger, in a shaky sort of way, "when I wanted to join that choir at school? Why didn't you let me?"

"Because you would've made an ass of yourself. And of me." Lydia chuckled bitterly. "And you *did*, too! You went behind my back and tried it, and they kicked you out."

Paul just looked down to the floor.

"I've told you so many times–you're not gonna be a singer. You're already fruity enough as you are without going out and singing all the time. Don't you wanna do anything *normal*?"

Paul was silent, as if he were thinking hard about it.

"No," he finally said. "I don't."

Lydia looked at Harvey, who nodded. Time to bring out the artillery.

She stood up, went to the counter, and picked up the manila folder lying there. She set it on the kitchen table and opened it.

In the folder was an application to join the Canadian Armed Forces.

Paul stared at the form. His expression did not change.

"If anything can help you become a real man, it's the army," said Lydia, in as close to a supportive and encouraging tone as she was capable of imitating. "They pay good, and they'll train you and work you until you build yourself up into a man. With the grades you been getting at school, I bet they'd even make you into a Sergeant or a Corporal!"

Paul visibly shuddered.

"And if we get another war–like if we go back to Eye-Raq and fight that Saddam fella again–maybe you can come back home a hero."

"If I survive," he said, "I guess."

"Don't be a goddamn wimp. Here's a pen. Just fill out the form and become a soldier. Every mom and dad are proud to have a soldier for a son. Isn't that right, Harvey?"

"Yes, m'love."

Paul sat and stared at the form as Lydia stood over him, antsy and eager, holding out the pen.

He picked up the form.

After a short beat, he tore the piece of paper in half, right in front of Lydia's face.

She gasped. "You piece of shit," she said.

And she walloped him right in the face. He fell off his chair.

"Get up, you little bastard," she said in a low voice. "Get up like a man."

But there was one outcome of this confrontation that Lydia had not counted on. She knew that Paul would get back up on his feet upon being ordered to do so. What she had *not* expected was for her son to follow through on her old advice about fighting back.

CRACK. With a clumsy swing of a fist, Paul Shoreditch knocked his mother to the floor.

He left the kitchen, he left the house, he left Mississauga, and he did not see his parents again for more than twenty years.

He made sure to stomp all over the Shoreditch lawn as he left.

NEIGHBOURS SHOCKED BY BRUTAL ASSAULTS ON WOMAN, GRASS! Cheesy old-movie headlines continue to entertain Jackie, but Mrs. Shoreditch is not amused. It is difficult for Jackie to imagine Mrs. Shoreditch shedding one tear, but the old woman seems to be on the verge of crying now, although in an angry, bitter way.

"To hit his own *mother*!" she sniffs. "Think of it. To strike his own goddamn mother. After all I did to help the boy. What the hell did I do to deserve that treatment?"

Jackie chooses not to answer.

"It wasn't long after that that Harvey and me moved here to Cambridge. Mississauga was getting too expensive and besides, there were too many goddamn Indians moving into the neighbourhood." She sips from the new mug of coffee that Harvey just brought her. "We didn't know what happened to him. Just before he came back, we heard he was living somewhere in Toe-Ron-Toe, working at some awful job at some store, stocking shelves or something. Maybe he was doing queer stuff too. I hear that's popular with you big-city folks, eh?"

Jackie picks silence again, for a different reason.

"Somebody told us they saw him at a bar once," Mrs. Shoreditch adds, "singing at one of those 'Carry Okie' nights."

"At what? Oh—karaoke."

"Yeah. The Chinese singing thing. They told us he sounded as bad as ever. Awful." She takes a deep breath. "I guess we really did fail as parents, didn't we, Harvey?"

"Yes, m'love."

"You got dirt on your face. You look stupid. Go clean it up."

"Yes, m'love."

Jackie clears her throat. "And you said he came back, eventually?"

"Yeah. About six years ago. After he got in trouble."

"Trouble?"

"On the computers."

It takes Jackie a few seconds to realize Mrs. Shoreditch means the Internet.

"Yeah. I don't know anything about it 'cause I don't do computers. But he came to hide out with us; we let him stay in the upstairs room. Until he went back to the city that day, and..."

Jackie is about to ask what spurred Paul to return "that day," then glances at her phone.

"Oh, sh—" She had no idea how long she'd been listening to Mrs. Shoreditch's stories. "I have to go if I'm gonna catch the last bus back."

"Are you sure you can't stay for a coffee?" asks Mr. Shoreditch with a timid smile.

"She has to go, Harvey!" snaps his wife. "Idiot."

"Yes, m'love."

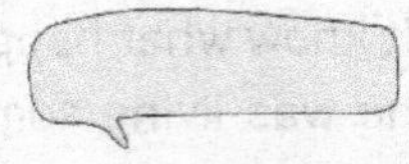

Monster, Jackie scribbles into her notebook on the hour-long Greyhound ride back to Toronto. *She's a monster. Maybe that's how Paul became a monster too? She's also a galaxy of stupid. Father such a doormat you want to rub your dirty shoes on his face.* Jackie thinks for a few seconds and realizes, to her annoyance, that she still knows next to nothing about who Paul Shoreditch really was, jack squat about what he did to generate so much online hatred, and *way* too much about his parents. *Like mother, like son? Or father?* she writes, then crosses it out and gazes out the window at the trees and fields whipping past as the sun sets behind the bus.

Jackie puts the notebook and pen on the empty seat beside hers, leans back, closes her eyes, and wonders what she would have turned out like if the Shoreditches had raised her. Would she have rebelled? Would she have become like Paul's mother? Or like his father? Would she have suppressed every urge to write, to read, to review, to care deeply about art and movies, to be anything she ever wanted to be until something inside her broke? *They stifled him. What a waste of potential. They stifled him until he just couldn't take it anymore. And he snapped. The poor—*

She opens her eyes, feeling a little queasy. *No. Don't.*

The phrase *waste of potential* sticks in her mind. It makes her think of Marlon Brando in *On the Waterfront.* She daydreams about that taxi scene with Terry Malloy brushing his brother's gun away with all the tenderness and delicacy of a lover and lamenting about how he coulda been a lot better, Charlie, and coulda had class, and how he ended up on a one-way journey to Palookaville instead, and so on. She remembers years ago, when she was living on campus at York University in north Toronto, how she and her dorm mate Sasha used to watch that movie all the time. *Whatever happened to Sasha? She loved Brando even more than I did.* She remembers how they snickered when Terry callously called Edie Doyle a fruitcake, watched in silent reverence during the cab scene, and came close to sobbing when Terry found out that the boy had killed all his pigeons. The Bernstein music wringing with unbearable pathos, the lifeless pigeon flopping past Terry, and the hopeless look on his face. How alone and useless he must have felt. Jackie wonders if Paul Shoreditch felt that alone and useless. *He must have, a hundredfold. Having to grow up wi—*

She jerks out of her half-asleep state.

Shit. No. This is wrong.

She grabs her notebook and pen and jots down: *Be careful. DO NOT SYMPATHIZE. Do not even EMPATHIZE. You know nothing about him, and it might be bad. For all you know, this motherfucker was running around punching random old ladies in the face like a maniac for years.* She pauses, thinks, and adds, *At least wait till you find out more.*

Jackie looks out the bus window and realizes the sun has gone down. She can barely see anything but her reflection.

FOUR

Jackie boots up her desktop when she gets home and goes straight to F**kPaulShoreditch.com.

Since Sunday, her request for interviews in the "Forum" community has triggered a staggering avalanche of exactly zero replies. She posts an identical message in "Stories".

On her other message from Sunday, Avenger_of_the_Weak has answered:

> sorry hildy. i don't do media interviews =(
> good luck with the story =)

"Some help *you* are, you freaks," she groans.

Exhausted, Jackie flops into bed. She lies awake for hours playing scenes from *Some Like It Hot* and *La Dolce Vita* in her head, in a desperate attempt to knock Mrs. Shoreditch's cranky voice out of there. Finally succumbing to sleep, she does not wake up until nine-thirty the next morning.

Jackie decides to go full out on breakfast, as she has eaten barely anything since grabbing a bagel with cream cheese and a water bottle at the Bay-Dundas bus terminal yesterday morning. Bacon, eggs, toast, a bowl of cereal, a banana–she has all of them at hand, and it is time to treat herself. Not all the healthiest choices, but who cares.

She watches her favourite *Mad Men* episode–*Commissions and Fees*, the one in which Lane Pryce offs himself–as she cooks and eats. After it ends and she puts the dishes in the sink, she realizes that she has not been on Spitter for a while. She boots up the desktop and calls up Bogie's face, then covers him with the site's home page. "Time to Give the World a Spit Shine!" reads today's slogan as she logs into the site.

She has a reply from Tuesday that she missed from the fuzzy beagle puppy.

No. I'm about 99.9999999 percent sure we've never met in person, @nagging_conscience_42 has written. ***If we had, I'd remember it. But I've been following your Spitter account for a while. I've been a devoted reader of your reviews and essays for some time. You're a smart and talented writer with a lot to offer. Pity that you're so arrogant too.***

Jackie feels queasy. *A devoted reader?* She cannot remember having one of those before, other than Rick Pevere. She does not know whether to feel flattered or stalked.

She ponders for a minute but cannot think of a comeback she likes.

Arrogant how? she replies. ***Is it arrogant to stand up to assholes? To stand up for social justice in your own small way? In a world full of privilege and ignorance and hate, I think complacency would be a huge, irresponsible mistake.***

She winces after she posts it. *In a world...* makes it sound like the beginning of an old Don LaFontaine movie trailer.

Jackie opens a new tab and checks her e-mail, then checks her blog for comments. A few new compliments on her *Do the Right Thing* piece–***Nice work!*** and ***Dead on, Jackie. I want to watch it again.*** On the other hand, somebody called SillyMommy has written

Stanley Kubrick's movies look great but they have no soul on her old essay about *Barry Lyndon*. She responds ***You sound smart, but you have no taste,*** then flips back to Spitter. @nagging_conscience_42 has already replied.

Of course we should stand up to assholes. But we should also check ourselves to make sure WE'RE not being the assholes once in a while.

"What's that supposed to mean?" Jackie says aloud. Before she has a chance to think of a reply, another post from the puppy appears.

Sometimes I get the impression that you're just looking for excuses to be a contrarian. I could be wrong. I wonder if you really consider people's feelings.

Jackie reads it a second time, then responds, choosing her words less carefully than she feels she ought to: ***You make it sound like I'm running around telling small children that their parents are dead. Of course I respect people's feelings. But the people who troll me seem to be asking for it. If their feelings are so fragile, they shouldn't start shit in the first place.***

She posts the comment, then thinks of a follow-up: ***Not that I care, but how well are you considering MY feelings?***

She stares at the screen waiting for the puppy's reply.

I think you're strong enough to take what I'm dishing you. And maybe you're right (about the trolls asking for it, etc.). As somebody who suffers from chronic depression, and who's reacted badly to other people's bullying before, I'm a little sensitive to these things sometimes.

Jackie tries to think of the right response. She does not want to sound insensitive to somebody's depression, but she sure as hell does not want to come off as apologetic or weak. *What does he mean by "reacted badly"? Or is it a she?* It hits her that she does not know this person's gender.

She sits and stares at the screen. And sits. And stares.

Nothing comes to her.

She opens a new tab and calls up her latest post on

F**kPaulShoreditch.com. No replies yet.

Jackie flips back to Spitter. Again, the appropriate answer does not come to her.

She is still staring at the puppy's last post when an irritating electronic whistle sounds from her purse on the floor. She jumps and reaches to grab her cell phone.

"New message" it reads.

Just got here. Booth by the Zapruder wall, says the text from Natalie.

"Oh, *fuck*." Jackie was supposed to meet her for brunch at 10:30.

The Greasy Knoll is quieter than usual, even for a weekday late morning. It proudly boasts to the public–on its menus, its outside windows and presumably its website–that it is the world's only JFK-Assassination-themed diner, although Jackie suspects there might be something in Dallas along those lines. She once had an idea for a sister pub called The Three Tramps but knew few people would get the reference. Each booth is designed like the bloodied seats in the presidential limousine, but with the front and back facing each other and a tabletop in between. Along the wall where Jackie and Natalie's booth is located are blown-up pictures of frames from the Zapruder film; the wall on the other side is decorated with Lee Oswald's mugshot, the pic of Jack Ruby shooting Oswald, and other familiar images. The female servers dress in cheap reproductions of Jacqueline Kennedy's pink suit and fake pillbox hats, and the male ones dress in Oswaldian white T-shirts. For the first time, Jackie has noticed the door of the men's room has a large image of the Texas Schoolbook Depository on it, and that the ceiling is a large mural blow-up of the Presidential Motorcade Route map that ran in the *Dallas Times-Herald* three days before the assassination.

Jackie has been meeting with Natalie for brunch here since they were dating, but she now notices details in the restaurant that she never thought about before because she has no meal to distract her.

Full from breakfast, she has ordered nothing but a glass of water. Natalie is stuffing her face with Sixth Floor Scrambled Eggs and a Magic Bullet Burger. She is not in a chatty mood, so Jackie has been off on a monologue.

"And they still believe that 'back and to the left' crap, too," she rants. "Go on any JFK message forum. All those silly conspiracy theories that were debunked *decades* ago, the Internet brought them all back. I blame Oliver Stone, too. Great director, terrible historian. He heard Jim Garrison's stories and bought them all wholesale. So naïve."

Natalie continues to eat in silence.

"Amazing what people believe, huh? Not just Stone, the people on the web too. They just believe the bullshit they hear without thinking. You can shove all the hard, solid evidence in the world right in their faces and they still ignore it. They believe what they choose to believe."

Natalie swallows.

"Why the hell do we always come to this place, anyway?" she says.

"What—here? The Knoll?"

"Yeah." Natalie wears an unusually sour expression. "This place is in such sick taste. So what if the food's great? We could go just about *anywhere* else. Don't you ever have doubts about it? About turning a national American tragedy into a silly breakfast menu?"

She sighs and starts eating again. Jackie takes a sip of her water and thinks. Yes, Natalie has a point. Something has always bugged Jackie about the Knoll, although she will not admit it out loud. The place is almost as tacky and tasteless as those Bodies exhibitions in which they display dissected human cadavers that may or may not be executed Chinese prisoners. And yet that sheer unapologetic crassness is why she finds the Knoll amusing. A Holocaust or 9/11 diner? Way too far. But she can handle the Knoll. It is located an easy walk from the HPO call centre and conveniently halfway between her and Natalie's homes. And the food *is* great. If she were not already so stuffed, she would be enjoying a serving of Mannlicher-Carcano Muesli, or maybe a David Ferrie Frittata.

"So," Natalie says, her mouth full, with all the enthusiasm of a dead worm, "you mentioned a thing. A thing you're doing for the website you write for."

Jackie nods. "Yeah. I don't know what my editor's thinking. It's so stupid. I'm thinking of telling him to shove the whole assignment, except he's the only editor in this city who'll pay me anything to write film reviews. And that's a bridge I wanna leave un-burned, for now."

"Uh-huh," says Natalie, glancing away. "What's the assignment?"

"Researching an asshole."

"Hm?"

"I had to go out to the boonies yesterday to interview this horrible old lady about her dead asshole son. Just trying to find out how he became such an asshole." Jackie emits a bitter chuckle. "Like I'm trying to find out what the guy's Rosebud is, only I can't imagine why anybody would care."

"Find out what his what is?"

"Rosebud. From *Citizen Kane*."

Natalie stares blankly at her.

"Oh," she says, remembering. "Right. They made us watch that in high school. God, what a boring movie."

Jackie does not argue. She is reminded once again of why she and Natalie never worked as a couple. "Anyway. I'm still not even sure what the editor wants. Am I supposed to write about the dead guy or the way everybody's reacted to his death? Or both?"

"Sounds more interesting than *my* life," mumbles Natalie, sipping her coffee.

"You really ought to see this bizarre website about the guy. I wasted a big chunk of my weekend looking through it. Couldn't believe some of the crazy, nasty shit I was reading. Just pages and pages of people complaining, nitpicking about him, and I *still* don't get it. What did the guy *do*?"

"Do?"

"To make everybody hate him that much."

Natalie does not answer. She takes another bite of her burger, distracted.

Jackie takes a breath.

"You... don't really care, do you, Natalie?"

Natalie looks at her. She appears to be thinking about it.

"No," she says. "I don't."

Jackie laughs with a cynical snort. "Okay then."

Natalie shakes her head and sips her coffee again. The table is quiet for a while.

"Well," says Jackie, "that was awkward."

Natalie does not reply.

"Doesn't mean you have to go all Boo Radley on me, though."

"Boo what?"

"Radley." She pauses. "From *To Kill a Mockingbird.*"

Natalie shrugs.

"You know—the neighbour. The mute guy. Robert Duvall played him in the movie."

Natalie sighs. Jackie thinks she hears a groan hidden underneath.

"What?"

"For fuck's sake, Jackie. Does *everything* have to be about movies with you?"

"I..." Jackie tilts her head in confusion.

"It's like, every time we talk, it's movies. It's like your only language, your only means of communication, is fucking movie references. Every time we meet like this, it's you and your movie references. When we were going out, all we did was watch movies. All you wanted to do was go out to movies or watch DVDs at your place." Her voice has raised a little, and a few people at the diner counter glance in their direction. "What makes you so sure anybody else gives a flying rat's ass about your Boo Radisson?"

"Radley."

"Whatever. What makes you so sure people even know who that *is*?"

"It's not that obscure a reference, Nat."

Natalie rolls her eyes. "That's not the point." She leans forward and buries her head in her hands. Jackie stares in bafflement. She has not seen Natalie act like this in years. "I don't know *why* we keep meeting up like this. We have no reason to hang out, even to keep in touch."

Because... we're friends?

"Do you know," Natalie goes on, "that I've been unemployed since June?"

"Seriously?"

Natalie puts down her hands and nods.

"But–the warehouse...?"

"Company let go of a bunch of people this year. I've been scraping by on unemployment insurance for months. Looking and looking for a new job, but I'm not qualified for much."

"Jesus." Jackie clucks her tongue in sympathy. "Sorry. I had no clue. Why didn't you tell me?"

"Because you never asked. And I knew you were never *going* to ask. Because all you ever want to do is talk about *you* and your stupid movies, movies, movies. And you come today, you're like forty-five minutes late—"

"I *said* I was sorry for that."

"—and all you want to talk about is JFK and your stupid writing thing. I only asked you about the writing to be polite. I wanted to tell you, but I knew you wouldn't care."

"Of course I care!"

"No, you don't. You're so cut off from everything, you don't see anything around you except your fucking *movies*."

Jackie is about to reply that there is far more to her than movie references, but the *Midnight Cowboy* theme in her purse interrupts her.

She answers her cell.

"Rick Pevere passed on your number!" The voice is female, loud and a little screechy. "It's Kathy McDougall!"

"Who?"

The voice on the other end laughs, with a minor note of contempt. "Don't tell me you don't know who I am! Kathy McDougal."

"Oh, right. *Kat's Korner*."

"You bet. So you wanna interview me about that little creep, eh?"

"Which little creep?"

"Paul fucking Shoreditch!"

There is an undertone of gleeful, hateful relish when the voice says his name.

"Of course!" *Duh.* "My apologies, Kathy. You caught me at a weird time. When're you free?"

"How about right now?"

Jackie chuckles uncomfortably. "Not really free at the moment. Having brunch with a friend, then I've got to get to my day job."

"Tomorrow morning? Ten?"

"Um... sure. Where can I meet you?"

"Sure you wanna do this in person? We could just do a phone interview."

"Uh..." *Shit. Of course. Real journalists often do interviews by phone, right? I'm an unprofessional idiot.* She hopes Rick reimburses her for the Greyhound ticket.

"No worries!" the voice says with a laugh before Jackie has a chance to respond. "Come to my place if you're not scared of a trip to Etobicoke!"

"That sounds fine." Jackie jots down the address and directions on a November 22 Napkin.

"Awesome! I can't wait!" The voice hangs up without a goodbye.

"Right," Jackie says, putting her phone away. "Sorry, Nat. That was—"

She finds herself talking to nobody. Natalie has taken off. A twenty-dollar bill sits by her mostly empty plate.

Huh. She suspects that these brunches with Natalie have come to an inglorious end. Or, at least, a long hiatus.

A grotesque wailing rings from the back of the cafe, and Jackie hunches her shoulders in deep irritation. *Great. Another screamer.* A crying baby has launched its tirade–a deafening symphony that rings throughout the Knoll, drowning out everything else–threatening not to reach its final movement for hours. Few things irritate Jackie like a screaming baby, or even a noisy preschooler. She does not mind children when they are quiet. But those moments seem tragically rare.

Thank fuck I never had one of those things. It's a blessing for the world. Can you imagine what a bad parent I would've been? "Stop squealing, you little monster. Just go out and play while Mommy watches the rest of this old Ida Lupino flick." She would laugh silently at the image if she were not getting so overwhelmed with anger. If she stays in this joint much longer, the noise may well drive her to march right up to the little bastard and scream back in its face–just hurl a cacophony of incoherent babbling nonsense at the kid. *Ha. See how you like it.* What a surreal sight that would be. Worthy of David Lynch, or maybe Luis Buñuel?

Stop making that noise! she wants to yell.

Then: *Holy shit. That sounded like—*

"Should I bring change?" a voice asks with transparent fake cheeriness. Jackie jolts in her seat, then looks up and sees one of the pink-clad, pillbox-headed servers standing over her.

"No, thank you," Jackie replies, reaching for her jacket.

"Have a good day," the Mrs. Kennedy clone says, taking Natalie's twenty. Jackie thinks she detects hidden hostility in the server's voice directed straight at her. *Well, of course.* Because she did not even order anything besides the water.

Jackie sighs. She may be a terrible journalist, she thinks, but she has not lost her unique gift for inadvertently pissing everybody off.

Damn. Maybe the puppy's right.

An uneventful day at the call centre. HPO season subscriptions are mostly sold out, so customers are interested mainly in single tickets and smaller concert packages. When she gets home, around ten-thirty as usual, she boots up the computer. But she avoids Spitter, at least right away. Her first stop is JackieRoberts.com, on the lookout for trolls. Another nice comment on the *Do the Right Thing* essay. ***Brilliant Jackie. A great analysis of a great movie,*** writes someone called Brokeback_Munchkin from whom she has heard before. But she finds what she is looking for on her glowing tribute to *Mr. Smith Goes to Washington* from several years ago. Another Anonymous, though more literate than the last one, has posted: ***The fact of the matter is that Frank Capra's movies are so full of cliches even by 30's and 40's standards. You would see that if you were a more perceptive critic.***

Jackie shakes her head in amusement. Sometimes these people make it too easy. She types back ***I hate clichés too. Especially "The fact of the matter is."***

Then she checks her e-mail. Confirmed: another interview for the Shoreditch story. Some dude named Chuck McMahon, who claims he knew Paul Shoreditch in grade school–and who Rick says was an attendee at the aborted funeral–is available Sunday. She replies, asking for a phone number and offering hers, making sure to do things properly this time.

Jackie logs out of her e-mail account. Then she tries to think of anything else she should be checking as she stares at the screen. Nothing comes to mind. *Fuck it. Let's get it over with.*

She calls up Spitter and logs in. The beagle puppy has not posted anything since this morning. Jackie remembers that it was her turn to reply when she left the conversation. Now, with a fresh look, she takes a different tack.

Why are you so interested in me anyway? she writes. ***I hope you're not some creepy stalker weirdo. Hope I'm not wasting my time arguing with some fedora-wearing incel shithead in his parents' basement. If that's what you are, I fear the worst implications of your "reacting badly."***

Jackie logs out of Spitter and heads back to

F**kPaulShoreditch.com hoping to get a little last-minute research in before meeting with Kathy McDougal. Still no response to either of her queries. She scrolls down the links on the "Stories" page looking for a clue, for something good, *anything*. Now, one heading jumps out at her: **"He Scared Me Even In Grade One!"** She noticed it before, but never thought to click on it until now. According to user JasonWoods73:

> Paul Shoreditch attacked me at recess in grade one once! It was almost 40 years ago but I still remember it vividly. I was just playing in the sandbox minding my own business, when he comes along and starts punching me in the head. Just out of the blue, no reason, I didn't do anything to provoke it! He didn't really hurt me, he wasn't very strong and couldn't punch very well tbh, but it still scared the shit out of me, why would he just attack me like that. It doesn't surprise me that he grew up to be a bastard too. At least that's the impression I get from this website [...]

Well, okay then.

One of several replies below reads,

> I remember that! I was in school with him too.

At least that part of Mrs. Shoreditch's story was true, and it is fascinating to see a couple of third-party confirmations, but Jackie is disappointed that it adds virtually nothing to her info.

Realizing that she has not checked out much of the "Miscellaneous" section yet, she goes there and clicks on a random entry titled **"A Prayer"**, wondering if this is going to be the first pro-

Shoreditch write-up she has seen. The post is written by the user Rikka_Braga:

> I am not very religious, I was brought up Presbyterian but it didn't really take. I'm not an atheist or anything, I think God is out there and watching us, but I just never got into the habit of going to church or reading the Bible much.
>
> There is one exception I make, though, and even my husband doesn't know I do this. But sometimes when I'm by myself, in the morning or shortly before bedtime, I will kneel by my bed and offer this prayer of thanks. I don't know if God is listening, but it sure gives me comfort and I would recommend this if you think it's for you. My prayer goes like this:
>
> Dear God,
>
> I thank you that I am not like Paul Shoreditch. I thank you for my moral, social, and cultural superiority over Paul Shoreditch. Please continue to grant me the wisdom, strength, and courage to be better than Paul Shoreditch, and please bless me with the humility to correct myself if I ever fall into Shoreditchian ways, and the patience and clarity to correct others who succumb to Shoreditchian temptations. Deliver us all from evil, dear God. Amen.

This post has more than fifty responses, calling the prayer

> inspiring, powerful, deep

and

> a perfect call 2 our selve's 2 look @ the man
> in the mirror and become the best u that u
> can be! =D

Jackie stares at the prayer with her jaw hanging.

This is the most fucked-up one yet. I want to go out and get a drink.

But she has to get up at a decent time tomorrow, for a trip to Etobicoke.

FIVE

"Spitting Is Always Bolder than Action!" reads the new slogan. Jackie makes a quick visit to Spitter before embarking on her epic subway and bus journey to the west borough of the city.

You've got me all wrong, Jackie. First of all, I wear a trilby, not a fedora. =P, writes the beagle. ***Seriously, you have nothing to worry about. Even if I *were* a creepy weirdo, you'd be the last person I'd want to stalk.***

She shakes her head. *Is there any need to lay it on so thick?*

What troubles me, @nagging_conscience_42's next post continues, ***is that you appear to see people in black and white terms. Everybody on the Internet is an idiot, or an asshole, or a creepy stalker, or an uncultured hick, or a decent person who likes your writing or agrees with your viewpoints. People are complex, Jackie. Even the most annoying of us have our own unique dreams and vulnerabilities and passions and [...]***

"Yeah, got no time for a lecture, dude," Jackie gripes out loud, closing the web browser. Sam Spade looks at her from the computer screen with those sad Bogie eyes.

"Wish me luck today, kid," she tells Sam before shutting the computer down.

"Isn't it beautiful?" Kathy McDougal says, beaming as she shows off her baby, *Kat's Korner*, on her bedroom desktop. "I love how the web gives people like me such *power*. Without my site, I wouldn't be able to reach so many people, every day, so *easily*, and change lives. Before, only the privileged–the male, the white, the conventionally attractive–only they could wield this kind of power in society." She grins like a mischievous kid. "This is a Golden Age!"

Jackie can see every exclamation point as if everything Kathy says calls up huge subtitles floating in the air in front of her. At one of Kathy's louder bellows, a black blur shoots like a bullet out of the room from under the bed. Jackie jumps in her seat, realizing only a moment later that the blur was a cat.

Jackie is sorely tempted to file Kathy under the classic Cat Lady trope, but she owns only two of the animals–Garfield, an orange Exotic Shorthair, and Robert Smith, a black Bombay. Her large Etobicoke high-rise apartment has the same cat-litter smell that Jackie has experienced in the pads of other feline owners. But it is not just *live* cats that dominate the atmosphere of the flat. Kathy herself–who looks to Jackie somewhat like Björk, if Björk had bigger eyes and never went to a gym–is wearing a blue T-shirt with a photographic image of two Siamese kittens playing with a yarn ball, and messes of cat hair cling to her black sweatpants. A printout of the late, great Grumpy Cat is taped to one of her bedroom walls for decoration, and even the main logo of KatsKorner.ca is book-ended by two amateurishly drawn cartoon cats. Jackie does not respond much to it all as she is more of a dog person. Except, these days, for beagles.

Kathy has been showing Jackie some of her website's proudest achievements. She scrolls through past *Kat's Korner* stories and stops on another headline. "This one, from two years ago!" she says, beaming. "Valeria Jensen–she's one of our most popular contributors–she found out about this incident at a grocery store in Calgary. A Sobeys, if I remember right. One of the managers was harassing the teenage girls *constantly*."

"I bet." Jackie winces. She has had a couple of bosses like that.

Kathy frowns. "Disgusting! Of course, most of the poor girls there wouldn't report it to the higher-ups because they knew the store was run by a classic Old Boys Club that wouldn't take them seriously. But one of them–she knew about *us*!" She grins with pride. "She sent an e-mail to Valeria, who's always looking for stories like this. Valeria had the girl film the manager with her phone secretly while he was saying some really inappropriate things with one of the cashiers. And *voilà*! We named and shamed the creep. Even posted the video–see? Right here. Wanna watch it?"

"No thanks. I get the gist."

"Within a week, the store fired him!" She beams as if bragging about curing AIDS. "There was no way the shitface could talk his way out of that one. Video doesn't lie. It's great to see justice and accountability in action! Isn't it?"

"It is." Jackie nods.

"Or how about this one?" Kathy navigates through the website stopping on another story. "We did a thing about a lawyer here in T.O. You've heard of Melissa Heinlein?"

"Sounds familiar."

"Awful, awful woman. Big, high-profile defence lawyer. Liked to post on Spitter a lot about 'due process' and 'presumption of innocence' and other archaic legalese crap. We gave her a hard time over that, but she couldn't get away with that racist post!"

"Oh–right." Jackie thinks she remembers the story, vaguely. "You guys broke that?"

"We sure did! Back in late 2014, the turd was going on about bad customer service she had when she went to pick up photo prints or something. She ended the post: 'I hate Blacks.'"

"Jesus. That's blunt."

"Yep. Oh, she *tried* to talk her way out of it! She kept telling other media that 'Blacks' was the name of the store—she even insisted the rep she dealt with was Asian—but do you think anybody believed her? No! They believed us!" Kathy grins. "Let's just say Melissa Heinlein's career stalled a bit after that. The things we can do, huh? The things we can do!"

Jackie keeps smiling, while trembling slightly. She cannot make up her mind whether Kathy McDougal is a heroine or a nutter. Maybe a bit of both.

Still... she cannot help envying Kathy. Jackie sees her almost as a mirror image, only a warped, curved one. Jackie will not admit it out loud, but she has had her own childish fantasies about playing Internet Vigilante—exposing the abusers, the corrupt, the regressive, the trolls, her weapon of choice being her own phone camera. If not in real life, at least in a movie. *Who wouldn't want to be a hero? These days, it's not that hard.*

Wait a minute. Blacks Photography? Wasn't that—

"In the medieval times," Kathy continues, "they used to drag troublemakers to the town square and lock them in the stocks! They'd stay in the stocks all day, and you could just go right up to them and throw food at their faces. Even rocks and stones! And everybody would walk by and yell at them, insult them, humiliate them." She pats the top of her computer monitor affectionately, like her first-born child having mastered a complex figure-skating move. "*This* is it. This is *our* stocks! And it's even better 'cause it's not always temporary. Sometimes they stay in the stocks forever!"

Slightly closer to nutter?

"And you do everything from here?" asks Jackie.

"What, *Kat's Korner*?"

"Yeah."

"Oh, of course not! It started out that way, but then the site got really popular, and I started getting advertisers and hiring other writers. Now we have a small office downtown."

"Uh-huh."

"But I still prefer to work from home most of the time! So convenient. Just me and the kitties! And nobody else. Not a big fan of people." Kathy reaches down to pet Garfield, who is rubbing himself against her desk leg. "Are we, Garfy? No, we aren't!"

"Anyway," says Jackie, clearing her throat, "let's talk about Paul Shoreditch."

Kathy goes silent.

"You were part of the mob at the funeral, right?"

Kathy nods slowly.

"I take it you knew Paul, then?"

Another nod.

"Garbage human," Kathy suddenly spurts.

"Sorry?"

"Garbage. Human. That's what he was. A smelly little tit." She sports an odd expression that somehow mixes amusement and raging fury. "And that's what we wanted the world to know. That's why we marched on the service. Our consciences wouldn't let us sit back and let him rest in peace, let anybody give him a fucking memorial service to *permit* him to do so."

Jackie coughs. "I see. Well. I've been doing some research, and while I see there's a lot of anger aimed at Paul's... *existence*, it seems... what I still don't understand is, *why*."

"Why?"

Kathy laughs.

"If you want to know *one* reason," Kathy says in a low, steady tone, "it's very simple. All you have to do is ask Fiona."

"Fiona who?"

"I never got her last name."

"But..."

"All I remember," says Kathy, through her teeth, "was the sight of her on the floor, half-passed-out. And the way that little shitbag *smacked* her... and squeezed his arms around her... and..."

Jackie almost stops breathing.

Oh my fucking God. I don't like where this is going.

"Right in my living room, over there. While a dozen other party guests were looking on. It was so sudden, and we were so shocked, we couldn't even react!"

"What..." Jackie swallows. "What are you saying?"

"She was only twenty-three, you know. A fucking *baby*! I barely knew her–one of my old friends from Vancouver, Megan, brought her along. Drank a little too much, and that little fuckface..."

She looks as if she's about to detonate, and Jackie trembles again.

"What did he *do*?"

She expects Kathy to start screaming like a demon based on her expression.

"You *know*, Jackie. You know exactly what he did."

Oh no.

"Are you *sure*?"

Kathy looks at her, stone-faced. "I know what I saw."

"And... others?"

"I could give you the names of other witnesses." A pause. "She was taken out of here by ambulance afterwards."

Oh Jesus. "That bad?"

"Her head smacked on the floor. There was blood on the carpet. I can show you the stain."

Jackie feels a deep, painful sinking inside her stomach. She wishes on her life that she had told Rick to stick this ridiculous assignment up his ass.

"Did you notify the police?" she asks. "Didn't *anybody*?"

"Oh, yeah–*I* did. And they investigated... for like two fucking *seconds*! And they dismissed it. Just like that." Kathy lets out a guffaw that sounds almost like a growl. "I knew I was wasting my time. Cops are useless in cases like this. So are trials. Everybody knows that!"

"Uh," Jackie stammers. "And this happened... when?"

"About six years ago." Kathy takes a breath to calm some of the suppressed rage out of her voice. "And I launched *Kat's Korner* about a year later. You could say he inspired it."

"Really?"

"Every man who's ever treated a woman like shit, every man who's ever used a woman and discarded her like a fucking sandwich wrapper, every man who can't see how lucky he is to be a man–*they're* the reason I started *Kat's Korner*. Paul's behaviour was just the final kick I needed."

There is a long silence. Garfield meows. Jackie scans her notes to see what she should ask next, but then a glance at her phone stops her. It is already quarter after eleven.

"Shit," she says.

"What is it?"

"I have to go."

"But we've barely started!"

Of course they have. Jackie arrived late because the TTC does not stop anywhere near Kathy's building, and they spent too much time chatting about Kathy and her website.

"I start work downtown at one," explains Jackie. "And I want to grab something for lunch before I get there."

"Why did you schedule this for now?"

"*You* did. Remember?"

An uncomfortable pause as Jackie wonders if Kathy is going to start an argument. But Kathy just laughs.

"Of *course* I did!" she says. "My bad. Sorry about that."

"No worries." Jackie starts gathering her things together.

"Guess I caught you at a bad time yesterday, huh?" Kathy picks up Garfield and lays him on her lap. She pets him with a bit of what Jackie perceives as a Don Corleone vibe. "Tell you what. I'll shoot you an e-mail tonight. We'll reschedule, or we'll even do the interview by e-mail. Cool?"

"Cool."

Kathy grins. "Thanks so much for dropping by!" She waves the cat's arm at Jackie. "Say bye bye, Garfy!" Then, in a squeaky voice, "*Bye bye Jackie!!*" Jackie notes Garfield struggling to break free of his owner's grasp.

She leaves Kathy's apartment in a daze. The sky seems to be threatening rain, but only a few drops are spitting down for now. She wishes it were a thunderstorm to match the current feeling in her stomach. When she reaches the bus stop after a fifteen-minute walk, she realizes she never turned the Olympus on to record any of the conversation with Kathy. *Fuck me. I'm a prize idiot.*

A tough day at the call centre. She cannot keep her full focus on the calls, making fewer sales than usual. And she does not care. How can she concentrate? She simmers with rage and confusion that she can barely hold back. Those images of Paul and the young woman on the floor, the smacking, the blood on the carpet, will not leave her head. When she forces it away, she can only see that goddamn web pic of the teenage Paul in her mind's eye.

Jackie's lifetime experience with sexual misconduct has been relatively limited. She has dealt with her share of obnoxious stares and handsy creeps but has never let it bother her much. She has never been raped or traumatized, although she has known women who were, and of course, she has received the occasional half-baked rape threat on the Internet. She likes to think nothing can trigger her about this subject. *Yes, I'm one of the lucky ones. I know.*

The more she thinks logically about Kathy's story, the less sense it makes.

And yet...

There is something about Paul Shoreditch and this Fiona person that makes her nauseous, even frightens her. There is something so ugly and alien about this strange man whom she still knows so little about, that the thought of him being a predator seems too perfect.

What do they say these days? Only two percent of allegations like this are false or mistaken, or is it eight now? One out of five women are assaulted before they leave college, or out of four? Twelve out of seven men admit to having groped a woman? I'm no expert on this stuff. Maybe I'm a little naïve. All I know is, they tell you to believe.

Always believe. If you don't, if you doubt anybody's claim, you're part of the problem yourself. That's what they say, anyway.

As she works, she hears an argument in her head between Brain and Gut. Brain has the voice of the middle-aged Gregory Peck. Gut has the voice of the young, virile Clark Gable.

Brain: Kathy McDougal is a bit of a loony.

Gut: Even a loony's got no reason to make up a story like this.

Brain: Why wouldn't she? People far more credible lie about all kinds of things, or at least jump to wrong conclusions. We're all human.

Gut: You're out of touch, old man. We're living in a new world. Too many victims have been disbelieved in the past. We've gotta correct that. Now.

Brain: Fair point. But we mustn't over-correct. Let's approach this with some reason.

Gut: No.

Brain: Yes.

Gut: No. Go stab yourself with a fork, Brain.

Brain: Get lost, Rhett Butthead.

Then Gut materializes as Gable in *It Happened One Night*. He gives Brain a middle finger and then slowly proceeds to take his own shirt off revealing his bare chest underneath, and even though she is not usually attracted to men, Jackie wants to run to him and make hot, steamy consensual love to him. Not because it would be more fun, but because it would be so much easier. And safer.

She arrives home that evening still in something of a daze and turns on the desktop out of habit. Bogie pops up on the background again. "Go to hell, Spade," she mumbles at the pic, wondering if it is time to replace it with Katharine Hepburn or Jane Fonda.

She heads to Spitter. Almost no notifications as she has not posted anything today. The beagle puppy's lecture, which remains partly unread, still dangles before her, awaiting a response.

Fuck off, she shoots back to @nagging_conscience_42.

She considers blocking him (or her? Them?), then decides that this person is not worth the gesture. Then she thinks about blocking every single male who follows her on social media, or at least replying ***fuck off*** to every single comment or reply from a man.

Fuck you, Paul Shoreditch. I want to hate you so much right now.

She tries to shake all these nasty thoughts out of her head. *No. No. Come on, Jackie. Stay objective. At least until you know for sure.*

She is not hungry even though she has not eaten since breakfast, having decided she had no appetite for lunch after all. She is thinking of calling Rick Pevere tomorrow and telling him she cannot do this stupid assignment anymore. *I'm not a real journalist, and neither are you, dude. We're just two thirty-something kids playing grownup.*

In the morning, messages await her.

First, Spitter.

Really? asks the beagle puppy. ***Really, Jackie? I gave you all that material to work with, and the best you can come up with for a comeback is "Fuck off." That's beneath you, Jackie. I expected better. You're smarter than that.***

She chortles.

I *am* smarter than that, she types. ***And in my great wisdom, I deemed that you were worth no deeper reply. So, from my superior brain to yours, I repeat: Fuck. Off.***

Then Jackie checks her posts on F**kPaulShoreditch.com. Still no replies.

And she has received an e-mail from Kathy McDougal. The subject heading is "Hey!"

Jackie does not click on it. She experiences the same nausea and simmering rage she felt yesterday during and after the interview. She steps away from the computer for a few minutes to collect herself. Then she picks up her phone and dials Rick without taking a moment to consider if he will be awake at this time on a Saturday morning.

He answers after six rings. She hears him yawn.

"Sorry, did I wake you up?"

"Nah. I was already up." He sounds as if he is chewing something.

She takes a moment to think about why she is calling. Then she stalls anyway.

"Rick? If I do a long-distance phone interview for the story, you can reimburse me, right?"

A pause. "Huh?"

"The *Indie Voice* can pay me back, right? If I do a long-distance interview?"

"Mmmm, for what?"

"For the story. The Paul Shoreditch story."

No answer.

"You know. The funeral riot. 'Society and that type of thing.'"

Another silence, and then Rick coughs. "Oh! Right. Of course. I forgot about that."

Moron. "So...?"

"Just bring me the phone bill or e-mail it to me or whatever. We'll figure it out."

"Good."

"And any other expenses. Reasonable ones, anyway."

Jackie almost smacks her forehead, suddenly remembering she threw away the Greyhound ticket to Cambridge. She does not know what she did with the receipt. "Thanks."

"That all?"

She hesitates. "To be honest, Rick, I'm having doubts."

"About what?"

"This... story. I don't think I can do it. It's going into some disturbing territory."

"Meaning?"

"I could be wrong. I... think he may have been a sexual predator. Paul Shoreditch."

"Seriously?" A sudden peak of interest in Rick's tone.

"That's what Kathy McDougal told me."

"Man."

"She says she saw him do something to a woman."

"Do what?"

Say it, Jackie, whispers Gut. But she cannot.

"And," adds Rick after a pause, "does she have any, like, evidence of this?"

"She says so."

"Not that it matters. I'm sure Kathy wouldn't lie about something like that."

Of course it matters! snaps Brain. *Due process matters! Don't be a fool.*

Clam it, Brain, says Gut.

Shut the fuck up, BOTH of you!

A weird silence, and then Rick says, "This could be interesting."

"What do you mean?"

"I mean, that kind of explains the whole thing, doesn't it? Like, maybe this was a big open secret among this online community. Another whisper campaign. The way so many people knew about Weinstein and Cosby and that, but it still wasn't public knowledge for years."

Jackie does not answer.

"I mean–think of it," says Rick. "You're Ronan Farrow."

She snorts. "Huh?"

"You've exposed a predator. This is a real news story. You're a real journalist now, Jackie!"

For fuck's sake. "No, I'm not, Rick. And I don't want to be. I'm just a movie critic, and maybe not a very good one. I don't have a clue what I'm doing here–and now, with this nasty little plot twist, I don't think I have the stamina to keep on going. That's why I'm calling you right now. That's what I'm trying to express."

"Bullshit, Jackie. You're awesome."

She rolls her eyes.

"Why do you think I picked you for this? You show so much talent and enthusiasm in your reviews that I wanted to see you doing something more challenging. You don't wanna waste your whole life getting twenty bucks a review, do you? I know you like doing it, but I feel bad because I know you can do so much more."

Jackie sighs. *Why is it always so much easier online? Why do the real-life debates and arguments never seem worth the trouble to win?*

"Speaking of money," she says, "we never got around to discussing how much you were going to pay me for all this."

"All what?"

"This. This Shoreditch thing. This whole ridiculous news piece I've been devoting so much of my free time to when I could be doing anything else."

Rick pauses, then laughs. "Of course. Sorry."

"Well?"

"Drop by the office whenever you get a moment. We'll talk."

"When works for you?"

"Just anytime. I'm almost always there."

"But—"

"I gotta go. Mom's got breakfast ready." He hangs up.

Jackie just stands there holding the phone. *Wasn't he already eating breakfast?*

Slowly, groggily, she makes her way back to her desk. This is one of the rare times when she has no desire to check anything on the Internet.

Let's get this over with.

She clicks on Kathy's e-mail.

> Hey Jackie! I'm so sorry we didn't get to chat longer this morning. =(I blame myself. We should have planed better. I thought I'd send you some background stuff about Paul which might help you and then, when you're ready, we can get together again for another chat or just do it over the phone.

> So I met Paul about 2013, I think, when we were both working at FunMart Drug Emporium which is

That's the second time you've typed "which" without a comma before it. She wonders how somebody with such careless spelling and punctuation manages to edit a popular news website, if *Kat's Korner* counts as a news website. Kathy must have a good proofreader on staff.

> Drug Emporium which is a big food and drug store in Scarborough. Again, this was before I launched Kat's Korner. I was a cashier, he was a full-time stock clerk. At the time, I had no idea what a Garbage Human he was! I just thought he was a shy and awkward guy. He didn't seem to have alot of friends or anything. To be honest, I just sort of felt sorry for him. He was kind of ugly and awkward, but also kind of articulate and smarter than he let on. I was like, howcome this guy is only a stock boy at a shitty drug store? He seems brighter than that. So I got to know him a little.
>
> We had this one thing in common. We both wanted to be musicians when we were younger. I wanted to play guitar, and he wanted to be a singer, but of course those were dumb pipe dreams. I never had the time to apply myself to the guitar. I could only do a few chords. And Paul, he was the worst singer you ever heard! XD He had no voice, no range, nothing! Anyway, we kind of bonded over that, at least as much as you could bond with somebody who had pretty much no social skills whatever.
>
> He told me he was a virgin. Can you believe that! He was the real 40 Year Old Virgin! =)

> I didn't know men that age could still be virgins in real life, I thought they used their privilege to get every bit of sex they could get by then. Well, I've always been a very generous person, generous to a fault. So I decided to give the guy his first time. I kind of regretted it though! =(It was soooo bad. The worst sex I ever had. He had no idea what the fuck he was doing! Of course, I should have expected that from a 40 Year Old Virgin and all that, but still. lol. He could barely even get his dick hard, and when he did [...]

What follows is a long, detailed, graphic and unpleasant description of Kathy's awkward first sexual encounter with Paul Shoreditch. Jackie scans down the lengthy paragraph, looking for the spot where the story ends, catching bits of way more than she wanted to know along the way. Something about Kathy's writing style gives her a stab of *déjà vu*, but she ignores it as she keeps scrolling.

> [...] even a teenage boy can figure out how to make a girl come without too much trouble. Come on! Anyway, I made sure to tell him we weren't boyfriend and girlfriend or anything, we were not a couple. We were just fuck buddies, friends with benefits, that sort of thing. I told him if he wanted to go and fuck any other women, he could, I wouldn't mind, I wouldn't be offended. Not that I expected him to! I wasn't *that* stupid. I just wanted to make sure the little freak didn't have a crush on me or anything, he wasnt going to go jump in a lake or something when I told him the truth. But he was OK with it. I said I would still fuck other guys, and he was OK with it.
>
> And now I'm so ashamed and embarrassed

about it all. What a terrible mistake! =(The biggest mistake of all was when I invited the crepe to my birthday party and he attacked that poor girl. Weird how his libido suddenly took off like a rocket at that point. I didn't think he had that in him, to be honest. When I told him to fuck other women, that was certainly not what I had in mind. But I guess you can't really communicate with a sociopath.

I don't know how to get in touch with Fiona. I don't know her at all. Even my friend Megan who brought her, we had a bit of a falling out, and she's blocked me on all the social media =(I could give you her name, but even if you track her down, she won't want to help you if she knows I passed her name on. Sorry. Maybe try my friend in Brampton Vanessa Darby, shes at (905) 555-0499 or vanessa.d@flymail.com But, feel free to quote any of this info in your story. Call me if you want more. I showed you my site. Dishing the dirt is almost a career to me now, and also a full-time hobby. I can give you idiocies and weirdness about that pathetic little man that will make your brain melt!

Lots of love,
Kathy
(Garfy says bye bye, so does Robert Smith =)

Jackie cannot help wondering if she is missing something stupidly obvious about the e-mail but decides she has had enough idiocies and weirdness for the past day and a half. She has not been out to a movie in more than a week, and she needs an escape badly. She checks the online listings. *Singin' in the Rain* at the Fox, at two o'clock? Good enough for her.

SIX

A bright orange room with erotic paintings all over the walls. Paul Shoreditch is in the centre, singing and tap-dancing. Jackie has never seen a photo of him as an adult, yet she knows it is him; the same mousy face, the same stupid, blank near-smile. But Paul is wearing a white jumpsuit with a large beige cricket codpiece on the outside of the trousers with suspenders, a black bowler hat, and a long black cane in his hand. There is a large black eyelash on his right eye. He is tap-dancing while singing "Singin' in the Rain" and leering at her lasciviously. Of course. Alex in *A Clockwork Orange*. The only Kubrick film she could not watch a second time.

He keeps dancing and singing and moves a step closer to her. And the dancing seems to go a little faster, and the singing quickens too and raises in pitch like a three-dimensional hologram recording being jacked up to a higher speed. And he moves a step closer and then the dancing is even faster, and he is closer, and now the dancing is so fast that he is just a blur in an uncontrollable frenzy, and he moves closer again, and she is on the verge of screaming—

She opens her eyes. Back in her room again, staring at the ceiling.

Fucking Christ. Why can't I dream about Mary Poppins for once?

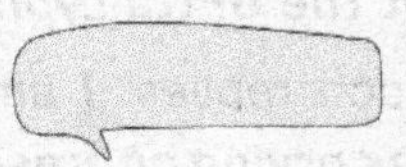

Sunday afternoon. Jackie sits at her computer, scrolling through Spitter while waiting for Chuck McMahon to call. She is prepared: her cell phone sits right on her desk to the left of the keyboard, with the Olympus and her notebook right beside it. No nonsense this time.

She tried to go through F**kPaulShoreditch.com again this morning but did not have the stomach to search for what she really wanted to find, although she suspected it was there somewhere. She half-heartedly skimmed over the usual headings–**"what a freak"** ... **"Did that creepy little shithead NEVER shower???"** ... **"I saw him at the karaoke the other night, man it was like hearin a bear cub being tortured"**–and then decided she was done with this part of the job for the day.

"Spit Happens!" reads the slogan at the top of the Spitter page. To Jackie's disappointment, the conversation with @nagging_conscience_42 has continued:

I was just rereading a couple of your old blog essays, the beagle puppy has written. ***The one about "Bicycle Thieves" and the one about "The 400 Blows." Very well done. I've never seen either of these movies, but you've made me eager to look them up.*** All this reply is doing so far is make Jackie sickly eager to write about movies again. ***But what I really find interesting is the contradiction between your tone in these essays and your tone on Spitter and in your website's comments sections. When you write about films, you express a lot of compassion, which seems genuine. You appear to have a sincere empathy for the underdogs and the misunderstood. And it makes me wonder: What if Antonio Ricci replied to your "Bicycle Thieves" essay and said you'd missed the point of the whole movie? What if Antoine Doinel commented that your praise of Truffaut's "phallic imagery" was utter bullshit? How would you respond? Would you tell them to fuck off too?***

Jackie responds: ***Are you a professional psychologist, buddy? I don't think I can give any credence to your speculations about my motives until I see a degree on your office wall. Until then, please invest in some training at the Getta Lyphe Institute.***

To which the puppy soon replies: ***I am no psychologist, and I didn't mean to come off as prying or presumptuous. Sorry if that's your impression. Although I do find it fascinating that, once again, you won't give a direct answer to my question. You just go on the offensive and toss out a smart-ass, hackneyed comeback. What are you hiding, Jackie? What are you afraid of?***

The nerve, Jackie thinks as she rereads the last response. If she was afraid of anything this person had to say, she would have blocked him (her? them? it?) by now. If she had anything to hide, she would never have signed up for a Spitter account. She wants this bullshit conversation to end, but there is no way she is letting this person get the last word.

She mulls over the last response, trying to think of the right way to answer, when the *Midnight Cowboy* theme bursts from the phone. "Fuck!" she yelps, then answers the cell and puts it on speakerphone. "Hello?" she says as she flicks on the Olympus.

"Sorry I'm late. Had to do some stuff." Chuck McMahon's voice is deep, rough yet resonant, with a laid-back vibe. It could be a radio announcer's voice if it were not so casual and urban-accented. It also sounds familiar.

"Anyway," she says after the standard polite introductions are out of the way, looking over her scribbled notes, "you knew Paul Shoreditch."

"Yeah. A *long* time ago. The Croucher."

"You were a friend?"

A mild chuckle. "I guess so. As much as you could be, with Paul."

"And you came to his funeral?"

"What there *was* of it, yeah."

"And..." A voice in her head–Gut's voice, full of all that Gable smartassery–nags her to leap right to the point. "Did he ever abuse women?"

"Uh," he says, taken aback, "not that I know of. But, like, I haven't seen him since we were kids. In the '80s." Another short pause. "I couldn't tell if he even had the slightest *interest* in girls, never mind abusing them. Why would you ask *that*?"

"No reason."

An awkward pause. "Anyways," Chuck goes on, "I ran across a small obituary in the *Star*, just by accident, and felt it would be good to be there. At the funeral. It was weird seeing that in the paper 'cause I hadn't thought about the guy in, like, thirty years." Another pause. "I've hardly thought about *anybody* in school since the music career took off."

Jackie feels as if she has just been smacked across the mouth with an iron pan. Now she remembers where she has heard this voice. "Holy shit," she says.

"What?"

"Excuse the language," she adds, as if it matters, "but you're Angry Chuck M."

He laughs. "Of course. Didn't you know?"

"I do now." *Why didn't Rick mention it?*

Jackie was never a fan. She never got into hip-hop music, and she remembers getting really sick of hearing Angry Chuck M music blaring here and there at her high school. Thankfully for her sanity, it did not last long. His career had a brief peak in the late 1990s and early 2000s, when he reigned as the nation's top Caucasian rapper, while the critics and much of the music scene dismissed him as an inferior Eminem clone with a laughably fake Ebonics accent and even faker street cred. He had a few charted hits in Canada (among them "Mack Dat Slut", "Party Party Party Party Party" and "Punk, I'mma Kick You in da Head, Yo") before he quickly faded into obscurity.

"And what are you doing these days?" Jackie asks out of the mildest curiosity.

"Ever been to McMahon's, by the Lakeshore?"

"Heard of it. Sports bar, right?"

"I own it. Bought it when it was still the Freak & Firken. Got rid of all the Anglophile crap and installed a shitload of TV screens. Blue

Jays, Leafs, Raptors, Argos, the Olympics, even curling—we screen 'em all. Drake stops by once in a while. You ought to drop in sometime."

"I'll keep it in mind." *Yeah, right.*

"Also," he adds with a self-deprecating laugh, "I gained back all my childhood weight. More than that, even. That's why fans don't recognize me anymore. If I still have any."

Jackie chuckles to be polite. "Back to Paul. You first met him in school?"

"Softball. He was on my team in Mississauga. I think it was the end of grade... six?"

"So you played too."

"Me and my friends, we all did." He laughs again. "My friends bullied him a lot. And I'm sure it continued after I moved away."

Jackie wishes he would not talk about Paul being bullied. The last thing she wants right now is to feel sorry for the little creep. Assuming he *was* a creep.

"So boys bullied him," she says. "What about the girls? Did *he* bully *them* instead?"

"Actually, I think he was bullied by some girls, too."

Shit. Why does she feel disappointed?

Jackie closes her notepad. "How about just telling me about Paul in general? What was he like? How did you interact with him? That sort of thing."

"Like, the whole story? Or just—"

"Why not. I've got time." Jackie leans back in her chair and relaxes, daydreaming she is interviewing Michael Haneke or Barry Jenkins instead.

Years before he became Angry Chuck M, Chuck McMahon was known as "Beef". A childhood habit of Hostess potato chips, Oreos and

Pepsi had resulted in a bigger girth than the other kids had, and they had bullied him in grade school, calling him a "cow" and "Bessie". But after he demonstrated some fair athletic ability despite his weight, some of the bullies made friends with him, and his nickname evolved into the catchier "Beef". He started playing in the local softball league when he was eight and soon became friends with some of the league's stars: Russ Fullerton, Bobby Skatz, Chris Allen, Brent Hahn, Rick Emmett. As far as Mississauga little-league softball went, this was the A-list. It was not merely that they were good at sports; they were from more affluent families.

"It was the '80s," the artist formerly known as Beef tells Jackie now. "Greed was good, remember. And a lot of the kids I knew–the white ones, anyways–had fathers who worked on Bay Street as executives or whatever, and they lived with their families in the 'burbs while they commuted to the office every day downtown. Some of them were even vice presidents." He clears his throat. "I was the only one of the group who came from a working-class family. My dad worked in an auto factory in Brampton. The kids were rough on me at first, until they found how much I knew about sports and music and movies and stuff."

These boys all batted above .350 on the first softball team in which Beef met them–a team sponsored by the Erindale Lions Club–but Russ was the real star. He was a great hitter, but as a *pitcher*, he was a machine. With a right arm that spun like a propeller, Russ Fullerton could whip a perfectly aimed fastball past anybody making even his heavy-hitting buddies feel like idiots during practice sessions. People knew when they were hearing Russ Fullerton pitching, even when their eyes were off the field, because every softball pounded the catcher's mitt with a unique, loud, dusty *thud* that sounded like somebody pounding a sack of flour with a sledgehammer. Even baseball pitchers who threw overhand were impressed when they saw Russ's power and technique. Everybody in Mississauga softball was convinced he was going to be the next Dave Stieb.

The 1985 season put Beef on the little-league team sponsored by PayLess Food Palace, along with his buddies Russ and Bobby Skatz. They shared the same team with a short, skinny little boy with a flat nose, big ears, a horrible overbite, a conspicuous pair of snaggleteeth and dark, oily, messy hair that always seemed to be sprinkled liberally with dandruff.

"Shit. I've seen that kid before," Bobby said quietly to Russ and Beef when they arrived for their first practice day in May. Bobby was a short, dark-haired boy with a face full of freckles and a mean little smile. He pointed to one of the benches as Russ was practising his swing with three wooden bats at once, and Beef was sipping a cup of Kool-Aid from the coach's cooler.

"Which kid?" asked Beef.

"The Croucher." The boy in question was sitting by himself on the bench, hands loosely flopped onto his lap, staring out at the softball field with a blank face.

"What about him?" asked Beef.

"I hear he's, like, the biggest dork in the whole league. When he was little, he tried to beat up all the kids in his school. Nobody knew why. Then he stopped because he was a wimp who couldn't beat anybody up. Now he's just a big loser who *gets* beat up."

"We should beat him up," said Russ, taking another swing. "With these bats."

Bobby laughed. "Yeah. We should."

"Why's he called the Croucher?" asked Beef.

Bobby explained the Croucher's weird batting strategy. Then he laughed and pointed at Russ. "I bet even *you* couldn't strike him out."

"Bet I could," replied Russ, taking another swing.

"No way. He shrinks that strike zone down to nothing. It's not enough to throw fast."

"Fuck off. I can strike out anybody. Even that little dweeb."

"Bet you can't, asshole."

"Can too, shithead. Three straight pitches."

"Oh yeah? Let's find out."

Bobby strolled over to the kid on the bench, who was still staring at the other players tossing and catching on the field. Bobby did not notice the boy's smell until he was standing over him; it was not unusual for jock kids to smell a bit after some hard work on the field, but this kid had just been sitting on a bench and still reeked as if he had not bathed in a month. The sprinkles of dandruff in the boy's pillow-head hair also became visible to Bobby.

"Yo. Croucher," he said.

The kid continued staring, as if he had not heard.

"Hey!" Bobby grabbed the boy's shoulder and shook. "I'm talkin' to you, buddy."

The kid turned his head slowly to Bobby.

"Why're you looking at the other guys like that? You a fag or something?"

The boy on the bench shrugged.

"You don't even know?"

The boy paused, then said in a very soft voice: "My mom tells me I am, sometimes."

Bobby laughed. "I guess you are, then."

"But I don't know what a fag is."

"A gaylord. You a gaylord, Croucher?"

"I don't know."

Bobby laughed again. "Yeah. I bet you are."

The boy shrugged again.

"Anyways. Me and my buddy Russ over there, we got a bet. He thinks he can strike you out on only three pitches. I say you can get a walk by doing your crouching thing. Wanna show us?"

He shrugged yet again. Bobby handed him an aluminum bat, and the boy took it and stood up.

"Don't let me down, pal," said Bobby. "Make me look good."

The boy gave him a strange look. "Are... are you my *pal*?" he said, his voice cracking.

Bobby guffawed. "Are you fuckin' kidding?" He went back up to Russ and Beef. "We're gonna do it," he told Russ as he picked up his catcher's mitt. "And we're gonna make him look like the biggest asshole in the league, if he isn't already. He's already a prime candidate for Fag of the Year."

"Not sure if you're old enough to remember," Chuck now tells Jackie as if he senses silent shock from her, "but back then, boys used to call other boys they didn't like 'fag' and 'gay' and 'gaylord' all the time. It didn't necessarily mean homosexual. Sometimes, it was just the same as saying 'sissy' or 'asshole' or 'dickhead'. Although," he adds with a short laugh, "if they found out you really *were* gay, that only put you deeper in the shit."

The rest of the PayLess team stood by the field and watched. Russ took his place on the rubber slab in the pitcher's circle as Bobby got into position behind the plate, not bothering with a catcher's mask. The coach put on a mask and got behind Bobby as a temp umpire. The infamous Croucher stepped up to the plate slowly, shyly, wearing an oversized batting helmet that looked as if it might fall off any second. He raised the aluminum bat just an inch above his right shoulder as he bent down, *way* down, shrinking the strike zone down to next to nothing. The handful of people on the team who had never seen this act before, including Beef, laughed or scoffed.

"Strike him out!" cried one kid.

"Come on, Croucher!" shouted another. "Show Fullerton up!"

Russ Fullerton was a tall and thin, yet muscular young man with a long, goofy face that always seemed to be on the verge of snickering. Perhaps that comical face was what confused the Croucher, who smiled, perhaps wondering if the pitcher was going to be his pal too. Nonetheless, there was no way the crouching batter could have been ready for the bullet that whipped right by his elbows, smacking Bobby's mitt with a loud *thud*.

"Streeeeeeeeeek!" called the coach, and everyone laughed, including Beef.

The batter blinked as Bobby tossed the ball back to Russ. In seconds, the pitcher's arm whipped around again like a windmill set to Warp Nine, and the speed and force of the ball was so strong that the Croucher lost his balance and fell over backwards. Everyone laughed even harder.

"What a dorkwad! Can't even stand up straight," one player shouted.

"Finish 'im off," called another.

Bobby made the time-out sign, and he got up and approached the pitcher's spot as the batter picked himself up again. Beef watched as Bobby and Russ conferred privately for about ten seconds, wondering why Bobby was going to the trouble of discussing strategy with the pitcher outside of a real game, especially when Russ was betting against him–and winning. Whatever they were discussing, it made Russ giggle, and Bobby nodded and hurried back behind the plate with a weird grin.

Beef quickly found out why. So did everybody else. The last one to figure it out was the Croucher himself as he was lying on the ground, holding the left side of his head above his ear and grimacing in pain. His helmet had fallen off right after Russ' pitch had smacked into it.

The coach stood up straight, walked over to the batter's writhing form on the ground, looked down at him and said in a blunt voice, "Ball one."

Young Paul Shoreditch heard the laughter assaulting him from all sides. His face contorted, and the tears began tumbling down his face, and his mouth let out an infantile wail that was almost loud enough to drown out the boys' laughter. And the boys, as if they were in a competition, raised their laughter volume up a few notches.

"Crybaby!" shouted Bobby.

"What a little suck," another boy snickered.

"He's a sucky baby! Sucky baby!" chanted another.

And Paul cried all the more, and the boys laughed all the more, and all of them–except for Beef, who stood to the side and watched the show with mixed feelings–took turns coming up to him and applying a swift kick in his groin or the stomach. Even the coach did nothing to stop it. The softball practice was virtually abandoned at this point, and this kicking game went on until Lydia Shoreditch arrived to pick up Paul.

"Shit, let's get outta here," hissed Bobby to the others when he saw Mrs. Shoreditch arriving at the park. "I hear his mom's a real psycho."

And they ran away from the softball field, under the impression that the boy's mother would object to their treatment. But the elder

Shoreditch approached her crying, wounded son, glaring down at him with a mix of judgement, shame and bitter amusement, and croaked, "The hell's the matter with you? Couldn't even fight 'em back? They have *bats* here, stupid."

His mom's lesson made no difference at this point. Paul had lost whatever little shred of respect he might have had from the PayLess team and eventually, the whole Mississauga little-league softball community. He had graduated to a new nickname: Sucky Baby.

"I like to think I'm a compassionate guy," Chuck tells Jackie on the phone. She cannot tell whether he is bragging or just stating an opinion. "Yeah, some of my rap songs were pretty mean and nasty, back in the day, but that was what the kids were buying at the time. And growing up among all these privileged little assholes teaches you how to be hard when you need to be, and I used that when I was writing songs and stuff. But when I saw these kids wailing on the Croucher like that, something in me kind of froze. I couldn't make myself join in. Only a few years before, they'd been going after me the same way for being fat."

But conscience does not always bring action, so Beef stood by and watched every time the rest of the team laughed at Paul and called him Sucky Baby. They laughed whenever he played left field–*deep* left field–and, when pop flies came his way, he would panic and cover his face with his arms as if shielding himself from a pint-sized nuclear missile. They laughed and hurled verbal abuse when the crouching strategy did not work because the pitcher was too good. They laughed hardest when the crouching *did* work and he got to first base. Even when the bases were loaded and Paul drove in a run that way, it was all a joke to the boys. Paul Shoreditch was their Designated Clown.

There was a hot June evening when they were playing the Pizza Paradise-sponsored team. By the fifth inning (out of seven), PayLess was creaming Pizza Paradise sixteen to two, but both teams were so hot and sweaty that they wanted the game to end soon. None of the players were putting much effort into the game anymore except for Russ, who never relaxed his fiery, machine-like delivery. Even the parents watching the game, who were normally loud with cheers and chatter, looked indifferent.

Beef, playing shortstop that inning, assumed it was the heat mixed with carelessness when he saw Bobby drop the ball behind the plate. There was no runner on first waiting to steal, but Bobby still appeared distracted. He was staring in Beef's direction so intensely that Beef wondered if he had missed an important signal. Bobby called for a time-out, whipped off his catcher's mask and jogged up to Russ, still staring oddly in Beef's direction. With a grimace, Bobby whispered something to Russ and pointed past Beef.

Beef turned to look. There was Paul, in deep left field, with his usual dumbstruck expression. Beef turned back to the pitching circle where Russ was looking at Paul as Bobby giggled with a sneer. Russ turned back to Bobby and shrugged. Bobby pointed again, more urgently.

"Look!" Beef thought he heard him say in a hushed voice. "He's doin' it again!"

Russ looked again, shrugged, and said something to Bobby, who nodded and then headed back behind the plate, after which the game continued.

Two strikeouts later, it was PayLess' turn to bat. It was typical for the boys to sit on the bench in the batting order, with the one going after the on-deck player at the end nearest to the plate. But Bobby did not sit in his assigned place. He strolled behind the players, past Beef, past Russ, and stopped behind Paul, hands on hips, staring down at his dandruff-sprinkled PayLess cap.

"Yo. Sucky Baby," he said.

After a pause, Paul slowly turned his head to look at Bobby as if he had just remembered his new moniker.

"Tell me something," said Bobby. "Why do you jack off in the field?"

The other boys, including Beef, looked at Bobby and Paul. Some of them giggled; some looked confused. Paul looked the most confused.

"I asked you a question, Suck. Why do you jerk off when you're on the field?"

Paul shrugged. "What is that?"

"You know. You feel yourself up."

"I don't understand."

"Yes, you fuckin' do. You play with your wiener. I saw you. You rub yourself on your uniform pants where your dick is. Why?"

The boys giggled again. Paul just shrugged. "I didn't," he said.

"Yes you did, and you know it."

"For the record," Chuck tells Jackie, "I never saw Paul do anything like that. That doesn't mean Bobby was lying, although I know he'd spread mean gossip about kids he didn't like sometimes. But I never saw it, and as far as I know, nobody but Bobby ever did."

Huh. Guess he started early. Being a perv, that is. Jackie makes a note of it as Chuck continues.

"Well?" added Bobby, lifting his cap and wiping sweat off his forehead. "Why do you do it?"

Paul shook his head, his expression blank.

"I don't think he did," said Russ.

The others stopped giggling and looked at Russ.

"Huh?" said Bobby.

"I think he was just scratching himself," said Russ, his goofy face strangely straight this time. "Yeah. He was itchy on his balls, so he scratched them." He coughed. "That's what it looked like to me. Still pretty fuckin' gross, but not the same as jacking off."

The others laughed again, with less enthusiasm.

Beef watched Bobby stroll around the bench and position himself in front of Paul, who was staring at the grass beside his inquisitor's feet.

"First you're staring at the boys on the field from the bench," said Bobby in a low, controlled voice, "and now you're yankin' it in the middle of a game. You a fag?"

"No," Paul said, his voice cracking a bit.

"You better not be. 'Cause there's no room for fags on this team."

"I'm not."

"Well, just to make sure..."

Bobby whipped his fist into Paul's testicles.

Paul yelped and fell onto the ground in a foetal scrunch, bawling himself silly.

"That should keep you from getting your rocks off for a while," said Bobby.

All the boys laughed, except for Beef. Some of them clapped too.

"Sucky Baby's crying again!" shouted one.

"Bobby!" called the coach. "Stop screwing around. You're on deck."

Bobby went to grab an aluminum bat. He started towards the on-deck circle then stopped, turned, and marched back to the bench. He stood over Paul's body, still whimpering on the ground, and raised the bat as if he were about to smash Paul's head like a sledgehammer on a rotten watermelon.

"*No!*" screamed Paul in a piercing falsetto. "*Please!*"

The screams were so loud that everybody stopped–on the field, on the spectator benches–and gazed at the scene.

Bobby held the bat in position for a few seconds. Then he smiled and brought it down gently towards Paul's crotch.

"Remember," he said, "keep your hands away from there. This bat hits balls."

Again, everybody on the PayLess batter's bench except Beef laughed. So did some of the other players and spectators on and off the field, although they had no idea what the joke was. "No! Please!" a few of the boys shrieked, mimicking Paul.

Bobby went to the on-deck circle and practised his batting stance as if nothing had happened.

Beef was supposed to hang out with Bobby and Russ the following Saturday. They had planned to see *The Goonies* for the second time and then hang out at a nearby arcade until it closed. But he got a bad cold and had to stay home for a few days. He did not see his friends until he joined them before school on Tuesday morning. They were laughing near the back entrance.

"You missed the fun," said Bobby, locking his BMX on the bike rack.

"Good times at the arcade?"

"We didn't go," said Russ. "It was so nice out when we left the theatre, we just didn't feel like it. Guess what we did instead."

"What?"

Russ and Bobby looked at each other and then laughed again.

"What?" said Beef, starting to laugh too.

"We went to Sucky Baby's house," snorted Russ, "and called on him."

"Seriously?"

"Shit, I never saw a front lawn like that before," Russ added. "I was scared of stepping on it by accident. It couldn't of been real."

"So we go up and ring the doorbell," said Bobby, "and his mom answers. It's, like, four in the afternoon, and she's still in her robe, and her hair's all in curlers and shit. She's got a cigarette dangling from her lips and she's got this mean look, like she always does. And then Russ..." Bobby struggled to control his laughter. "Russ looks right at her with this sweet face and he puts on this whiny, kiddie voice and goes, 'Can Paul come out to play?'"

Bobby and Russ laughed so hard, they were almost crying. Beef affected a smile.

"And then what?"

"So she glares at us and says, 'What the hell?' And I go, 'We're his friends. We want him to come out and play.' And she's all surprised and goes, 'My boy has *friends*?'"

"She says he's not home, he's out shopping," said Russ. "And she slams the door in our faces. Doesn't even say goodbye. So then Bobby had the idea to wait for him. So we went around to the side of the house and waited. We saw him come home with this big cart packed with full, brown paper grocery bags. And we're like, 'Does he do *all* the shopping for this family?'"

"We stay hidden until he goes inside with all the groceries," Bobby continued. "And we heard some yelling inside the house. Then the back door opens, and we sneak around to the side. So he comes out, and he gets the lawnmower and starts mowing the backyard. And we get bored and shit, and we're about to take off, but then he brings the mower close to where we are, and it's louder, but we hear something that doesn't sound right. So we peek again. And he looks like he's talking to himself."

Bobby and Russ fell into snickering fits again. Beef gestured for them to go on.

"That's what we thought," said Russ, catching his breath. "We couldn't hear what was coming out of his mouth over the mower. But then he, like, turns the mower off for a second, and then we can hear it better. And..." He burst into laughter.

"What?"

"The little gaylord was *singing*!"

"All to himself!" said Bobby. "And that's not the best part. You know what he was singing? That really old song–'Girls Just Want to Have Fun'!"

Russ and Bobby succumbed to wild laughing attacks as if a person singing were the insurmountable peak of absurdity. Beef nodded and laughed too, for good measure.

"We were gonna surprise him," said Russ. "We were whispering and trying to decide what we were gonna say, but his mom beat us to it."

"His mom?"

"We saw something hit the back of his head, and he turns around, and his mom's there behind him. Still with the curlers and everything. And she's like, 'Stop that goddamn singing! The neighbours are gonna think you're a goddamn flit!' It was *way* funnier than anything *we* could've done."

"Stop that! Stop that! You're not going to do a song while *I'm* here," Jackie says in an atrocious Yorkshire accent, then chuckles.

"What?" says Chuck.

"You know. The King of Swamp Castle. *Holy Grail.*"

"I... don't understand."

"Never mind. Go on." Jackie cringes. Even she should have known better than to expect Angry Chuck M to get a Monty Python quote.

The laughter did not end when the bell rang. Bobby and Russ referenced the incident throughout the school day. In science class, they kept singing to each other in a Cyndi Lauper voice during a lab exercise until the teacher gave them a stern look. Outside during the lunch hour, they re-enacted Paul mowing the grass and singing and his mother throwing stones and sticks at him. In French class, the pair performed a skit in which Russ played "Monsieur de Suckybébé" and Bobby played "La mère fachée de Suckybébé". Even the teacher found it mildly amusing.

Beef laughed too, but only for show. This was Bobby and Russ's joke, not his.

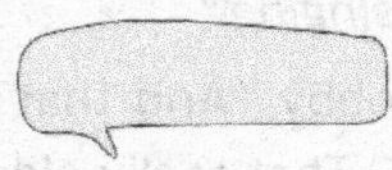

The next Thursday evening brought another softball game, and Beef found himself just ahead of Paul in the batting order. The coach had moved him way down the order due to a slump; Russ and Bobby had been performing as well as usual.

Sitting next to Paul on the bench, Beef finally understood what the other boys were talking about when they mentioned how he reeked. It was not just the body odour, but also the cigarette stink. Possibly from being shut up with a chain-smoking mother most of the time and not having the sense to shower on a regular basis.

"Hey. Sucky Baby," said Beef, elbowing Paul on the arm. "You smell like you've been rolling around in a mound of cigarette ashes. You smoke?"

Paul, who was staring down at the ground, paused as if he had not felt Beef's elbow, then looked up at him, puzzled.

"I said, do you smoke?"

Paul shook his head.

"Then why the hell do you smell like that?"

Paul pursed his lip and shrugged. Then he stared at the ground again. Beef decided he was not going to get much of a conversation out of the guy, so he turned his attention back to the game. "Go Brandon!" he hollered at the batter. "Knock it outta the park!"

He ignored Paul for a few more innings. It was during the bottom of the sixth–when Russ, Bobby and the leadoff boy had the bases loaded and the team slugger was up to bat, and the Grocery Haven team was beating PayLess by three, and everybody's attention was fixated on the game, and the air was thick with claps and chants–when Beef thought he heard music somewhere.

Somewhere turned out to be inches to his right. Beef turned to see Paul, sitting slouched, hands on his lap, staring out into nothingness, caught up in his own world. He was not singing to anybody or for anybody, but just for himself, in a weak, pathetic, reedy voice that could not sustain a note for a second. Beef recognized the song as UB40's "Red Red Wine", but Paul was messing up the lyrics, turning the song into a bizarre mondegreen salad. He sang about how red wine was the only thing that could make him boogie and then went on about a blue, blue harp.

"Hey!" said Beef. "Sucky Baby. What the fuck are you doing?"

Paul continued without a hint of a reaction.

"Hey! Wake up, retard. Why the hell are you singing?"

"Is he *singing*?" one of the boys further up the bench said.

"Sucky Baby sings?" another one said.

"Shut up," Beef snapped at the others. He turned back to Paul, who had stopped singing and was looking at Beef. There was no embarrassment or anger in Paul's face.

"Stop that shit," said Beef. "That's a crappy song, and you're singing the words wrong."

Paul blinked, then turned his attention back to the field. Beef heard the crack of a bat and turned in time to see a softball shoot deep into centre field, past the glove of the fielder. All of the parents and other players were on their feet cheering.

"And you're making me miss the game, dumbass," added Beef. "Thanks a lot."

"You're welcome," mumbled Paul.

Beef looked at Paul, who was staring out into the field without a trace of irony in his face.

And Beef laughed. He couldn't help it.

"You're all right, buddy," he said. "You're all right."

PayLess beat Grocery Haven, seven to six, and all the boys on Beef's team were high-fiving each other and saying things like "Way to go!" and "Great game!" Beef smiled and accepted every high-five and compliment that came his way. As the teams packed up their equipment, Bobby and Russ approached Beef.

"Yo," said Bobby, "Russ's dad is taking us out to Pizza Paradise."

Russ pointed in the direction of the nearest street. "We're parked over there. Let's go."

Beef thought for a moment.

"It's okay, guys," he said. "I'm not really that hungry."

Russ and Bobby each did a double-take.

"Are you *sure*?" asked Russ, goggling.

"Yeah," replied Beef. "I ate before the game. Plus, I'm kinda tired, what with the game being so crazy. Think I'm just gonna head home. Tell your dad thanks, though."

"Jesus," said Bobby. "Call the fuckin' *Toronto Star*. Call *CBC News*. Beef McMahon turns down free pizza! What's next, nu-kyu-ler war?"

They heard Russ' father blast the car horn, and Russ said, "Okay, see you at school." And they grabbed their equipment and headed off.

Beef picked up his glove as he gazed down the path through the park. He saw Paul Shoreditch strolling along the path, his own ratty glove dangling from his right hand. He had a strange, bouncy walk, Beef noticed. Like skipping, but without the joy.

Beef jogged down the path to catch up to Paul. It was in the wrong direction to Beef's house, but an odd hook of curiosity pulled him that way. When he started getting closer, he slowed down. Because he heard it again: that weak little voice that sounded like an animal being tortured while scratching a chalkboard with its claws. Again, the singing was not addressed to anybody, and it was out of step with the rhythm of Paul's bouncy walking. The song was "Relax" by Frankie Goes to Hollywood, and Paul was singing the filthiest part at that moment.

Jackie laughs.

"What is it?" Chuck asks.

"Oh–nothing. Just wondering why nobody ever thought to ask for requests."

"Requests?"

"You know... 'Hey kid, how about an old Satchmo standard? Or a Mozart aria?' I'd even have settled for 'Freebird.'"

Chuck clears his throat. "Did you ever hear the guy sing? I don't think it was something anybody wanted to encourage."

He goes on as Jackie thinks, *Jeez, tough crowd. And he thinks Paul was immune to irony?*

"Hey! Sucky Baby!" Beef called, running to catch up to him.

Paul froze in place like a stunned animal and stared forward.

"It's just me," said Beef, behind him.

Paul turned around and looked at Beef. His expression changed from mild fear to mild suspicion. "W-what do you want?" he said.

"Why are you singing?"

Paul looked ahead again and shrugged. He began walking, and Beef caught up beside him.

"And why *that* song?" pursued Beef.

Paul thought for a second. "I don't know. I used to hear it on my mom's radio sometimes, when she was out. I just felt like singing it."

"You really shouldn't sing that song. It's *so old* now, for one. It's, like, more than a year old! Nobody listens to it anymore. But also–it's by that gay band from England. Bronson Beat or something. They're all gay lovers, and it's a song about doing gay stuff." He snickered. "No wonder people think you're a faggot."

"Sorry," murmured Paul.

"Well, don't be *sorry* about it." Beef laughed. "You're not hurting anybody but you."

They were silent for a moment.

"Your mom didn't pick you up this time?" asked Beef.

Paul shook his head. "She said her and my dad were going out to play Bingo tonight." He paused. "I hope she wins. When she loses, she yells at my dad for days."

"Uh-huh." Beef coughed a couple of times. "And... why do you sing like that?"

Paul shrugged again. "'Cause I like it, I guess. It's the only thing I like doing."

"But you suck at it. You got no voice. Have you heard yourself?"

Paul thought about it.

"I don't care," he said. "I just like doing it."

"Buddy–you sound *terrible*. Trust me."

Paul sighed. "That's what my mom says. Maybe I'll be good at it when I grow up, though."

"No you won't."

"But if I work hard at it?"

"That only works for some things. With singing and that kind of artsy stuff, I think you have to have talent in the first place." Beef spat on the ground. "I think so, anyways. I don't know much about that shit. But why do you want to be good at that when you could be better at softball?"

Paul did not answer.

"I could help you get better at softball. I used to suck hard at sports too, but then I lost a bit of weight and exercised more. Then I joined the softball league and I practised more and worked hard at it, and I got good at it."

Paul thought about it. "I don't know. I'd rather get good at singing."

"But you can go further with softball. Look at me. I'm cool now–well, sort of. I have cool friends like Russ and Bobby. Other guys like hanging out with me. Even a couple girls had crushes on me at school this year. Don't you wanna be as cool as me?"

Paul did his standard shrug again.

Beef stopped and tapped Paul's arm to make him stop walking too. "Dude," he said, "look at me. I could help you. I've been where you are, and I can help you get out of it. Whaddya say we start hanging out?"

"Hanging... out?" As if sounding out a complex phrasing in a foreign language.

"This Saturday. I have your address from the team info. So I'll call on you and we can go out and do some stuff."

"Saturday's when I do the grocery shopping. And mow the grass. And water the flowers. And blow-dry my mom's Capodimonte figures. And—"

"So do all that stuff in the morning. I'll come in the aft. Cool?"

Beef raised his right hand for a high-five. Paul stared at the hand curiously.

"Anyways," said Beef, "I gotta get home. See you in a couple days."

Paul looked at him, paused and then nodded with an unsure expression. Beef turned around and jogged home in the other direction, stopping only once to ask himself, *Wait a sec. What the hell is a Capodimonte figure?*

"I knew I had my work cut out for me," Chuck tells Jackie. "Trying to make Sucky Baby into one of the cool kids would be like trying to make a world-champion kickboxer out of a nun. But maybe I could at least make him legit enough that he wouldn't get picked on so much. If he was never gonna be Prince, maybe I could still carve him into a passable Michael Jackson."

As promised, Beef called at Paul's house the next Saturday afternoon. After a moment of confusion from his robe-clad, curler-haired, cigarette-spouting mother, the boy emerged. Beef led him to the nearest strip mall, where they bought two large bags of Hostess potato chips and two bottles of Pepsi at the Smoke & Gift. Or rather, Beef bought them as Paul had no money on him.

"Don't your parents give you an allowance?" Beef asked as they sat on the curb by the parking lot, munching away. "Don't they give you *any* money?"

Paul shook his head. "My mom says I'd have to earn it," he mumbled with his mouth full of sour cream and onion chips.

"But it sounds like you already do a lot of chores and stuff around the house."

"That's just Earning My Salt."

"Earning what?"

"My Salt."

"What the fuck does *that* mean?"

"I... don't know." He swallowed. "I think it means I have to do chores and stuff to earn my stay in my mom's house. Or something like that."

"Jeez. That's fucked up."

"But for money," said Paul, stuffing his mouth with more chips, "I'd have to get a job and earn some murr rurr vurr rurr ruv vurra rurv..."

"I can't understand you with your mouth full like that."

"I said—" said Paul, and then he started choking.

"Woah! Dude," said Beef, and he slapped Paul hard on the upper back.

The slap worked too well. Paul spewed all the chewed-up chips onto the pavement.

"Ew! Gross!" said a couple of teenage girls in tank tops and short shorts passing by.

Paul took a minute to catch his breath.

"Fuck," said Beef. "Don't you know how to eat properly? You'll choke to death if you stuff your face like that. You've got to go slowly and *savour* the chips."

Paul nodded.

"And you shouldn't talk with your mouth full. In fact, you shouldn't even open your mouth when you chew stuff. It's totally gross. People can see the food in your mouth."

Paul nodded again. "I know. My mom tells me all the time, but I forget. She tells me I'm a savage. I'm a savage Indian from the western days, and a cowboy ought to shoot me."

"Well, that's an... *extreme* way to put it. But that doesn't mean she doesn't have a point." Beef stood up. "Let's go to my house. I'll show you how to eat properly."

"But," said Paul, pointing to the mess on the pavement, "shouldn't I clean this up first?"

"Why?"

"To Earn My Salt."

Beef laughed. "Dude, you're not on your mom's time. The salt is on me right now. And you might even get some pepper out of it too."

"What?"

"Never mind. Crap joke. Let's go."

Beef's parents were away that day, and his older sister was at a movie with friends, so Beef had the whole modest, one-storey house to himself. He set up Paul in the kitchen and cooked a small meal of bacon and eggs for them both, and the meal came with a free etiquette lesson. Beef showed Paul how to take his time when eating a meal, to keep his mouth shut while chewing and avoid speaking until after he had swallowed a mouthful, to rest his dirtied utensils on the plate rather than on the table, to drink his milk without slurping it and so on.

"I never thought I'd find myself teaching table manners to anybody," Chuck tells Jackie with a stifled laugh. "It's hilarious when I think about it now. If Russ and Bobby ever found out what I was doing, they'd have disowned me with a hundred punches. If my fans back in the day knew about this, they'd have made me turn in my Street Card. You never know what you'll end up doing."

"Another thing," Beef said to Paul as they were washing the dishes after the meal. "How often do you shower, Paul?"

He looked at Beef with a quizzical expression. "Shower?"

"You know fuckin' well what a shower is. You're not *that* dumb."

"Of course."

"You *do* shower, don't you, buddy?"

Paul thought for a moment, drying a plate. "I have baths."

"How often?"

"Every Saturday night. After dinner."

"Not good enough. You still smell."

"But that's what I've been doing as far back as I can remember."

"From now on, Paul, you're gonna have a shower every morning before you come to school. And you're gonna wash your hair thoroughly each time. Alright?"

Paul looked at Beef as if Beef were a drooling madman. "*Every* morning?"

"Yeah. And one other thing..."

Beef rinsed and dried his hands, told Paul to put the glass he was drying on the counter for now and pulled him over to the bathroom. He opened the cabinet above the toilet and pulled out a rectangular stick with a green cap. *Speed Stick* the logo read.

"Deodorant," said Beef. "Get this for yourself the next time you go grocery shopping. Okay? Deodorant is your friend."

"Deodorant is my friend."

"That's right."

"And..." Paul looked at Beef with utter seriousness. "*You're* my friend, too?"

"Well, what the hell do you *think*?"

Paul nodded. "Thank you, Beef."

"No prob. Next week's lesson is gonna be basic socializing. Now let's go out and see if the barber shop is still open."

"If Paul was gonna be on a softball team," Chuck tells Jackie, "the least I could do was teach him how to actually *like* the goddamn game. I wanted him to understand the excitement and pleasure I got from it–the drama, the tension, the glory of a home run or a game-winning catch. The appeal of the loud *crack* of a bat on a ball. The warmth of the sun on your neck and arms as you're waiting in the outfield. The smell of the grass. That kind of stuff." Pause. "Am I boring you?"

"Hm?" says Jackie. "Oh, no. I don't do sports, so it's all kind of foreign to me."

"Might as well have been to Paul, too. At least, I wanted him to see the game could be *fun*. If nothing else, maybe it would distract him from that stupid singing. Maybe I could get him talking about Damaso Garcia and George Bell instead of fuckin' Cyndi Lauper."

There was a softball practice scheduled the next afternoon at three, but Beef had agreed to arrive at the park early with Paul. "If we get an hour or two of extra practice beforehand," Beef had said, "maybe you can make some progress without the other guys laughing and making fun of you the whole time." So Beef brought his own bat and a bag with a few softballs in it, along with his glove, and called at Paul's house a few minutes after one. Again, his mother answered in her nightwear and curlers, a cigarette dangling from her mouth. This time, her face was an ocean of bafflement.

"The hell did you do to my boy?" she said. "He looks almost... *normal*."

Out came Paul with the same weird face but cleaner, and with a bold new hairstyle: parted in the middle and feathered. He looked like a miniature Luke Skywalker in the first *Star Wars* movie, but his face had been deformed in a lightsaber accident. He still smelled, but not quite as much.

They went to the park where Beef tried to get a light game of catch going. But Beef ended up doing all of the catching. Every time Beef tossed the ball to his partner, no matter how softly, Paul would raise his hands to cover his face or crouch down as if avoiding a gunshot, as he often did in games. Then Beef would have to stand and wait as Paul chased after the ball and then brought it back, giving it a weak toss that bounced along the ground back to Beef.

"You're afraid of the ball, Paul," he said. "It's not gonna work if you're afraid of the ball."

"But it hurts," he whined. "It hurts when it hits you."

Beef sighed. He could not blame Paul. He knew more than anybody else in the league what it was like to be smacked on the side of the head with a racing softball. Even with a cushioned helmet on, it had to hurt like a motherfucker.

"Let's try something else," he told Paul. "Come to the infield with me." He jogged towards his equipment, which lay by the fence by home plate, and told Paul to go where the shortstop position would be. Beef tossed his glove by the fence, grabbed another softball and his bat, and approached home plate. "I'm gonna hit a few grounders to you," he said.

Paul tensed up. "What if it bounces and hits me in the face?"

"It won't. Just try to catch the ball, or at least stop it from getting past you."

Beef hit a soft grounder directly to Paul, who jumped out of the way as if it were a speeding car. The second one also got by him by a few feet. "Don't *avoid* it, buddy! Go right towards it and catch it!" A third grounder, slower and softer, went under Paul's legs; he leapt up as if he'd just seen a snake. The fourth was so slow that it was almost a roll. *That* grounder was safe enough for Paul, who hesitated for a split-second, then stayed and scooped up the ball.

"I got it," said Paul, raising his glove. "See?"

Beef rolled his eyes. "Great," he said, then pointed to left field. "Now go get those other balls that went by you."

When Paul returned, he rolled all four balls back to Beef. "Can you hit them all like that?" he said. "Just soft and slow. I can get those."

"That's not how they're gonna come to you in a game, Paul."

Paul just did his usual shrug.

"Okay, fine. I'll hit a slow one to you right now. Are you ready?"

In the second that followed, Beef wondered if he was making a huge mistake. As he tossed the softball in the air, he wondered if he was about to traumatize Paul for good, if not physically cripple him.

As he whipped the bat around to smack the airborne ball, he wondered if he had already succeeded in terrifying Paul away from the sport for life. As the *crack* sounded in the air and the ball shot as fast as a bullet towards Paul's face, he had a quick mental image of himself explaining to Lydia Shoreditch what had happened over Paul's unconscious body, and Paul's mother ignoring Beef and kicking at Paul's inert form, yelling at him to wake up.

But Beef's plan worked. Even better than he had expected. Paul's physical reflexes kicked in before his mental panic mode did, sending his gloved hand up to block his face. And that was where the ball landed–right in the webbing of the glove. And it stayed there.

Beef dropped his bat on the ground and watched as Paul opened his eyes, looked at his glove, and kept staring at the ball sitting in it. He seemed to turn to stone in that position, except for his eyes, which kept getting wider, and his jaw, which fell as if someone had dropped it.

"You okay, Buddy?" asked Beef, with a friendly chuckle.

No answer.

"Paul?" Beef approached him. "You alright?"

Paul took a breath. He looked at Beef.

"I caught it," he said softly. "I can't believe I caught it."

"You sure did." Beef gave him an encouraging smile. "I knew you could."

"I caught it!"

Again, Beef could not help laughing. This was the first time he had seen Paul express any strong emotion other than physical fear or bawling. Paul was not quite smiling, but something had clicked inside of him. Although Beef was not a big *Star Trek* fan, he was reminded of an episode he had seen once in which Spock had burst into joy when he found out that Kirk had not died after all. Paul was like an emotionally repressed alien, in a way.

Paul was gazing at the ball in his glove again, and Beef said, "Don't stare at it too long, buddy. Your head might turn into a huge softball."

"I caught it," he said again.

"I know." Then, on a whim, Beef added: "Do you wanna keep it?"

Paul looked up. "What for?"

"Well, as a souvenir. A reminder. Your first catch." Beef reached into his pocket and pulled out his switchblade. "Here," he said, taking the ball from Paul's glove. With one of the blades, Beef carved the initials "PS" on the ball, then handed it back to Paul.

Then, out of the corner of his eye, Beef thought he saw a familiar-looking boy treading down the path in the park. "Shit," he said. "Paul, can you go away and come back at three?"

"Huh? Why?"

"Just... I don't want the other guys to see me with you." He spat. "I should've told you this before, but I don't want the others to know we're friends."

"Why not?"

"'Cause they'd think I was a loser and they wouldn't be my friends anymore."

Paul's face fell a little. Beef could see a sense of betrayal in it. But there was also a note of acceptance too, coupled with an infinite lack of surprise.

"Look," Beef added, "I'll see ya later. We'll do this again, I promise. But when you come back for practice, don't let on we hang out together. Okay? Same thing at games."

Paul nodded, then turned to go.

"This way," said Beef, pointing in the direction opposite from the path, and Paul took off that way carrying his glove and the carved softball.

"It never occurred to me he was gonna keep the ball for *that* long," says Chuck. "When I found out what happened at the funeral with the minister, I was like, 'What the *fuck*?' I'd totally forgotten all about the ball until then. Like, thirty-four years! It must've meant a lot to him. Sad, huh?"

Jackie thinks for a moment.

"I don't know," she answers. "I still have the old VHS tape of *E.T.* my parents gave me for my sixth birthday. A sentimental keepsake. It was the first movie I ever loved."

"*E.T.*?" Chuck laughs. "That sappy old kids' movie? God, I hated that shit."

"Carry on." Jackie bites her tongue softly, imagining how she would respond if Chuck were an anonymous online idiot. She also realizes that she *still* has not called her mom.

The boy arriving at the field was Martin Knuth, another member of the team, but not a popular or conspicuous one. He had misheard the practice start time as two o'clock and thought he was late, so Beef played catch with Martin until the rest of the team showed up, including Paul.

Paul's new hairdo got laughs from the other boys—"When the fuck did they invite Princess Di on the team, huh?" smirked Bobby—but that died down quickly. Nobody commented on Paul's slightly reduced smell. Beef saw it as a battle victory in a long, bloody war.

It was too bad, Beef thought, that he did not have a family as well-to-do as his friends'; otherwise he might have taken it upon himself to buy Paul some clothes. The smell, the hair, the singing and the other weird behaviour—those were only part of why the other kids felt such revulsion towards Paul. When he was not wearing his baseball uniform, he was clad in old, faded blue jeans and striped or even plaid shirts that were already a little too small for him; sometimes he would also wear dress shirts with oversized collars, and on a cooler day, he even wore a large V-necked sweater with clashing blue and green stripes. It was as if the fashion curve in the Shoreditch household had never progressed beyond 1977. His shoes were white sneakers that were now grey from dirt and when Paul walked, they squeaked loud enough to turn heads twenty feet away. And, of course, there was always a smell. Paul apparently never washed his own clothes. Beef wondered how this was possible as the Salt-Earning regimen that Paul's mom oversaw *must* have included laundry at some point.

"A big problem," Chuck says, "was that I was no expert in fashion myself. I couldn't afford the cool duds the other kids wore. And in the '80s, man, image was *everything*. The way you looked, the clothes you wore, the way you styled your hair–*these* defined who you were above anything you said, anything you did, anything you wanted to accomplish, anything you believed in. It was a problem for me, though much more for Paul."

Despite Beef's own ignorance, he knew something needed to be done about Paul's clothes. He wondered how best to bring it up as he invited Paul to his house for the following Friday evening, which turned out to be an evening of pizza, popcorn, Cokes and TV. Beef's parents were out again, and his sister was in her room yakking on the phone with friends most of the time, freeing up the living room for the little party. The entertainment lineup consisted of *Wheel of Fortune, Family Feud,* and repeat episodes of *Webster, Mr. Belvedere, Benson,* the second half of *Dallas* and everybody's new favourite, *Miami Vice*.

Paul was close to falling asleep by the end of *Dallas*, but the gunshots and violence in *Miami Vice* woke him back up. He spent much of the show trembling and either covering his eyes or pretending to look at the screen but really staring at the cable dial to the right of it. Beef had to fight himself not to laugh out loud.

"Come on, man," he said. "It's not *Friday the 13th*."

Paul ignored him, still staring at the cable dial.

"You know what I love about this show?" said Beef, trying to spark interest in Paul. "The clothes. The fuckin' clothes. Man, Sonny and Tubbs sure know how to dress."

"Uh-huh," Paul mumbled, his voice cracking a little.

"I wish I had cool jackets and shit like that. And those loafers! So rad."

"Right."

"You ought to get your parents to buy you cool duds like that. You know how much the other kids would like you? You'd get more friends. Girls, too. Girls like boys who dress up smart."

"They do?" Paul's voice peaked a little. "Why do they like it?"

"I dunno. They just do." Then a commercial break came on, and Beef got an idea. "You free tomorrow, Paul? I mean, after your chores and stuff?"

"I think so. I guess I can do them all in the morning again."

"Let's go to Square One."

"What's that?"

Beef laughed. "Come on! The big shopping mall. Don't tell me you never been there."

Paul shook his head.

"Aw man, you *got* to go. They got all these big clothing stores. Let's go and see if they have clothes like that for kids our age."

"But I don't have any money to buy them."

"Neither do I. But we can *look*, can't we? We can dream about buying them. And maybe one day, we'll have the money, and we can go back and buy them and be cool. Okay?"

Paul paused, then gave his familiar shrug, which Beef took to mean "yes".

He called on Paul at about one o'clock again, and they took a couple of buses to Square One. Beef paid bus fares for both of them, and he had a sinking feeling that he would be buying at least a snack or something for Paul at the mall. *Fine. Whatever.*

Paul looked amazed at the huge, noisy shopping paradise that surrounded him. Beef wondered if Paul had even been to a large mall before. His eyes bugged out at all the stores and the crowds of people passing by in spring clothes, and at the bland white décor. Even the smell of the popcorn from the movie theatre, or of sizzling burgers and pizza from the food court transfixed him at certain moments. The overhead muzak played tinny recordings of recent hits by Madonna and Bryan Adams and Phil Collins and Tears for Fears, and Paul hummed along to some of them, although it never lasted long as Beef would snap, "Cut that shit out, Paul! I told you, you have no voice."

"Is that a record store?" Paul asked timidly as they passed the Sam the Record Man shop. Corey Hart's "Never Surrender" blared out of the store, and teenagers in denim jackets and band T-shirts were scattered inside, flipping through the records and cassettes.

"Sure is. Wanna go browse?"

Paul nodded with a faint smile. He rarely smiled, and Beef was not sure whether it was a good or a bad sign.

Beef led Paul to the record racks in the store. "Last time I was here," Beef said, "I got that new Slayer album. They have a pretty cool metal selection here. You like heavy metal?"

Paul shrugged again while shaking his head. Beef wondered if he should be giving him a lesson in metal appreciation. But a few seconds of Slayer might have given Paul a stroke. Even Def Leppard was probably too heavy-duty for this kid.

"I guess you don't buy records or tapes much, huh," said Beef.

Paul shook his head as he looked over the records on the stacks in wonder. "I used to have a record player," he mumbled, almost to himself, "when I was really small. But my mom took it away. She said it was a distraction from Earning My Salt."

"Holy shit, dude. You don't even have a tape player or a ghetto blaster?"

"What's a ghetto blaster?" Paul gazed over the records with the envious expression of a pauper examining a king's pile of gold pieces. "Wow!" he exclaimed, loud enough that it was a wonder all the kids in the store did not turn to look. He stepped over to the "W" section. There, staring from the shelf, were the relaxed, unsmiling faces of George Michael and Andrew Ridgely from the cover of Wham!'s *Make It Big*.

"You know Wham!?" asked Beef.

"I think so! They do that really happy song, don't they? I saw them sing it on the TV a few times!" And before Beef could stop him, Paul began to sing the chorus of "Wake Me Up Before You Go-Go".

"Shhhhh!" Beef snapped. A few customers and the cashier glanced in their direction. "I told you, don't sing."

"Sorry."

"And it's a stupid, gay song. I think those guys are gay lovers too. And it's *so old*, Paul. It was on the charts, like, last October."

"But it's such a happy song. It makes me happy when I sing it." Paul stared at George and Andrew as if he had found his musical soulmates.

Beef sighed. He peeked in his jeans pocket to see how much cash he had. "All right. Want me to buy you the record?"

Paul jerked his face to Beef in shock. "You... you'd *do* that for me?"

"Sure. I got enough money."

Paul's jaw fell. "But I don't have anything to play it on."

"You can play it at my house on my parents' old stereo. You can even *keep* it at my house if you think it would freak out your mom or something."

Paul's eyes bugged at Beef in amazement, hardly blinking.

"The usual thing," said Beef, "is to say, 'thank you.'"

"Thank you, Beef."

Beef took the copy of *Make It Big* to the shaggy-haired, denim-jacketed teenager at the counter. The cashier looked at the album cover, snorted, and mumbled, "Six ninety-nine," as he sulked over the cash register. Beef handed over seven bucks and exited the store, with Paul following like an obedient child.

"Thank you, Beef," he said again.

Beef was about to tell him in the nicest possible way to shut the fuck up about it, but he was interrupted by a familiar voice to his right, spouting, "Thanks for *what*?"

He turned his head to look. Russ and Bobby stood a few feet away, arms folded and big, nasty grins dominating their faces. Beef froze. Paul did too for a few seconds.

"We were just passing by," said Bobby, "and we couldn't help overhearing Sucky Baby giving a little concert. What's he thanking you for?"

"For the record," Paul said in a high voice, near a squeal. "He bought it for me!"

Bobby looked at the *Make It Big* album in Beef's hands, then at Beef's face, which was staring at the floor, blushing and wincing.

"He *bought* it for you?" said Bobby, trying to suppress laughter. Russ was already giggling like a tickled baby. "Why would you do something like that, Beef?"

Beef just shrugged and closed his eyes.

"Because he's my friend," said Paul.

Oh fuck, Beef thought. *Here it comes.*

"Your *friend*?" said Bobby. "I didn't think Sucky Baby had any friends. Just gay lovers."

Russ approached the shaking Beef and yanked the album out of his hands. "Look at these two gaylords," he said to Bobby, pointing to the picture of Wham!. He tore the clear shrink wrap off and slipped out the record from the cover, which he dropped carelessly onto the floor. Then Russ held the record in both hands and lifted a knee right into it, cracking it in two. Bobby fell over laughing, and Russ turned to him with a self-satisfied smirk as if he had just delivered the cleverest aphorism in the history of wit.

"Why did you do that?" said Paul, shaking.

"Faggots," said Bobby, and he sent his right fist into Beef's gut.

Beef toppled over onto the floor and crouched on his side, his feet on top of a few broken record shards. A few passersby turned to look at the scene but continued on their way.

"Beef!" gasped Paul. "You okay, Beef?"

"Punch the geek in the balls again," said Russ. "Like you did before. That was hilarious."

Paul looked at Bobby and then down at the floor, and he sniffled, and the tears began flowing. Paul let out a howl, louder than a screaming baby that had just bumped its head on the floor.

"Ha ha! Crying little Sucky Baby," shouted Bobby. Russ nearly fell over laughing.

Paul howled again and then turned around and ran, screaming all the way. He almost knocked over a toddler trotting alongside his mother. "God damn it!" she snapped, watching Paul run heedlessly through the mall.

"We better take him outside and finish him off," said Russ, still giggling as he pointed at Beef, who was still clutching his belly and trying to catch his breath.

So Bobby and Russ picked up Beef from the floor and dragged him out the nearest mall exit, then carried him to a corner between two of the store entrances where few cars were parked. And they threw him onto the pavement and beat and kicked Beef as mercilessly as two twelve-year-olds could.

"Don't hang out with us anymore, you fat little faggot," Bobby said in a low voice, almost a whisper. "We don't want your gay cooties. Just stay the fuck away."

Beef struggled to speak. "I'm... not... even... gay... you... sick... assholes," he coughed.

Bobby glared at Beef's face for a moment. Then he slowly stood up, looked down at Beef, and kicked him one last time in the chest. Beef yelped out as Bobby and Russ ran away.

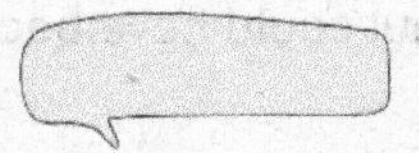

"That was it, for me," Chuck now tells Jackie over the phone. "I mean, no more softball. No more sports at all, even. I quit the team as soon as I got better. I knew Bobby was gonna tell the other boys I was doing gay things with Paul, and the kids would never let me forget it. Anyway, that was the last time I saw any of them. Russ, Bobby, even Paul."

A moment passes before Jackie realizes he has stopped talking.

"Uh," she blurts. "So... never again?"

"Never again."

"So you never, you know, stood up for Paul? You just abandoned him?"

"Didn't really get a chance to connect with him again. My family moved to Willowdale not long after that; they were super-freaked out by what happened at the mall. I went to middle school there, made new friends, nicer ones." He clears his throat. "The next year, I heard Run DMC for the first time, and it blew me away. I knew the only thing I wanted to do was rap. So I chucked the jock shit for good, worked to lose weight, and devoted myself to music."

"And the rest is history."

"You know," says Chuck, with a contemplative tone, "I never really thought about it before, but I probably owe that kid a lot."

"Paul Shoreditch?"

"Yeah. Him and that weird fucking singing of his. I mean, maybe subconsciously or something, maybe it was *him* wanting to be a singer that inspired me to go into music. Not just Run DMC, I mean. On some level, I think the fact that he just sang and didn't give a shit about it made me realize I could do rap if I wanted to, and to hell with what the jocks and normals all said."

"But you told Paul you needed talent for music. Work wasn't enough."

Chuck laughs. "Well, I had no talent, so I guess I proved myself wrong."

"I see. Do you think Paul could have become a good singer if he'd worked at it?"

The speakerphone explodes with laughter, which goes on and on and on.

"But," Chuck finally adds, after catching his breath, "I'd like to think I did other good things to help him. Even though the friendship didn't last long, I showed him a little about how normal people work, how the real world operates and all that. He must've got something out of it. I'm proud of how I helped him."

"Yeah. You're a real hero," Jackie says, rolling her eyes.

"Just before the funeral, I looked up Russ Fullerton and Bobby Skatz online, see what they were up to. Turns out Russ is a big corporate executive now, right here in T.O., downtown. I forget the name of the company. I'm actually surprised he didn't end up a pro ball player; he really was that good. And Bobby–wanna know what happened to him?"

No, no, no. "Sure."

"He's in Switzerland or something. He's a fuckin' *priest*! Seriously, he found religion! A real Catholic priest." He laughs. "I never would've guessed in a billion years. Man. I was thinking of contacting both of them, but—"

Jackie looks at the Olympus and realizes that it has shut off. It must have maxed out its recording space a while ago. She feels dumb for not having noticed–*God, I'm so shitty at this*–but also surprised at how focused she was on Beef's story.

"Anyway," she interrupts, "I'm out of time."

"Sorry?"

"I have to go." She forces a smile, as she does every day at the call centre, hoping it can add some politeness into her voice. "But thank you so much, Chuck. This was so helpful. And it was... an honour to speak to you."

She has to pee, badly, so she dashes to the bathroom as soon as the line is disconnected. Then she re-enters the main room of her pad and sits on the bed.

Another fucking wild-goose chase. Jackie has learned nothing about Paul's sins, except that he *might* have had a public-stroking problem when he was twelve. She knows far more about Chuck McMahon and Lydia Shoreditch and Kathy McDougal than about her main subject.

The only thing she got out of the Angry Chuck M interview was a rash of bad memories. She recalls the tall, smirking girl in her Grade 4 class–*Kim Kirby? Was that her name?*–who always called her "Freckle-face" and "Loser", and who told the rest of the class that Jackie had rabies and, of course, most of them believed it. She remembers the time in Grade I when her friend's older brother took her favourite Cabbage Patch Doll right out of her hands and held it up in the air, laughing as Jackie tried to jump to get it and then gave up in a crying fit. She remembers how humiliated she felt when her secret girlfriend broke up with her in the eighth grade by hiding a note in her locker telling her how boring and ugly she was. Not that any of this was anywhere near as bad as what Paul apparently went through. As bad as her pain was–or at least, as bad as it felt at the time–she cannot help imagining how much worse it must have been for Paul. And how happy he must have been when he finally found a friend in Beef, and then how completely humiliating it must have been when that was cut off. *Jesus. The poor guy. The poor little...*

She stops. And her body fills with anger, all directed at herself. Before she even thinks about it, she slaps herself in the face. Hard.

"Stop it!" she screams out loud. "STOP! IT! He's a CREEP!"

She winces–first, at the sting of the slap, then in embarrassment as she wonders if any of her neighbours heard her. She is quiet for a while, then shakes it off.

I've been going about this all wrong. Or stupid Rick has put me on the wrong path or something. I don't know.

All she knows is these random trips into Paul Shoreditch's past are going nowhere. She has to dig shallower, not deeper, to get at these incriminating bones.

She goes back to her desk, where Bogie stares at her from the computer background again. His eyes now seem less sad than disappointed.

"Well?" she asks him. "What leads do *you* have?"

SEVEN

Three in the afternoon the same Sunday. Jackie stares at her phone on her desk, the Olympus beside it as before. *Get it over with.*

She sent an e-mail to Vanessa Darby—the witness Kathy had cited—yesterday, but it bounced back earlier today. It seems the address no longer exists. Now she has transcribed her interview with Chuck McMahon and deleted the recording for space. Nausea and restrained rage have returned. She may be about to hear more details of a story she does not want to know.

Jackie lets out a long, heaving breath and dials the number.

The voice that picks up is a harsh, low croak.

Jackie flicks on the recorder, confirms the responder is Vanessa Darby and explains who she is.

"I was wondering if you had a few minutes to talk about Paul Shoreditch."

A lengthy silence. "Who?"

"Paul Shoreditch."

"*Who?*"

"Paul. Shoreditch. I understand you witnessed an incident involving him in 2013."

Another pause, followed by a hacking cough.

"Who the hell is Paul Shoreditch?" Vanessa sounds as if she has been smoking six packs a day for decades.

"I apologize if I've been unclear, Ms. Darby. I'm sort of new at this kind of reporting. I got your name from Kathy McDougal. She referred you as a witness to a... an incident at a private party at her apartment. Can you remember the party?"

Silence again. *Why do I get stuck with the special ones?*

"Kathy *who*?"

"McDougal. Editor of the website *Kat's Korner*." A beat, then Jackie adds, "Also used to work at a store called FunMart."

She braces herself for another epochal pause, but Vanessa replies with a weird change in tone. "Kathy *McDougal*?"

"Yes."

"Holy cow. From *FunMart*?"

"Yes."

"The hell's she givin' my number out for?"

"So you know her."

"The hell's she even *got* my number for? I better get it changed."

"Ms. Darby, can I ask—"

"Tell that bitch to go to hell!" Vanessa's voice is loud and shaky. "Keep that nut job away from me! I don't wan—" The rant takes a sharp turn into a long, revolting coughing fit.

"Are you okay?"

Jackie never finds out because Vanessa hangs up.

That wins the BAFTA for the most surreal moment of the day. She stares at the phone. What was that all about? Why would Kathy give out contact info for such a random person–one who clearly wants nothing to do with her?

Jackie gets an odd feeling that Kathy was not expecting her to follow up on the witness but rather, to believe everything she said without backup.

I warned you, says Brain inside her head. She imagines the Peck figure in black and white, bespectacled and clad in a three-piece suit–the spitting image of Atticus Finch in *To Kill a Mockingbird*–hands at his hips, shaking his head.

Leave me alone, Jackie answers.

In the name of God, Jackie, do your duty.

And that would be...?

No reply. Nobody wants to give her a straight answer today and it is pissing her off.

About ten-thirty in the evening. Jackie has been staring at the computer screen for hours, with only the odd bathroom break. She checked Rick's old e-mail with the links and names, then looked up Morty Bozzer, the fourth attendee at Paul Shoreditch's funeral. He was a manager at the FunMart store where Paul and Kathy McDougal worked. Jackie shot a note to him asking if he was up for an interview. Since then, she has been scouring the "Stories" section of F**kPaulShoreditch.com for anything useful. But nobody has responded to her queries, and most of the entries she now reads are either about Paul as a kid or extremely minor pet peeves. All sound the same after a while.

One entry titled "**sucky baby lol**", authored by Andy_Jelan_73__, piqued her interest briefly, only because it told her what she had already heard.

> i remember sucky baby. i was on his softball team in '85, what a little dweeb. if you threw a ball at him he would start crying and it just made you want to kick his ass. he used to jack off when he was playing

> in the outfield too, whip it out and jerk it in front of everybody. its funny how you grow out of your petty childish dislikes after a while but, man, this website brings back a lot of disgust. i fuckin hated this kid. another thing [...]

Jackie stopped there.

This website makes her feel icky. Much of it is a high-school Vicious Circle, a *Mean Girls* rip-off without the Lindsey Lohan character. As if all of Paul's old school bullies have teamed up for one last virtual wedgie. Other times, it is like slowly sinking into a mud pit of other people's bitterness. She wants a long, warm, relaxing bath. And she would take one if her teeny little pad had a bathtub. Instead, she goes back to Spitter.

Today's slogan is "Spit and Shine Will Save Nine!", whatever that means. And behold, another reply from the beagle.

Not that there's anything to be ashamed of in being afraid, @nagging_conscience_42 has written. ***Everybody feels fear sometimes. It's a healthy emotion. It's kept me from doing something really drastic to myself a couple of times. Like Hamlet said... "But that the dread of something after death, the undiscovered country, from whose bourne no traveller returns, puzzles the will, and makes us rather bear the ills we have than fly to others that we know not of?"***

Jackie buries her face in her hands, snorting with contemptuous laughter. *Seriously, dude? A Shakespeare quote?* And why is this person getting so upfront with her, hinting at these dark personal details? What makes the puppy think she wants to know about that? There is something wrong about this conversation, something that creeps her out.

She clicks "Reply" and types with a smirk: ***If you're pompous enough to quote "Hamlet" in your messages, maybe the world doesn't really need you anyway.***

She is about to post the response, her finger right on the mouse, ready to click—

No. God, no. What am I doing? WAY too far.

She sits and stares, thinking about her response. She cannot send it, knowing how it could be misconstrued, but something will not let her delete the text either.

Oh, come on! He's not gonna take it literally, is he? It's not like he'd actually go and do something. Would he?

She emits a forced laugh. But the situation does not seem funny.

Jackie takes her hand off the mouse and uses her hesitancy as an excuse to go to the bathroom. When she gets back to her desk, she looks over the unsent message again.

"Whatever," she says as she clicks back to the tab with F**kPaulShoreditch.com.

She gazes over "Stories" for what seems like the quadrillionth time, then realizes she is sick of looking at the list and tries "Miscellaneous" again. *There's got to be plenty here I haven't seen yet, for shit's sake. Such a long list.* She scrolls down the list. One title catches her eye, buried between **"Screw him"** and **"so ugkly i cant look at his face ahaha"**.

Dated May 7, 2014, the entry is titled, **"He saved my life."**

Say WHAT?

The author's username is "WRIGHT". She clicks on the link and reads the modest content.

> Paul Shoreditch saved my life. If nothing else, he did that one thing. I find this website unfair and really harsh. Paul may have had his personal faults, like all of us, but he does not deserve any of this. Please take down this website.

Jackie is not surprised to see dozens of replies. Headings include **"LIES LIES LIES LIES!!"** and **"youre a stupid liar, he would never do that"** and **"Come on Paul this is so obviously you. Get off the site shitface!"** She does not bother clicking on them.

She sits back and thinks. *Wow. Fucked up indeed.* This is the first positive online comment she has ever seen about Paul Shoreditch, and she does not know what to make of it. It seems sincere, but so did *Mein Kampf*. It might be true. It might be a troll. Or it might be an extremely deluded person who did not get to know Paul well.

Or maybe people are complex beings with good *and* bad in them, and a guy can be a sick bastard one minute and a lifesaving hero the next?

She shakes her head and tells herself she will go back to that entry later. After a few seconds of scrolling the "Miscellaneous" section, she happens on another entry she does not remember seeing before, from 2015. *Wow, I suck at this deduction stuff.*

The title reads, **"Holy shit! Did u know P.S. has a Spitter account?!"**

I certainly did not. Jackie clicks on the entry. The only text is a link to said Spitter account. This one also has plenty of replies, with headings like "**omfg this is gonna be hilarious!**" and "**HAHA DUMMASS**" and "**Is this guy 4 realz?**" and "**what could he possibly Have to say? LOL.**"

She clicks on the link. On her screen is a Spitter profile page with a plain blue background and a default "anonymous" user pic, which is just the silhouette of a head and shoulders. The name on the account is simple, plain "Paul Shoreditch" with no bio, no cover image.

Jackie reads the most recent entry on the account.

Don't pretend you feel bad about this. This is what you all wanted, and you know it.

Huh. No idea what you're on about, Paul.

She scrolls down to another entry that makes her giggle stupidly.

I wish I could sing as good as George Michaels. He has a really beautiful voice.

An unexpected yawn interrupts her laughter. One quick e-mail check, and she'll hit the sack early. She bookmarks Paul Shoreditch's Spitter page.

Her e-mail notifies her of two new comments on

JackieRoberts.com: one on a post from more than ten years ago titled **"Ten Reasons Why I Love the Cinema"** and the other on her 2015 essay about David Lean's *Brief Encounter*. She checks out the first one, scrolling down the post, wincing at what a bad writer she was in her twenties.

DominickThePoet has written: ***You don't understand that film is not a legitimate art form. It is not, and every educated person knows this. There are two distinct reasons. First, it is not an art form in itself but infact is a combination of all the other different art forms. Drama, writing, music, photography, and so on. The second reason is that film doesn't last. It does not stand the test of time, the way music and poetry do, but it dates instantly. Ok maybe there's the odd exception like Casablanca, but for the most part, films always have early best-before dates. [...]***

She reads no further, replying: ***Hey Dominick. You don't sound like you've seen many films. I would suggest starting with the "Police Academy" series, which I would argue has stood the test of time far better than the logic of your argument will. Also, I suspect that your sexual history had an early best-before date.***

She groans. *Does that last bit even make sense?* Far from her best effort, but it will have to do. Then she looks up the reply to the *Brief Encounter* post.

IMHO, the comment from HappiestGilmore reads: ***you are SO pretentious. You are the most pretentious film writer on the web, and that's saying quite a lot. This essay reads like you've swallowed three college textbooks with a side of thesaurus. Just showing off knowledge and no substance. Nobody believes you're that smart, Jackie. I can see through you like you're made of glass.***

She takes a deep breath. Then she closes her eyes and takes another one.

Normally, this is the kind of cheap trolling that she loves. This should be inspiring her with another cutting comeback, another attempt to silence the witless. But if there is one thing she loathes being called, it is "pretentious".

Especially after hearing it a few too many times in university. If you mentioned Hitchcock or Scorsese, they were okay with it, but

God help you if you compared something to Ozu. *Anytime you make some cultural reference that one person out of a hundred might not get, that one person is sure as shit going to label you "pretentious". You don't know if it's jealousy or ignorance or what.* Jackie does not hesitate to call others pretentious if she thinks they deserve it, but when someone flings it at her, she wants to scream at top volume, raging at the sick, glaring injustice of it.

HappiestGilmore's comment is so deep under Jackie's skin that she stands up and paces around the apartment. She wants to shoot back a devastating comeback, but this attack has left her mute. *Why do they think I do this, anyway? Why would I take the time to write all these essays for no money, no glory?* She does not write about film to show off. She does not do this just to look like an intellectual or an expert. She does this out of a pure love of cinema and a profound desire to share it with others who care about the art form—and to teach those who want to learn.

Pretentious? Who the fuck is pretending anything? I'm as true as you're ever going to find, you feckless twit. Not like a lot of others. Certainly not like some creepy, pedantic Spitter douchebag quoting Shakespeare randomly to—

She stops. She sits down and flicks back to the tab with the puppy's last Spitter comment.

Still there. Her un-posted reply sitting in the text box.

If you're pompous enough to quote "Hamlet" in your messages, maybe the world doesn't really need you anyway.

She looks it over again. And again. *No. That's not right. I can't post that.*

So she puts the cursor at the end of the word "really" and deletes it. She is aware, after all, that she overdoes unwarranted adverbs in her writing. Good editing practice.

Click. With a tap of the index finger, the comment is blasted out into the world, waiting to hit its yapping beagle target. And in Jackie's mind, some sort of justice is served. She is not sure how, but she can feel it, and that is good enough.

He's not gonna do anything. If he expects me to take what he dishes me, he can take this.

EIGHT

The beagle puppy has invaded her sleep again. Staring at Jackie with the same blank look and this time, she senses not judgement but deep, irredeemable sadness. With a touch of disappointment.

What is it? What do you want from me?

No answer.

Further away is a dark, blurry figure waving its arms and hands. It appears to be dancing. The figure comes closer, rapidly and smoothly, as if a film camera is zooming in on it. It looks like an African American man wearing a dark suit, swaying from side to side to a beat, singing in a strange, scratchy voice. She cannot make out the words, but the tune sounds familiar. She cannot see the beagle now but senses it is still there, looking at her.

The singing and dancing figure comes closer, and the lyrics become clearer. *I'm a-comin' / Sorry I made you wait / I, I'm comin' / I hope and trust I'm not late / Mammy, mammy...*[1]

---

[1] Lyrics from "My Mammy" by Al Jolson, public domain work.

And Jackie now recognizes the figure, or thinks she does: Al Jolson, in blackface, singing onstage in *The Jazz Singer*. But as the figure comes closer and the singing gets louder, it hits her that this is not Jolson's voice. It is off-key and reedy, with no sense of rhythm. The figure finishes the song and waits for applause, but there is none. *Mammy,* the voice calls, *why didn't you want me to sing, Mammy? Maybe I could've gotten as good as George Michaels.* And now she hears the audience laughing. The figure's head sinks in shame, and the laughter grows louder, and Jackie thinks she hears individual voices in the crowd shouting *Sucky Baby!* and *Fag!* and *Loser!* She does not need to look at the figure's face to know who it is. The laughter fades out slowly like the end of an old pop song, and a loud, booming, echoing old woman's voice, a familiar one, explodes with, *I! HAVE! NO! SON!!!*

The scene fades as the last voice echoes, but the beagle puppy is there staring at her, sadness and loss and regret emanating from its face like a foul odour.

What? What is it?

The puppy bares its teeth and snarls.

Jackie yelps as she wakes up in the dark.

She catches her breath and waits for a moment, shaking. When ready, she turns her head slowly to her old digital clock radio. 4:34 a.m.

Way too early. But she is not getting back to sleep now. And she has to pee.

On the toilet, she starts feeling a sense of dread.

When she flushes, she feels a desperate, pulling urge to get the hell to her desktop and log onto Spitter–an urge so strong she almost neglects to wash her hands.

As soon as the modem connects, she goes straight to Spitter. A new notification, presumably a reply or a "like". *Please. Please be the puppy. Please.*

There has been a reply to her last Spitter message to @nagging_conscience_42, but it is not the puppy.

haha way 2 tell of that pompous ditchpig,

@RoughRidersFan8487 has written and posted. ***maybe he'll take ur advice and jump of a cliff rotflmao***

A shiver runs up her back. *Calm down. Maybe he—or she—hasn't even read it yet. Maybe the puppy logged out and went to bed before I posted that message. Maybe I'll get another condescending lecture tomorrow, this time on my insensitivity.* And maybe, for the first time in her life, she will be relieved to get a condescending lecture.

She takes a breath and thinks for a minute. She considers deleting the post, but that feels cowardly and dishonest, and anybody who has seen the conversation will be aware of her dishonesty. If she fucked up, then she fucked up, and maybe the best action plan is to own it. She clicks to post a second reply to the puppy's venture into Shakespearean soliloquy: *I was just kidding, of course. I don't advocate suicide.*

She posts it. Part of her feels dissatisfied with such a bland, ordinary comment without a trace of bite in it, but she cannot think of anything better, not before five in the morning.

I have to get my mind off this shit. Jackie closes the web browser and turns around, looking over her DVD collection for something happy or escapist. *Indiana Jones?* No, she watched the two good ones just a few months ago when she was on a Spielberg kick. *E.T.* is out for the same reason. Pixar? No, too many dark moments. *The Wizard of Oz*? Maybe.

She gets the *Wizard* disc from the case and pops it into the computer's DVD drive. She sits back on her old hand-me-down couch as the black-and-white MGM lion roars and the familiar notes of "Over the Rainbow" from the overture wash over her. But she cannot surrender herself to the charms of the classic she has seen dozens of times since childhood. She can see the phoniness of the sets too clearly, and the theatrical affectations of all the actors, and the corniness of the writing, and the fake quality of the special effects. All she can think about is the real world and how messy it can get, and how you cannot always fix it.

I wish I had a goddamn cyclone to take me away from here.

A few hours later, Jackie is dead tired but knows going back to bed will be fruitless. Instead, she is back on the computer. Still no reply from @nagging_conscience_42. She has repeatedly checked the account's Spitter profile page, but there has been no post since the *Hamlet* lines. She can see the page while logged into the site, so she has not been blocked. There is no evidence of any activity. Either the puppy has not been on the site since last night, or.

Or.

She has looked over the profile page, partly out of curiosity. It turns out this person is (*was?*) from Ottawa, too. The background image shows the goofy green tongue-wagging planet from the covers of the *Hitchhiker's Guide to the Galaxy* books, and the bio reads, ***Don't Panic. I'm a hoopy frood, and I know where my towel is.*** That explains the "42" in the user ID. She skims down the entries and sees that @nagging_conscience_42 is a frequent poster. Typically four or five Spitter posts per day, not counting replies. The vast majority are mundane reports like ***Out shopping, in the mood for a ham dinner,*** or ***New Final Fantasy game totally sucks. What were they thinking?*** or ***Finally, finally get to see the Good Omens series. =D You rock, Pratchett.***

But once in a while–randomly and infrequently–it gets more serious. ***You're not alone,*** the puppy wrote on Bell Let's Talk Day, a corporate attempt to cash in on mental health awareness. ***If you're thinking of suicide, or know someone else who is, this is the number to call.*** Another post: ***Sometimes I just want to climb up to the top of Peace Tower and just walk off the edge. But then I play Weird Al again and realize that laughter is one reason to keep going on. Thanks, Al.*** Yet another: ***Fuck it. Fuck everything. I want to give up now.***

Then, almost a year ago, a series of posts in response to a news story about a teen suicide in Virginia, apparently a result of online bullying. The victim had angered a wide range of Spitter users by posting pictures of herself wearing a Japanese geisha costume at a

Halloween party, and they had sentenced her to merciless shame over cultural appropriation. ***You people make me sick,*** the puppy wrote. ***Literally sick. An innocent young life lost because you assholes had to feel so self-righteous. Why? What did you gain? What did the world gain? Is this what you wanted?***

Jackie feels queasy. The post seems to be screaming it right at her.

Fuck me. Am I a murderer now?

She stands up and starts pacing in slow, dizzy circles around the apartment. *Holy shit holy shit holy shit holy motherfucking shit. What have I done? What the hell have I done?* Jackie does not cry often but feels on the verge of collapsing onto the floor and bawling like a slapped baby. But it does not happen. Maybe due to a lifetime of trying to come off as a strong woman and suppressing any appearance of weakness. Maybe it has less to do with guilt and more with selfish worry about potential consequences for herself. Or maybe it is just a mental image of Lydia Shoreditch walloping her in the face and ordering her to stop "that noise".

After several minutes of pacing, she sits back down at the computer and looks at that older post by @nagging_conscience_42 again. ***Is this what you wanted?*** The question is eerily familiar. After scrolling back up to the top of the profile and seeing, to her frustration, that the puppy *still* has not responded, she goes back to Paul Shoreditch's Spitter profile. *At least I'm not responsible for what happened to him.* She looks at his last post again.

Don't pretend you feel bad about this. This is what you all wanted and you know it.

She notices the date of the post for the first time. October 15. Then she opens another tab and calls up one of the news stories about the Peace House fiasco that Rick sent her.

Yes. October 15—the same day that Paul Shoreditch fell to his demise.

Jackie has goosebumps on her arms.

Did he? Could he have? Come on. You don't know that, it could be a coincidence. It could mean anything else. She sighs. *Why do I feel like I'm responsible? I'm not.* Then she realizes what she is doing and groans, wanting to slap herself again. *What does it matter? Maybe he was a perv. Even if he wasn't, he's clearly done something to piss everybody off. Maybe his conscience finally caught up with him. His Nagging Conscience.*

But a knot in her stomach pokes at her, telling her she is missing something.

She looks at the second-last post, dated three years earlier. ***If there is a God then he must be real sadistic***, Paul wrote. ***I didn't ask for this awful life but he gave it to me anyway.***

The one before it is dated December 12, 2013. ***I hear so many lies and the more I hear them, the more I start to believe them. Maybe I really am what they say and the lies are true.***

Then a couple of months before that: ***How I wish I had a voice like Streisand. Except it would be a man's voice but just as good.*** The posts get far less sparsely spaced from then on—weeks or days—and most are bland, trite statements about singers he likes. Sinatra, Celine Dion, Julie Andrews, even Placido Domingo—anybody with a great or unique voice seems to get a mention.

Jackie shakes her head. The ramblings of a maniac? Or a deeply troubled soul with a bizarre music obsession?

Why didn't it occur to me before that he had a social-media account? Maybe my research should've started here in the first place.

Then she notes the replies and forwards Paul's Spitter posts. Almost every one has dozens of each. The last one has 86 replies. Jackie clicks on the replies and sees comments like ***Rest in Pain you useless piece of shit*** and ***haha good one Paul, nobodys ever gonna feel bad about anything that happens to you*** and ***Yes. Yes this was exactly what we wanted. Thanks for doing the I good thing you ever did in your life........... Croaking!!!***

It is as if they all know something but will not say it openly. As if some quiet, secret plan has been fulfilled among a group of conspirators and now they have come together in triumph.

Then Jackie scrolls through the comments further and spots two familiar names.

One appears in an early reply which reads: ***fuck you, paul shoreditch. =D fuck you and the horse you rode in on, you shitcunt. XD you're a loser and you'll always be a loser. if there's a hell out there, you're surely in it now XD XD XD***

The reply is from the user @avenger_of_the_weak_81. Jackie is not surprised to see that I.D. associated with that post.

The other familiar name appears in the text of another early reply, from a user she has never heard of, @PunkFeministBitch1996. This post reads: ***See u in hell Shoreditch. U r going to pay steep 4 what u did to Kathy McDougal. We know what u did and we're not gonna forget it. Never forget. Never never never.***

"What...?"

She reads the post again. Then she scrolls up some more, and like a pouncing feline, Kathy's name leaps at her from another post. ***Kathy MacDougall is literally laughin her head off right now*** reads the message from @tiffany_porter, ***and so am i. Speakin as a long time Kats Korner reader, i hope you felt lots of pain when you fell. Ass hole.***

A few posts later, from @Babyface857: ***You were an abuser, Paul Shoreditch, and you died an abuser. Kate McDougal has attested to that. She has spoken her truth, and the truth never dies.***

About ten posts later: ***KATHY MCDOUGALL GET HER REVENGE!!!!!!!!!!!!!!!!!!!! HAHA***

Kathy's name is in only a handful of these replies, but something is not right here. Something Kathy has omitted in her story. A huge omission.

After a few minutes of hesitation, she posts a reply to @Babyface857, who appears to be the most literate of the bunch: ***Hi. Please forgive my ignorance, but I'd really like to know what Paul Shoreditch did to Kathy McDougal. In what way was he an "abuser"?***

Then Jackie goes back to check the puppy's account. *Shit*. Still no reply, still no new posts.

I just don't know what to do.

She turns off the light and collapses onto her bed. She does not expect to sleep. Her head whirls with guilt and confusion and stress and exhaustion. She tries to distract herself with trivia. *Academy Award winners. Best Picture. 1928*: Sunrise *and* Wings. *1929:* Broadway Melody of 1929. *1930:* All Quiet on the Western Front. *1931:* Cavalcade. *No, hold on, it was the other "C" one...* Cimarron. *1932:* Grand Hotel. *1933: That was* Cavalcade. *Duh. 1934:* It Happened One Night. *1935:* Mutiny on the Bounty. *1936:* The Great Ziegfeld. *1937... 1937... 1937... come the hell on. 1938 was* You Can't Take It with You. *Don't skip 1937, it's cheating. 1937...*

It is not working. Normally, she could rattle them off like the Seven Dwarfs or the alphabet. And she feels dizzy with conflicting emotions that she wants to forget.

Fine. Let's try Beatles albums. She thinks through her parents' old record collection. *1963:* Please Please Me. *1964:* With the Beatles. *1964:* Beatles for Sale. *1965: soundtrack from* Help!. *1965:* Rubber Soul. *Shit, I think I missed one. Another soundtrack.* Hard Day's Night, *also 1964. Of course. Then 1966... 1966... 1966...*

Jackie does not remember dreaming this time. She opens her eyes and hears raindrops hitting her apartment window. Then she sees the time 12:01 on the clock radio. She jerks up in a panic. *Fuck! Oh, fuck me hard. I'm such a loser.* She forgot to set an alarm. She has less than an hour to get to work.

She leaps out of bed and grabs the nearest T-shirt, pair of jeans, bra and panties from wherever they happen to be—on the floor or in her dresser. No time for a shower, no time for breakfast or lunch. She senses that her hair is a frightful bedhead mess but fails to care.

Her desktop is still on, the screen gone black, and she remembers why she was awake for much of the night. *One last peek,* she thinks. *I don't want to, but I have to.* She shakes the mouse to wake the computer up, and the first place she goes is the puppy's Spitter page. "Oh, come on! Come on!" she gripes out loud. Still no reply, still no new posts. The profile page is still completely visible, so

@nagging_conscience_42 has neither blocked her nor deleted the account.

Stop worrying about it. It may mean nothing. She grabs her purse and her fall jacket, slips on her shoes, and runs out of the apartment as if a cop is chasing her.

Her rush, it turns out, is for nothing. The subway line is closed down today, with shuttle buses running for the next six stations. After waiting in the rain with a small crowd for five minutes, she boards a bus, too late to get a seat. The bus fills up with people quickly, and she is stuck standing in the middle of a mess of wet, grumpy people, barely able to move. She smells bad body odour mixed with strong perfume and what may or may not be urine. Raindrops keep pelting the windows, which are too fogged up for her to see anything outside. And she is pretty sure the shrimpy, middle-aged, shaven-headed dude sitting a few feet from her is ogling her ass when she is not looking.

The driver is nowhere to be seen. Probably using the washroom or running to the nearest Tim Hortons for a coffee. Or beating off somewhere. *Who knows.* The bus doors are open and Jackie hears music from a car stereo in the vicinity, pumped up loud enough for her to recognize the song–if one can call it a song. She forgets the title and wishes she had long forgotten that the song existed, but there is no doubt she is hearing one of the less successful singles by Angry Chuck M, one nevertheless played ad nauseam by many white wannabe rappers who went to her Ottawa high school.

I don't care what people think of me / Bitch, I don't care what people think of me! / I'll kick you in the nuts if you don't agree / 'Cause I don't care what people think of me! / I do what I want / I do what I want / I do what I want, bitch! / I do what I want! / Don't fuck with...

The tune, or what there is of one, for this section is an obvious rip-off of the chorus of Eminem's "The Way I Am", but the lyrics have none of Marshall Mathers' relative wit or poetry. Many of Angry Chuck M's lyrics revolve around threatening to kick the listener in the head or the testicles, for some reason. Jackie finds it next to impossible to make any connection between this nasty, hateful rapper and the dorky, overweight, middle-aged bar owner she spoke with on the phone yesterday–or the chubby softball kid from his story. Sometimes she is amazed, sometimes not, about the different masks people wear, showing you only what they want you to see.

The Angry Chuck M song is soon joined by a new and arguably worse one. A young woman and her four or five-year-old daughter stand near her. The girl, who is holding a half-eaten oatmeal cookie dripping with saliva in one hand and her mother's finger in the other, has begun singing "The Song that Never Ends" loudly, with the complete absence of self-consciousness and shame typical of a small child.

The mother smiles and nods along to the beat as the girl starts the same verse over. A few other nearby passengers smile, charmed by the scene. Nobody else on the bus says anything, and the only sound remains the child's high-pitched lyrical squeal.

Jackie has to chew on her lips to stop herself from damaging her front teeth with grinding. She hated this song when she was a kid and that old Lamb Chop puppet woman used to sing it, and she hates it even more now. There is something so meaningless and banal about it that irritates her on a deep level, maybe a subconscious one.

But it is not just the song that makes her want to punch something or someone. It is the grating, nasal whine of the girl's voice. It is also the lack of sleep. It is the fact that her period has started. It is the stress of being stuck on a shuttle bus that is not moving and probably never will, and the stress of being late for work again. It is the intolerable weight of guilt for what she has done to @nagging_conscience_42 *if* she has done something to him, or to her, which makes her wonder, which boosts her stress more. It is her doubts about Paul Shoreditch and her strange feeling that his demise may not have been an accident on his part and her guilt about caring either way about such a scumbag, *if* he was a scumbag. It is the growing realization that he might not have been a scumbag and something terrible has been going on. It is the awful, inept rap song playing outside, and the mental picture of a group of jock bullies beating the shit out of a wimpy kid who does not belong on their softball field, and of a bitter old woman calling everybody a "fag" and smacking her son for crying, and that bald old bastard gaping at her ass, and the bus never moving, and the rain coming down, and the wetness of her messed-up hair, and that obnoxious brat and her stupid, repetitive song going on and on and on...

And something inside her reaches a detonation. Every thought and emotion that has been whirling through her mind collide in a massive twelve-car pileup over a hundred lit fuses.

"SHUT THE FUUUUUUUUUUUCK UUUUUUUUUUUUUUUUP!!!"

Every pair of eyes on the bus stares at her. They cannot believe what they have just heard. Even Jackie barely realizes what has happened. The little girl has stopped singing.

"What the hell did you just say?" the mother growls, her face aghast.

It is too late. Like a stolen car tumbling over a cliff in an old Chicken Run contest, Jackie's meltdown has gone too far to stop.

"I'm sorry! But I can't listen to that!" she yells at the mother, taking an aggressive step forward. "What kind of mother *are* you? Nothing in the world has *ever* been more annoying! Can't you just make your kid *shut her fucking pie hole*?"

The woman's reply is a sharp, vicious smack on Jackie's left cheek.

As Jackie loses her balance and tumbles backwards, falling into the legs and crotches of three other passengers, she hears what seems like dozens of loud, insistent echoes of the smacking sound all around her. She looks up and realizes that all the other passengers are applauding the mother and laughing at Jackie.

"What the fuck is *wrong* with you?" one man shouts at Jackie.

"Who *does* that?" a millennial woman with purple hair says. "I mean, what kind of person just screams about a random kid like that?"

"Get off this bus," another man orders. "Just get off. Now."

Some of the passengers start clapping again, while others agree out loud that Jackie has no place on this shuttle bus. Jackie picks up her purse, stands slowly, turns, and heads towards the front exit of the bus, shaking and stumbling as others move out of her way.

As soon as she steps off the bus and back into the rain, the driver arrives, giving her an odd look before he steps on board, gets into position and drives away. Another shuttle bus waits behind where the first one was and Jackie boards it. This bus is also overflowing, and the driver has gone MIA, so everybody has to wait for several minutes.

She grasps a ceiling pole with one hand and closes her eyes.

It takes her several slow, deep breaths to calm down. When her body is calm and her mind is clearer, she goes over what just happened in her mind. The whole scene feels like something she has watched staged on TV, not something that has actually happened, or that even involved her.

Jackie hangs her head in shame. She hopes the little girl is okay and feels relieved that she aimed her tirade at the mother instead of the girl. Then she winces as she remembers the other passengers' responses again.

Fine. Fine fine fine fine fine fine. I deserved that.

She stares down at the wet, slightly muddy bus floor.

But come on, people. It really is an annoying song.

Jackie is more than an hour late for work, soaking wet and unaware her hair is a worse mess than before. As she arrives, Sam glares at Jackie, her jaw hanging, as if she does not recognize her. "TTC," she mouths silently at Sam, then goes straight for her desk.

For an hour, nothing happens. Jackie makes no ticket sales. Not even the Christmas concert series, a popular HPO staple every holiday season, is getting any bites. Her leads either ask her to call back on another day or tell her they are not interested this year. The day is so dull, Jackie feels almost relieved when she senses Sam standing behind her.

"Jackie," she says. "I need to see you in my office. Now."

No polite smile this time.

Jackie takes off her headset and follows Sam into the small room. Once again, Patty sits there, holding the clipboard and pen. She wears a serious expression too.

For fuck's sake. What the hell did I do this time?

Sam closes the door, everybody sits down, and Sam turns her computer screen to face Jackie. "Jackie," she says, barely making eye contact, "could you please explain what we're seeing here?"

The screen displays a short article on TruthSerumNews.org, an American website Jackie knows well. It used to be a respected source of progressive political and entertainment news but in recent years, it has devolved into more of an online scandal sheet for which journalists just out of college write hatchet jobs about celebrities saying "offensive" things. Jackie still visits the site now and then, with a tiny morsel of guilt hidden in the corners of her brain.

The article is dominated by an embedded YouTube video, and the fuzzy preview image shows a crowd on a bus. The title of the article is "**YOU WON'T BELIEVE HOW POSTAL THIS WOMAN WENT ON A FIVE YEAR OLD GIRL AND HER MOM.**" The title of the embedded video is "**Psycho Bitch chews out kid for singing on bus in Canada lol.**"

Jackie gasps.

She winces hard.

Then she drops her head into her hands.

As if she cannot wait, Sam immediately clicks on the video and "The Song that Never Ends" starts playing in an irritating child's voice.

"Turn it off," Jackie says, her voice muffled by her hands.

But Sam lets the torture go on. After a few lines, the song is interrupted by a loud, screaming voice. It sounds like Jackie, and it also does not. It sounds like Jackie's mouth and vocal cords have been possessed by some demon–a tired, fed-up demon that just cannot hack it with humanity anymore, that no longer cares what it says or does.

"SHUT THE F—"

"Please!" Jackie cries. "Please turn it off!"

Sam does. There is a silence in the tiny office–Jackie cannot tell how long, a few seconds or a minute or longer–a silence that rings louder than any demonic shriek she can imagine. She lifts her head from her hands. Sam glares at her. Patty, as always, jots notes aggressively onto her clipboard. The YouTube video is paused on a frozen image of an angry, raving woman in a wet T-shirt and fall jacket, with hair so wavy and messy that it should be declared a danger zone. Jackie realizes for the first time how crazed and unbalanced she must have looked to the other passengers. She probably *still* looks like that.

Sam finally breaks the silence. "Well? Can you explain this?"

Jackie cannot stand Sam's stare. Her eyes wander to the motivational poster on the wall above Sam's computer. "ATTITUDE", the poster reads in giant capital letters, accompanied by an image of a silhouetted person stretching on a beach at sunrise.

She clicks her tongue.

"I… was having a bad day," she replies in a small voice.

"Everybody has bad days. Is that an excuse?"

Jackie looks at the floor. "No."

"Jackie, I know this didn't happen at work, but I can't help being troubled by it. If this is how you behave on your own time–and in public!–how can we be assured you won't behave like this *here*? How do we know you won't snap at a customer on a call? Or at another employee here? Do you think I'd have hired you if I'd known who you really are?"

"I'm not really like that."

Sam raises an eyebrow with a skeptical glance that appears to say, *Aren't you, though?*

"That's *not* who I am," Jackie says. "I swear. That's… a *part* of me, I guess." She swallows. "You know what these websites are like. They sensationalize; they only show part of the story."

"And what's the other part?"

"I…"

She thinks. *How can I explain what it feels like, when everything in your head comes crashing down so hard, all at once, that you just don't give a rat's ass anymore? How can I explain it so that she would understand?* But Jackie has nothing.

"I was just having a bad day," she mumbles. "And... now it's worse."

A short silence, and then Sam lets out a sigh, and then a longer silence. Patty keeps jotting notes on the clipboard.

"Jackie, take the rest of the day off," Sam says. "Make sure you arrive *on time* tomorrow–and calm and professional. And do something about that *hair*, for God's sake."

Jackie nods. She stands up and turns to leave the office.

Then she turns back to Sam, who is closing the web browser. "Uh," she asks, "am I still being paid for the rest of today?"

Sam closes her eyes and looks ready to burst. "Just go home, Jackie."

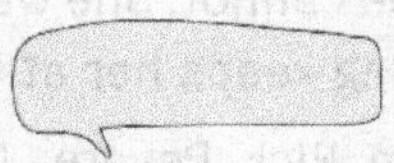

Now she wishes she did *not* go home. She wishes she could have stayed at work all day, all night, all week, and never gone home again. Or at least, never opened a web browser again.

Somebody, somewhere, has identified her.

More than a thousand new messages sit waiting in her e-mail inbox. Many have come directly from the contact page on JackieRoberts.com. Some are notifications of replies to her blog entries, some are replies to her *Scarborough Indie Voice* reviews, and some are replies on Spitter. Almost all hurl some level of abuse at her.

You misopedist piece of shit. I hope you die in pain.

I dont hit women but I sure wish I was there to slap you to. Then I would punch you in the face haha. How does it feel

kill your self you worthless shit

What kind of person are you Jackie?? You've probably scarred that poor child for life! Don't you have the slightest empathy for anybody but yourself?? No I don't think you do, I think you're a sociopath who likes to hurt people!! Shame on you, you vile worm. For shame.

WHY DON'T U GO AN KILL URSELF.

Misopedia is a horrible thing, I say its' just as bad as racism and misogyny and homophobia. I feel sorry for you for being such an ignorant woman.

lol you are a bitch and your writing sucks too. i do better on my blog XD

you should kill yourself

kill yourself

kill yourself

kill yourself

kill yourself

Jackie is so numb she can barely move. She wants to take her eyes off the screen, but she cannot. She wants to go to bed and stay there forever, but something keeps her at the computer.

An e-mail arrives from Rick Pevere. No subject heading. She opens the e-mail and sees the message: "Please call me as soon as you get this, thanks." Jackie grabs her phone and dials his number, feeling like a newly hired circus assistant sticking her head into a lion's mouth.

His voice sounds odd. A bit muffled and with a hesitant tone. She hears a chewing sound. Of course, he's eating something again.

"How are you, Jackie?" he says through a mouthful.

He has never asked her this before. Not in such a sincere way.

"I'm okay," she lies.

"Are you? Just... I see you've been making the rounds today."

"I'm fine. This shit happens."

"Cool. Glad to hear it." A pause as she hears him take another bite. "Because that makes it a little easier to say what I've got to say right now."

"Which is...?"

"Jackie, you know how much I love your writing. You're one of the best movie reviewers out there–better than some of the ones in the big newspapers. You've been a great—"

"Rick. Don't be a flake. Just spit it out."

Several seconds of silence. Rick swallows.

"I don't think it's a good idea to let you write for the *Indie Voice* anymore."

Jackie closes her eyes. Her heart seems to beat slower but harder.

"Because some douchefuck filmed me on a bus," she says. "Is that why?"

"Look. The *Indie Voice* has an image to maintain—"

Despite how she feels, despite everything that has happened, she cannot stop herself from doubling down into loud, nasty laughter.

"An image, Rick? Really? What kind of image is your dinky little website trying to project, anyway?" She hardly sounds like herself in her bluntness, she realizes. "How do you think everybody sees you? You think you're Ben Bradlee or something?"

"Ben who?"

"He was... never mind."

More chewing noises, mixed with unsteady breathing. "I just don't want the website associated with your name anymore. I'm sorry."

"Well, that's great. You know that writing reviews for you is really the only thing I have, right?" A tear wells up in one eye. "I mean, the only thing that makes me feel like a legit film critic–even a minuscule bit. And you want to take that away from me. Because of a stupid video."

"I'm sorry," he repeats, more faint. "You're a very talented and smart person, and I'm sure you'll find something. Eventually. I wish you luck. Honestly."

I'm not gonna cry. No. I don't cry. I'm strong enough to handle this.

She sits down. A lengthy interlude of deep, unsteady breathing from her end and careless chewing from his.

"So... you don't want the Shoreditch thing anymore, I take it," she asks.

"The what?"

"Paul Shoreditch."

"Who?"

She wants to hurl her phone against the wall and scream.

"Paul. Shoreditch. The crazy funeral and the website. The fucking news feature you asked me to do. The hate story." Pause. "Which I've been spending so much time working on."

A short silence, then, "Oh! Right. I forgot about that. I'm an idiot."

Yes. Yes, you are.

"Yeah," he adds, "don't worry about that anymore."

Jackie clenches her teeth.

"Rick," she says, "that was just another one of your whims, wasn't it."

More chewing sounds, though slower, as if he has to think about it.

"Yes," he says. "I guess it was."

"Go fuck yourself."

She pounds her thumb on the disconnection icon, wishing she were using an old-fashioned rotary phone she could slam down on a receiver.

The strangest thing: this may be the worst day of Jackie's life but having the balls to tell Rick to go fuck himself has given her something of a buzz. One she rarely feels.

Shit. That felt good.

But the buzz fades rapidly as she looks at the computer screen again. Twenty-three e-mails have popped up during the conversation. The latest one has the subject heading, **"U R A SHIT WRITER Y DONT U JUST QUIT"**. The second newest: **"I bet *my* five-year-old could kick your ass"**.

Jackie flicks off the web browser and sees that same cold stare from Sam Spade's face. Now it looks disappointed.

"I know, I know," she says to Bogie. "I'm sorry."

She falls into bed and, for the first time in years–she cannot remember doing this since high school–collapses into a long, hard, aggressive bout of bawling.

NINE

Jackie rarely leaves her bed for the next fourteen hours. Some of that time is spent sleeping, out of pure exhaustion. Some involves lying awake, either crying like a beaten child or staring blankly at the ceiling wondering if this is it, if her life is over now. Sometimes, she closes her eyes and fantasizes—not seriously but vividly—about killing herself. What would be the best way? Wrist slashing? Pill overdose? Jumping off the CN Tower?

I'd rather do something painless, but maybe I deserve the pain.

She gets out of bed for keeps at about seven the next morning. She has not eaten since yesterday afternoon but is not hungry. Pouring herself a glass of water, Jackie ponders. She cannot think of anything to do but go back to the computer and delete all the new e-mails.

There are thousands. Jackie does not read the vicious subject headings. But scanning through them, she cannot help but be reminded of F**kPaulShoreditch.com—all the endless lists of nasty posts, and all the replies.

In the midst of deleting the unread messages, she notices one from a Susie Glendenning, with the subject heading, "**Your question about Paul Shoreditch and Kathy McDougal.**" Still groggy, she clicks "Open the Message" out of habit.

Hi Jackie, the e-mail reads. ***This is @Babyface857 from Spitter. See below. I guess you've never seen this? It's been circulating for years.***

The e-mail includes a forwarded message from 2016, with a second forwarded message. The latter was apparently sent to Susie Glendenning from a name Jackie does not recognize with the subject heading: "**FW: Must Read This Shocking Account Of What Happened To The Editor Of KatsKorner.ca!**" Jackie feels a brief flicker of *déjà vu*.

The sender of the original is Kathy McDougal's e-mail address from KatsKorner.ca. The receiver line shows Kathy's address again, implying this was initially sent to a number of BCCs. The date of the original e-mail is October 12, 2013, and its subject heading is: "**WARNING: Do not trust this man! He is dangerous and sick =(**".

The only content of the original e-mail is "**PASSWORD: oaeirghksfyd3478–DON'T SHARE OUTSIDE BBB!!!**" and a link to a post on BlahBlahBlog, or BBB, a popular blogging site. Jackie has a BBB account she has not used in ten years; she never liked the bitter drama and fighting and flaming that always went on among the other users. She has to log into the site to see the private post, and it takes her a few moments to remember her old personal password.

When she gets into the BBB site, a large window pops up onscreen demanding another password. Jackie has seen this before–it is a site feature used for *very* private blog entries. Realizing that the weird letter/number jumble in the e-mail is for this step, she enters it.

The post is also dated October 12, 2013, and the account username is k.mcdougal. The user photo is one of the sketchy cartoon cats from the *Kat's Korner* logo, but much smaller.

Please forward this message to as many BBB users as you can, the post begins. ***If we can reach alot of people then***

"What the hell am I doing?"

She has forgotten that she does not have to work on the Paul Shoreditch story anymore. She is no longer required to interview anybody, to research anything, to *care*.

She flips back to the other tab and moves the cursor to delete the e-mail, but then stops. Curiosity? A misplaced sense of duty? It could be both.

She stares at the "Delete" button for a while.

Then she gets up, goes to the kitchen area of the apartment and gets another drink of water. Then she sits back down at the computer. *I'm gonna regret this, aren't I?*

> Please forward this message to as many BBB users as you can. If we can reach alot of people, then we can stop alot of pain, maybe even save a life or two. Also, here is a Trigger Warning for those who can't read stories about abuse, violence, imprisonment, and sexual assault =(
>
> There is a man in Toronto, Canada named Paul Shoreditch, who I was dating for a while. At first he seemed harmless, but then started getting abusive. It was a gradual thing. First he was fine, then he started calling me names now and again. He would call me bitch or slut or whore sometimes. I thought he was just kidding around and let him do it just for fun. There seemed to be no danger. How wrong I was! =(After a while, it was clear that he was not kidding. He really meant it. Then he started hitting me. Every time we had sex, he would insist on hitting and punching me. I said no, please don't, but he would do it anyway. And the sex would get rougher and rougher. He was like an animal. Not even a human being anymore! =O I got real scared but didn't have the courage to stay away from him.

On September 14 of this year, Paul Shoreditch invited me to the house he owns in North York, which is a borough of Toronto. He said we were going to just hang out and watch movies or something. I said OK. So he takes me to his basement, tells me he has to go to the bathroom and would be right back. He went up the stairs–and then locked the door! =0 And he kept me prisoner. He kept me prisoner in his basement for about five days, I think. I barely had anything to eat. He would come down and hit me and overpower me. He would torture me and assault me repeatedly. =(He is a very strong man and can overpower a woman very easily! It was torture. I felt like I was being held captive by terrorists. If there is a Hell, it has to be better than what Paul Shoreditch put me through.

When it was all over, he said to me, Don't you ever tell anybody about this. If you do, I will hunt you down and kill you, he said. So until today, I have not told anybody about this. I don't even feel like I can tell the police, because we all know how useless they are in these cases! But now I've changed my mind as far as you are concerned. I am risking my life to tell you all that Paul Shoreditch is an evil sadistic fucker of a man. =(Stay away from him. Obviously, I am not the first person to suffer at this crepe's hands, because I see there is a website now, http://www.F**kPaulShoreditch.com, where people are welcome to tell their horror stories about him.

Paul Shoreditch is the living epitome of privilege. Of white, male, straight, hateful misogynistic privilege. Let's do the right thing, and the kind thing, and spread the word about him! =)

Lots of love,

Kathy McDougal

Editor of KatsKorner.ca

Jackie reads it over again.

Holy shit. This makes absolutely no sense.

Then she reads it for a third time.

How the hell would Paul Shoreditch even have a house? He was a stock boy in a drug store! I doubt he made as much money as I do, and I can barely afford this tiny flat. This story makes Kathy's other one about the birthday attack seem believable.

Jackie goes back to her inbox, where the nasty e-mails are still coming in, and searches for her previous message from Kathy. She moves it to another folder so she can find it again without having to sort through the dreck and reads it again. It sounds like a second version of the same person, or the same person from parallel universes telling alternate stories.

Jackie tries to make sense of it. But that would take a special kind of mental gymnastics. If this actually happened, surely the police would have found out somehow? Paul would have been in jail for years, right? He may or may not have been a bad person but forcing somebody to be a sex slave in a cellar seems well beyond the impotent loser from Kathy's other story.

She looks up Kathy's number from Rick Pevere's e-mail.

"Hmmmmmmm?" answers a sleepy female voice. "Whoizzit?"

"Jackie Roberts. Did I wake you?"

"Yeah, but it's okay."

Jackie has forgotten that it is still relatively early but does not care right now. She tells Kathy about the BBB post. "Did you write that?"

A substantial pause on the line.

"No!" Kathy answers. "Of course not."

"You didn't."

"No. I've seen that post–I mean, I've seen a *copy* of it–but it's not from me. I'm not even on that site!" Beat. "That's what I tell everyone. I mean, when they ask me about it."

"It sure *sounds* like you."

"That's what they say. Guess I have an easy voice to imitate, huh?"

"So nothing like that ever happened?"

"No!" Kathy laughs. "Oh my God, it's such a silly story! If Paul ever tried to do something like that to me–not that I'd put it past the little creep–but if he did, I'd've snapped his back in two. And then he would've cried like a baby!" She laughs again.

"Then who wrote it?"

"I don't know. Honest. Somebody who hated Paul too, I'm guessing. Maybe somebody who knew what he did to Fiona and made up a new story. You know what people are like!"

"But why is your address in the original e-mail–the one forwarded to me?"

Kathy laughs again. "Well, *obviously*, whoever sent out the first forward, they wrote my address in there. My e-mail address is public, you know. It's right on the *Kat's Korner* site. It could have been anybody. Somebody who also knew Paul, knew Paul knew me, and used me to get revenge on him."

"You don't sound like you *mind*, though."

"Mind?"

"Somebody stole your identity. Made false accusations with it."

Kathy laughs again, with a deeper, harsher tone. "Why should I *mind*? Even if it's all made up, the creep deserved it all!"

"Huh."

"Anyway. Now that I'm up, I've got a couple of kitties to feed. Anything else, Jackie?"

Jackie is not sure what her next tactic should be. "I... guess not."

"Are you sure?" Kathy clears her throat. "Nothing else you've... seen online lately?"

What?

"Not sure what you mean."

"Never mind! Talk to you later. Garfield and Robert Smith say hi."

Then a sudden thought.

"Wait! Hold on," Jackie yelps at the phone. But Kathy has already disconnected.

Shit.

Because it just occurred to her: How could Kathy's *Kat's Korner* e-mail address have been public when she had not even started the website at the time? *Or maybe I'm remembering wrong?*

She turns back to the computer and looks over Kathy's long e-mail to her about Paul, scanning through it, skipping over the bad sex. But she cannot find what she is looking for. It must have been in the live interview. The one Jackie forgot to record.

Idiot. Idiot idiot idiot. Fuck me. Even though it doesn't matter now.

The alleged Fiona incident happened about six years ago. That was what Kathy said in the interview. The date on the original e-mail is about six years ago. "I launched *Kat's Korner* about a year later. Paul inspired it." Was that what she said? Something like that. "About a year later" would have been sometime in 2014. So how does the *Korner* address appear in an e-mail from October 2013? How would anyone know about the existence of that e-mail address if the website did not exist yet? Unless the sender of the first forward wrote in a fake date too. But *why*?

Either Jackie has a bad memory, or Kathy does.

Jackie opens a new Internet tab and calls up KatsKorner.ca, then clicks on the contact page. A poorly etched cartoon black cat with a wide, overzealous grin says in a dialogue balloon, "Hey Krazy Katz!! If you've got something to say to our editor, fill it in the comment box below!! Meeeyow!!!" There are text boxes for a visitor's name, e-mail address and message. No specific e-mail address is given—not Kathy's, not anybody's. Another lie. *Or another mistake?*

She goes back to the homepage. On the right sidebar, beside the latest articles, is an "Archive" list with links to various months of past stories. She scrolls down. The dates go all the way back to May 2013. Jackie clicks on that first month, and there is a page with just one story, dated May 16, 2013. **"Hi! Welcome to Kat's Korner!"** is the title.

Then she goes back to the BBB post and clicks on the author's username. The long post about Paul is the sole entry in the entire blog. It has attained more than three thousand replies, which Jackie has not even viewed–she already knows what their content is like.

Jackie clicks off all the Internet browsers. And there is Sam Spade again, staring at her, his mouth shut tight, waiting for her frail excuse for a reply.

"I know it's ridiculous, Bogie," she tells him, "but a small, irrational part of me *still* feels obligated to believe her stories. I don't like creeps. I think people like that should be put away forever and punished until they can't take it anymore. And the web, even some of the media, they've yelled at me for years–always believe, forget evidence, forget logic, just take everything as the gospel truth. But I can't do that anymore. What am I missing here?"

No response, as always.

Jesus, I'm not even supposed to be doing this thing anymore. Jackie shuts down the computer and goes back to bed. She lies awake for a few more hours, not planning to get up until she has to go to work. In her mind, she sees Brain standing and nodding at her with an understanding yet triumphant grin. Gut is nowhere to be seen. Maybe Gable is off to find another conquest.

She was dreading the commute, but to her profound relief, nothing awful happened. Almost nobody seemed to recognize her. It may have been because she no longer had a case of messy, wavy bedhead to distinguish her from the non-crazies on the subway. It may also have been because she stayed quiet and kept as low a profile as she could, forcing her eyes on her library copy of Michael Wolff's *Siege*. At one point, she spotted a thin, ginger teenage boy a few seats away giving her a dirty look, to which she responded with a middle finger. Later, a woman's smug voice said above her, "Try to restrain yourself, eh? She's only five months old." Jackie looked up and saw a middle-aged woman with a gloating grin, pushing a baby carriage past her seat. A few minutes later, the baby started crying and screaming and would not stop. Jackie felt ashamed of her irritation this time.

Now she is back at work, failing to make sales once again. None of her colleagues is speaking to her, but that is far from atypical. Jackie has felt no urge to socialize with any of these people since she learned that she was surrounded by snitches, or at least one. Nobody mentions the bus incident, although it is hard to believe they are unaware of it.

As she waits for an answer from a past HPO ticket buyer in Oakville, she overhears a snippet of quiet conversation between Chris and Julia. They are talking movies. Jackie would be overloaded with chat envy if the speakers were anybody but co-workers.

"Can't believe I gotta wait 'til next year to see the Black Widow movie," Chris groans.

"*Another* superhero movie?" gripes Julia. "Holy shit, it's like we get one a month now."

"Didn't you see *Endgame*? It was amazing."

"I skipped it. I'll probably skip the Black Widow one too. Who needs another Avengers movie, for fuck's sake?"

Jackie purses her lips. *One more vulgarity, Julia. Just one more swear, honey, and I'm reporting you to Sam. Because no one else will. These two-faced assholes.*

"It's not an Avengers movie," Chris says with all the predictable pedantry of a young comic-book geek. "It's Black Widow. Only one Avenger."

"An Avenger movie, then," says Julia with a sarcastic cough. "I stand corrected."

"Well, *I'm* cool with a new Avenger movie every year."

"So next year, Black Widow is Avenger of the Year. One day, it'll be Avenger of the Week."

Jackie smiles and chuckles inwardly. *Avenger of the Weak. Now that would be a bad Marvel movie. The superhero who makes nasty websites about bad guys. Surely Kathy McDougal would go see it.*

Especially if they threw in the cat from Captain Marvel. And she'd write a rave review about it on Kat's Korner, *with lots of love in it. Maybe she'd even sign it off with "Lots of love," and—*

Jackie freezes.

"Hello?" a man's voice says on the line.

She hardly hears him.

"Hello? Anybody there?"

Jackie whips off her headset and dives into her purse for her phone. Telesales personnel here are not allowed to use the Internet for personal reasons, so she will need her cell.

She makes a dash for the women's washroom, barely catching Sam's confused glance. Relieved to find the washroom empty, she enters a stall, locks it, and opens a web browser on her phone. First, she looks up Kathy's e-mail about her aborted fling with Paul. Then she looks for the welcome page on F**kPaulShoreditch.com and rereads it, and she goes to Avenger_of_the_Weak's post following Paul's death. Then she flicks back to the e-mail again, and back to the website posts again.

> this is where we gather to bask in our dislike for this horrid, pathetic little man and all that he stands for...

in Avenger's intro.

> I can give you idiocies and weirdness about that pathetic little man that will make your brain melt!

writes Kathy.

> Malodorous tit.

Also in Avenger's writing.

Jackie now remembers Kathy saying "smelly little tit" in the live interview.

alot, Kathy writes. Avenger too.

Crepe. That appears several times, and not in reference to French pancakes.

The same scattered emojis. The same exclamation marks. The same general rhythm. Even the exact same ***Lots of love*** sign-off.

"For fuck's sake. How did I miss it?"

And Jackie smacks her head against the stall wall.

Any journalist or investigator who had the slightest shred of perception would have figured this out right away. Too wild a coincidence, even to an amateur like Jackie.

The only difference between the two online personas, she now sees, is that Avenger rarely uses capital letters. Avenger never uses them *properly*, in fact—only randomly, at the wrong times. And that suggests that Kathy is doing it on purpose, consciously disguising her writing voice and doing a half-assed job of it. Either she is confident that nobody would care in the first place or would think to check, or she is phenomenally stupid. Both conclusions seem valid.

Jackie sits on the toilet seat and ponders further implications.

So Kathy McDougal is behind the anti-Shoreditch website, and she is clearly the one who authored the BBB post and sent that first e-mail. Who knows how many people that e-mail reached, and may still be reaching; for all Jackie knows, it is still circulating out there in the ether, winning over new anti-Paul converts even when there is no Paul anymore.

And they all believed her. Every fucking word. Like I did. Or almost did.

Something else hits Jackie: if Kathy has no qualms about posing as two separate people online, how far has she gone with it—and for how long? How many of those hundreds of people posting on F**kPaulShoreditch.com could be her too? And how much influence could that have? Enough to rile up a real-life mob? It may be a longshot, but Kathy could be the sole force responsible for the massive antipathy against Paul Shoreditch.

Kathy McDougal has a lot of time on her hands, no question there. She also has an extraordinary amount of anger, much of it directed at Paul. But why? Why Paul in particular? What would drive somebody–even someone as batty as Kathy–to make a whole website bashing one person, to send out a mass e-mail spreading obvious lies about that person, to build a whole underground movement and encourage its members to denounce him and even riot at his funeral...?

"*Why?*" Jackie asks out loud. "What the fuck did you *do*, Paul?"

"Hm?" a voice asks from another stall.

"What?"

"Were you talking to me?"

Jackie recognizes the voice as Amanda's. "No, just thinking out loud." She mimes smacking her head on the stall wall again, having not even heard Amanda come in. *It's amazing how they sneak up on you like that.* She wonders if Amanda is going to tattle on her for swearing in the office again. If the washroom counts.

She flushes the toilet so Amanda thinks she was peeing and heads back to her desk.

The first lead to which the computer system sends her is named Fiona Morgenfeld. There is no answer, and during the pause between calls, Jackie remembers the Fiona from Kathy's story about the party. *Is there even such a person as Fiona?*

"Hello?" says a man's voice through the phone system.

I know I'm not even supposed to be working on this ridiculous news story anymore, but...

"Hello!" he says, harsher. "Anybody there?"

"Oh..." Jackie says, snapping out of her funk and jumping back into character. "Good afternoon, Dan!" she reads mechanically from the computer screen. "My name is Jackie Roberts, and I'm calling on behalf of the Hogtown Philharmonic Orchestra. We're calling..."

TEN

The next morning, a voicemail on Jackie's phone.

"Hello, Miss Roberts," the message begins. The voice is male and high-pitched, almost like a Muppet, like Bert or Fozzie Bear, but not affected that way. "It's Morty Bozzer. I just got your e-mail. Sure, I can do an interview for your story about Paul..." The voice is attempting a casual, businesslike tone, but the falsity of it is obvious. He strikes Jackie as a little boy trying to sound like a man.

Out of habit, she taps the callback icon but disconnects after a second. Again, she has forgotten that she does not have to work on this story anymore.

And yet...

Fuck it. I've come this far. And I want to know whatever this guy knows. Maybe I can post the story on my website, she thinks, *so it does not go to waste*. Although she no longer holds out much hope for anybody reading her blog anymore.

But even if I don't write or publish anything... I've got to know. For myself. After all, I may be the only one in the world who knows what Kathy's really been up to.

Hating herself, she taps the callback icon again.

"FunMart. How can I help you?" answers a sullen, disinterested young woman's voice.

So he still works there. "Is Morty Bozzer available?"

"Just a second."

After a minute, the Muppety voice comes on. "Morty here."

"Hi Morty, it's Jackie Roberts."

The fake professionalism is back in the tone. "Hello, Miss Roberts," he says. "Thanks for getting back to me."

"No worries. You're at work now?"

"Yes."

"What would be a better time to call?"

"Huh?"

"To do the interview."

Short pause. "Ah. I assumed it was going to be an in-person meeting."

"I prefer to do interviews over the phone, when possible."

"I see." Jackie thinks he hears him licking his lips. "Miss Roberts?"

"Call me Jackie."

"Can we do this interview in person, Jackie? I'd feel more comfortable."

"Um..."

"Maybe at my condo," he says. The business façade has been dropped. He is speaking quickly, with more informality than she wants to hear. "I've got a nice penthouse condo downtown. If you come by tonight, or another night, maybe I'll cook something for you? I'm an amazing chef."

She tries to think of the nicest way to tell him she would rather smack herself on the breasts with a boiling water pot, but he interrupts.

"Or maybe you could come by my office at FunMart? It's dead around here weekday mornings. I could use the distraction."

"I can do a morning."

"Good." His tone betrays disappointment. "Tomorrow? Ten?"

"Sure."

He gives her the address, with some of the false professional tone back.

What the fuck was that? Was he trying to hit on me or something? She hates the thought of having to go on another pointless field trip, but it is not nearly as far this time. FunMart is located in a strip mall in the middle of Scarborough, not far from the RT line.

Jackie has a few hours to kill, and she is unusually hungry but does not feel like making breakfast. After a quick shower, she strolls to a small, seedy-looking breakfast café down the street from her building, one she has walked past many times and whose name she never remembers. The air is cool and breezy, but the sun is out and for the first time in a long while, she is not thinking about her health. She orders a large combo with two eggs, plenty of bacon strips, hash browns, toast, fruit, and orange juice, along with a cup of coffee. She barely looks at the bill when she gets it–just drops her debit card on it and gives a fatter tip than she normally would. *Guess I don't need any lunch today.* She walks out of the restaurant, stuffed to the ears, feeling like a hippo. The coffee sucked, but that has only made her yearn for better coffee, at least mediocre. So she stops by the neighbourhood Sobeys on the way back and buys a large tin of Maxwell House. She almost trips over a dead mouse on the sidewalk on the way back to her building.

Upon arriving home, Jackie turns the desktop on. When Sam Spade comes onscreen, she moves the arrow to open a web browser but stops herself. Where will she go? She does not want to check her e-mail because there will be little new but more abuse. Same with Spitter. Same with her blog–more nasty comments on her articles, and she does not have any new material to post anyway. The last thing she wants to do is write anything. And she has no reason to visit the *Indie Voice* website anymore. She wonders if her film-writing career or "career" is over.

Retired at thirty-six. The world's youngest has-been, like Orson Welles, except that I barely even got started.

On an odd whim, she goes to *Kat's Korner.*

Jackie has never taken the time to read the articles on the site; she has merely skimmed it, doing lazy, half-baked research for the Shoreditch story. Now she browses some of the more recent headlines. **TWENTY-SEVEN MORE REASONS WHY NORM MCDONALD SUCKS ASS**, screams one. **AZIZ ANSARI IS BACK WITH A NETFLIX SPECIAL. WHY CAN'T HE JUST GO JUMP OFF A FUCKING CLIFF?** bellows another. **STOP LETTING YOUR KIDS WATCH TOY STORY MOVIES, JOHN LASSETER IS EVIL INCARNATE.** And then there is **JUSTIN TRUDEAU IS NOT YOUR FEMINIST HERO: THIRTEEN WAYS HE IS A SHITTY HYPOCRITE.** And **CANCEL QUENTIN TARANTINO PERMANENTLY, HE IS OBSESSED WITH THE N-WORD AND VIOLENCE AGAINST WOMEN.** Jackie snorts at the last one. *Because no men have ever died horribly in a Tarantino movie, right?* The opening paragraphs, listed under the headline links and accompanying images, all read as if they were scribbled by angry, precocious fourteen-year-old girls. For all Jackie knows, maybe they were.

Not all the stories are celebrity-bashing rants. Jackie spots one titled **AMY SCHUMER IS MY HEROINE, I WANT TO HAVE HER BABIES!**, as well as **TWENTY-THREE REASONS WE NEED A FEMALE RICK MERCER, RIGHT NOW.** Plus the occasional political screed, typically anti-Trump, anti-Trudeau, anti-Doug Ford, or anti-Andrew Scheer. And, of course, there are several examples of the investigative-type stories that Kathy showed her at her place, all aimed at naming and shaming an individual or group for some perceived injustice. **WE HAVE VIDEO FOOTAGE OF RANDOM ASSHOLE FAT-SHAMING HIS GIRLFRIEND**, one heading yells at Jackie. Also, **MONTREAL SMOKED-MEAT DELI BULLIES EMPLOYEE FOR BEING A VEGETARIAN. SHAME!** And **SHUT DOWN THIS MONCTON CHURCH, WE HEAR THE MINISTER HAS NEVER PERFORMED A GAY WEDDING.**

A sudden thought: How many of these writers are Kathy McDougal too? Kathy's name is credited on some stories, but all those childish, hyperbolic introductory paragraphs may as well have been written by the same person. How long could a website like this get away with using fake writers? Would the target audience even care? *I could be wrong, though. Just speculation.*

Jackie is surprised that she has not seen her own bus incident on the site. Then she remembers a recent heading about the TTC and scrolls back up near the top. *Well, der. Of course they have it.* The image is just a random TTC bus, but the article is definitely about Jackie's meltdown: **CHAOS ON TORONTO BUS, CRAZY WRITER TEARS NEW HOLE IN KID AND MOM.**

Writer? How would they...? She clicks on the headline and scans down the article, past raging ranting about the audacity of anybody telling a mother how to raise her own children.

> [...] Staff at Kat's Korner have identified the screaming lunatic as Jackie Roberts, a local writer who contributes movie reviews to ScarboroughIndieVoice.ca and posts long, boring essays on old movies at her blog at JackieRoberts.com. We're guessing that as a film buff, Jackie sure loves big scenes! [...]

Jackie drops her head onto the desk. *Fuck you, Kathy McDougal. You fucking traitor. But then, why should I be surprised?*

She looks at the screen again. On the right sidebar, between ads for tampons and leg razors, is a section titled "Past Faves", and the first item on the list catches her attention: **SEXIST SPACE D-BAG SHOOTS HIMSELF, MUCH REJOICING FOLLOWS.**

Shuddering, Jackie clicks on the heading.

Kathy McDougal is credited as the author. The image with the article, dated from 2015, shows a smiling Mark Taminer. Jackie has heard of him. Taminer was a Canadian scientist employed with the European Space Agency, who was involved with an international team project that landed a space probe on a comet or asteroid or something. She remembers that he passed away a few years ago, but that is all she knows.

Kathy's lengthy article begins:

> Hallelujah! The world is now Mark Taminer-free, and we are all the better for it. Yesterday the news broke that Canada's most misogynistic scientist asshole put a gun to his head and blew his brains out. I bet even the people who had to clean up the blood and guts in his home didn't mind much! Mark Taminer was definitely a liability to our society. And all those mansplaining man-babies out there try to defend him. "But he helped land a probe on a comet," they say. "He's a brilliant scientist." Well, you can be as brilliant as you want, but if you insult women, if you tell all those hopeful young women who dream of STEM careers that they are nothing but objects to you, then anything you achieve is negated. And we will tell you about it, and we will never stop telling you about it! We will hound you and hound you until your life is a waking nightmare and you cannot escape your sins and your conscience.
>
> Mark Taminer, you thought you could escape public rage with a phony apology. You thought you could escape by crying like a two-year-old at a press conference, begging for a forgiveness and an understanding that you should have known you'd never get. You even thought you could escape them by continuing on with your space career as if nothing happened! What a fool. What a sad, pathetic little man you were. We kept on hounding you with articles on this site and others, with Spitter, with nonstop coverage of you and your evils. Many of us sent you personal e-mails. But now, it looks like you finally got the message. And

> we can all move on with our lives, knowing that there is one less sexism enabler in the world [...]

Jackie wants to stop reading. She also feels a familiar mixture of nausea and hard curiosity; familiar because it is not much different from what she felt during her first few excursions through the F**kPaulShoreditch.com website.

What did he do? Kathy, what in hell did Mark Taminer DO?

She scrolls down a little, skimming the text, until she spots this bit:

> [...] talk about where they were when Kennedy was assassinated or during the Moon landing or whatever? For me, I'll never forget where I was, on November 4 of last year, sitting at my computer and sipping a coffee, when I saw that video interview and got a look at that fucking horrible tattoo on Mark Taminer's arm. He wasn't even hiding it! And that was when my world fell apart, when everybody's world fell apart [...]

What kind of tattoo could make somebody's world fall apart? Jackie skims through the article again, wondering if she has missed something. *No,* she realizes–*it was the tattoo.* That was what the fuss was about, and only that.

She opens a new browser tab, calls up Google Images and types in the search terms "mark taminer tattoo". She clicks Enter and finds a whole page of virtually the same image.

"Holy shit," she says out loud. "It's just *Betty fucking Boop*?"

It is indeed Betty Boop, but not just her. On Mark Taminer's right arm, as seen in the infamous November 4, 2014, online video interview, is Betty Boop giving a wink and a saucy, seductive smile, her right leg around a stripper pole. She is presumably nude–presumably, because there are two black boxes reading

"CENSORED" over the breasts and the vagina. Jackie initially assumes that the black boxes have been added to the image via Photoshop, but a quick glance of the other Google results confirms that the boxes are part of the tat.

"This can't be right."

She switches from Google Images to the main Google search, under the same search terms. Now she is deluged with articles, blogs, forums, Spitter posts and more about the tattoo. Jackie does not click on any of them. She scans the summary paragraphs reading random quotes.

Mark Taminer hates women. This is the proof.

Thanks 4 ruining the kuel comet landing u sexist freak.

My wife wanted a career with NASA but, sick childish people like you are stopping her. Why should she throw away her dream because STEM is full of pricks like you. Just die already.

It seems you men are good at conquering space but you still havent managed to conquer the misogyny in you're own heart. Fuck you all

i hope you fuckin commit suicide you fuckin perv

Jackie shuts off the web browser and rubs her eyes. *I can't take this anymore. What the hell is wrong with people?*

Then a sharp jab of guilt nails her between the eyes, and she reopens the browser and goes straight to the Spitter profile for @nagging_conscience_42.

No change since last time. No new posts, no replies to anybody.

Feeling like a kid trying to rub graffiti off a school wall before a teacher walks by, she deletes her last two replies to the puppy. As if that could make a difference now. As if anything could.

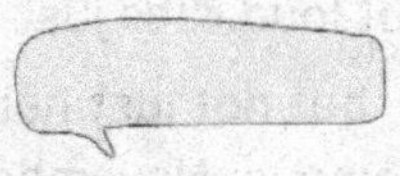

Jackie gasps loud enough to wake herself up. She stares into the blackness of the flat for a while, too tired to get out of bed, too freaked to go back to sleep. She peers at her clock radio. Two-thirty.

Terrible dreams this time, but she remembers only bits and pieces and random images. There was some floating for a while, and the puppy was there again, and Gregory Peck, and Bogie. She also recalls Kim Novak in *Vertigo*–or two of her, Madeleine and Judy, her two identities in the movie. But then Jackie looked away and back again and they had turned into two versions of Kathy McDougal, both laughing savagely at her, and then... she does not want to remember more.

She really needs to use the washroom, so she forces herself up and stumbles to the toilet. When she finishes, she staggers back into the main room of the apartment and flicks on the light.

As tired as she is, she refuses to go back to sleep. She remembers the large tin of Maxwell House in her cupboard. That should keep her awake for a DVD or two, and maybe through her morning interview with the store guy. She will have to buy another cup or three at Second Cup or Starbucks to keep her going at work, though.

Jackie gazes over her shelves and bookcase, over her massive collection, as she waits for the computer to boot up. Anything but *To Kill a Mockingbird*, she decides. Ditto *Vertigo*. And not *The Maltese Falcon* or *Casablanca* or *The African Queen*...

Her eyes travel over the first series of *Father Ted*.

A couple of shelves below that sits *Mystery Science Theatre 3000*.

Why not? I need to laugh again.

ELEVEN

"I could've gone to cooking school. I could've become a real chef."

Yeah, you coulda been a contender, Jackie thinks as Morty Bozzer babbles.

"But it just didn't work out that way, and I'm still here. Stuck at this scuzzy little discount store with scuzzy customers and dumb teenagers who can't do their jobs right. But that doesn't mean I can't try to reach these people with my impeccable taste." He points a thumb at the Frank Sinatra poster on the side wall of his office, a poster that serves as the only arguable sign of "taste" Jackie has seen in this store. "Once in a while, if they've got me in on a Sunday, I'll sneak a CD of Frankie on for the background music for a while, show these little Taylor Swift and Kanye addicts what *real* music sounds like. And if the stock boys have been doing a good job lately, I'll make a special little dish for them for lunch, save them a trip to the McDonald's or Pizza Pizza." He indicates the dish of Beef Wellington that Jackie is holding. "Good, huh?"

Jackie swallows the bite in her mouth. "Yes. Thanks."

She has no pretensions to expertise in high cuisine, and she concedes to herself that she may be missing some subtleties in flavour, but Morty's Beef Wellington tastes to her like nothing more than a sophisticated meat pie.

"Of course, it's good," Morty boasts with a self-satisfied grin. "I know it is. That's the kind of quality cuisine you always get from Morty Bozzer."

Jackie has not asked a single question about Morty's cooking passion or life story, but that has not stopped him from going on and on about it. If she felt more alert, she would count how many times Morty has used the word "I" or referred to himself in the third person.

Morty is a small, chubby frog of a man wearing an ugly, vomit-green sweater with fading blue jeans, because FunMart apparently has no budget for staff uniforms. He is in his mid-fifties, judging by the wrinkles, yet his clawing neediness and his quick, nonstop talking suggest an over-caffeinated teenage boy trying too hard to impress the adults at a swanky cocktail party. A chronic loneliness wafts from him like an odour, but not enough to make Jackie pity him. His small eyes peer at her through thick Poindexter glasses under a curled, receding hairline and over a forced wide smile that makes her cringe inside. It is obvious that he has the hots for Jackie, but she feels safe, sensing he would never have the guts to make any move on her.

As pitiful as Morty is, the store is a perfect match for him. FunMart is a sad wasteland. During Jackie's brief stroll from the front entrance to the back pharmacy, she observed a dusty, filthy, barely swept floor, along with cluttered, disorganized product shelves and scowling stock boys and cashiers. The few customers she saw looked as if they had wandered in off the street after looking for spare change or a drug fix. She thought she also caught a faint whiff of urine from somewhere. *How has this ramshackle shop stayed in business for so long?*

"Anyway," Jackie cuts in before Morty can start rambling on about himself again, "I wanted to ask you about Paul Shoreditch." She turns on the Olympus, mostly for form's sake.

Morty's smile broadens, and he starts giggling.

"Is... that funny?" she asks.

Morty cannot stop giggling, so he just nods.

"Yes," he forces out, catching his breath. "No. I don't know. That guy just made me laugh. Still does. He was *such* a little loser."

She wants to laugh too, at a different target, but stifles herself.

"Yet I couldn't stop feeling sorry for him," he adds. "I felt so bad when I heard he died. I really did. That's why I felt I had to go to that funeral. If you could call it a funeral." He clears his throat. "I mean, it's not the same as when Rob Ford died. *That* tore me to pieces, and I didn't even know the man. Same with Reagan, bless him."

Oh, for fuck's sake! Not another ultra-conservative. Paul was even more of a freak magnet than he was a freak.

"I mean, I sensed the guy was lonely. I know what that feels like. You probably think, 'Oh. Morty Bozzer's having a ball all the time, in that big penthouse condo, with that amazing view of the downtown area.' But it gets lonely up there." He grins again. "I bet you're wondering how I have such a nice, classy place like that when I work here."

"Not really."

He tells her anyway. "It belongs to my parents! They're pretty wealthy. They've got several houses and other property, and they bought me a penthouse condo. It's a great place. It would be great for parties except I don't really like big crowds of people much. Once in a while, I invite somebody up so they can sample my cooking, though. That's fun. There's also plenty of room for my wine collection–not just cooking wines, but also for drinking. A friend of my parents bought me an old Chateau D'yquem bottle, and I wish I had somebody to share—"

"Anyway," Jackie interrupts, "we were talking about Paul Shoreditch."

"Right. He worked here about... six or seven years ago, I think. I didn't hire him. The store owner did." Morty pauses to clear his throat. "He was a terrible stock boy. Smart guy–at least, I got the impression he was smarter than he seemed–but useless at his job. Careless, lazy, aloof. Even worse than the teenage grunts who did the same damn job evenings and weekends. I think the only thing he ever got right the whole time he was here was CPR, and he never had a chance to use it."

"CPR? As in cardiopulmonary resuscitation?"

Morty nods. "Actually, the Heimlich manoeuvre too. He did that even better."

"What do you mean?"

"Gary–he's the owner–he made us go to this health and safety training thing once. Even closed the store for the day. I just shudder at the revenue we must've lost that day, and all for some stupid hippie union bullshit."

"You think saving lives is stupid hippie union bullshit?"

Morty laughs. "It depends. My dad served in Korea back in the '50s, and I bet he saved a lot of lives. But if you ask me, training or no training, if you're dumb enough to get injured or killed while doing your job, you deserve everything you get."

Well, nobody asked you. "And what does Paul have to do with this?"

"He really mastered the Heimlich part. The fruity little guy leading the workshop, he made a big deal about how good Paul was doing it with the dummy. He had the right positioning, the right timing, everything. I think Paul was a little embarrassed about it, like nobody'd ever praised anything he'd done before, and maybe they hadn't." Morty laughs again. "Good thing he was using a dummy! Can you imagine if he had to practise on one of the other employees? Nobody would've let the freak touch them. Not with that ugly mug. And that smell! God, that guy smelled."

Jackie fakes a smile. "Right. Mr. Bozzer," as she cannot bring herself to call him by his first name, "I understand that Kathy McDougal worked at FunMart around the same time?"

Morty stops laughing, and his face sinks into a bitter little frown.

"Yeah," he says. "What a bitch."

"So you didn't get along."

"Not that I didn't try," he says, sulking in his seat like a naughty child after a lecture. "All I did was talk to her. Tell her about myself, you know, the usual thing. And you know what she does? Complains to Gary that I was harassing her! I mean–can you believe that? Can you believe somebody would accuse Morty Bozzer of something like that?"

"No. I can't believe anyone would accuse you of that," Jackie replies with a straight face.

"Well, Gary's a good guy, and he let me off with a warning. Not that I needed one. I stayed the hell away from her after that." He shakes his head, looking at Jackie with eyes begging for sympathy. "What a bitch, huh?"

"Do you know anything about a post on BlahBlahBlog about Paul?"

"About a what?"

"A blog post from 2013. Accusing Paul of some nasty stuff. Kathy McDougal is credited as the author, though she denies she wrote it."

Morty shrugs. "I rarely use the Internet. I don't even really know what a blog is. I go to the library to check my e-mail every so often, and that's it. That's why it took me a while to get back to you." He snorts. "And frankly, that's about the only thing libraries are good for."

Oh, for fuck's sake. She wonders if she will have another screaming meltdown, only this time, the target will deserve it. "Okay," she says, controlling her breathing, "what about the party?"

"What party?"

"Kathy told me she had a birthday party at her apartment back then and that Paul was there and behaved... inappropriately. Do you know anything about that?"

Morty shrugs with a patronizing half-grin. "I wouldn't know any more than you do. You don't think she'd have invited me to a party, do you?" He chuckles with a frown. "Or even if she did, that I'd have stooped to the level of going to it?"

"So you wouldn't know an acquaintance of Kathy's named Fiona?"

Morty shakes his head.

Why am I here again? Jackie thinks, imagining all the productive things she could have been accomplishing at home right now, like sleeping or binge-watching old *Twilight Zone* episodes.

"Mr. Bozzer," she blurts in a last-ditch attempt at journalistic professionalism, "do you think Paul Shoreditch would've been likely to sexually assault a woman?"

"Huh?"

"Or grope one, or abuse a woman in any way?"

Morty stares at Jackie for a long moment. Then he falls into another stupid giggling fit.

"Oh, come on!" he emits between giggles. "That guy? That little weenie? He barely had the guts to even talk to a girl! Unless she talked to him, and believe me, that never happened." He wipes his eyes. "Except for Kathy. And after dating that bitch, I doubt he'd ever want to speak to another female again."

"So they were dating. Paul and Kathy. They weren't just friends with benefits."

Morty catches his breath and thinks. "Well, kind of," he says. "I guess so. I'm not sure he understood how dating worked, but you could call it that."

"I see."

He furrows his brows with a blank stare. "Now that I remember it, there *was* something about a party."

"Hm?"

"Just some gossip among the staff. Shortly after he left the job. Everybody was talking about how he made a fool of himself at Kathy McDougal's birthday party."

"How?"

"No idea."

"Nobody specified anything?"

"If they did, I don't remember. Though I remember they were all laughing about it."

Laughing? That's it? "Did they talk about anything else he did?"

"Not that I remember."

What a shitty story. Not that Jackie seriously expected to hear about a sexual assault, but she cannot swallow her disappointment.

"Mr. Bozzer—"

"You can call me Morty, y'know."

She does not. "What can you tell me about Paul? And the whole thing with him and Kathy?"

Morty sits back, looks at the ceiling and says, "Lemme see what I can remember." And Jackie wonders if she is in for another long flashback full of nothing.

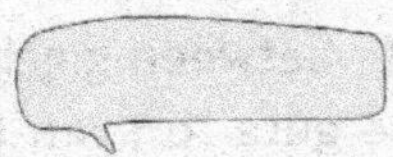

Paul Shoreditch began working at FunMart Drug Emporium on June 21, 2013, but Morty Bozzer was on vacation in Italy for two weeks–a trip paid for entirely by his parents–and did not meet his new underling until July 2.

"We've hired a new kid in stock, Monday to Friday daytime," Gary told Morty when he returned that morning. "Maybe 'kid' isn't the right term here. He's forty, but he might as well be a kid." Gary laughed. "A fat, shy, stupid little kid. You'll have a ball with him."

An hour later, Morty was building a box display of paper towels near the back of the store when Gary wheeled a work cart nearby, followed by another guy. "Hey Morty," said Gary, "this is Paul. Paul, say hi to your manager."

In front of Morty was a mildly overweight, balding little man, a little over five feet tall, with a face unlike anything he had ever seen. The mess of acne scars dotting this face almost distracted Morty from the prominent buck teeth and the snaggleteeth sticking out the sides of a mouth that seemed not to want to close fully, ever. Morty was briefly reminded of the Giant Mouse from the old cartoons or rather, the baby kangaroo Sylvester the Cat mistook for a giant mouse, but this guy had none of the cuteness. The strange man seriously needed a professional groomer: tufts of hair waved around from the back of his neck, and even from his ears and nostrils. Lifeless blank eyes stared ahead, not really seeming to see Morty.

"Hello, Paul," Morty said, deepening his voice and sticking out his hand.

The new guy shook Morty's hand, if one could call it a shake, as it barely clasped Morty's fingers. He said nothing and made no eye contact.

"I'm sending him to stock the diaper aisle," said Gary. "After that, he's all yours."

Morty thought he detected a silent snicker behind Gary's last statement.

After he finished the display, Morty went to the diaper section. Paul had barely progressed into his task. The diaper shelves were nearly empty, and the skid of boxes was full and unopened. The new kid was sitting on his cart, clutching his left hand with his right, a tear rolling down his face and a small trickle of blood dripping from the hand. An X-acto knife lay randomly on the floor nearby.

Morty sighed and grit his teeth a little. *Please, Lord, not another idiot.*

"What happened?" he asked.

The man jerked a little at Morty's voice. He wiped the tear away quickly with his right hand as he looked up.

"I think I cut myself," Paul said in a feeble, grainy voice.

"Oh, for fuck's sake," mumbled Morty. He took his time going to the back room to get a bandage from the First Aid kit and coming back to attend to the wound.

"Ow!" griped Paul. "That really hurts."

"Shut up," said Morty as he carelessly wrapped the bandage around Paul's hand. "It's not that bad. It'll heal pretty qui—" He shuddered from the blast of odour that seemed to be coming from the new kid's armpits. *My Lord, is that smell even human?*

When Morty finished, he stood and waited for Paul to start filling the shelves with diapers. But the man just sat on the cart staring at the bandage on his hand.

"I'm sorry about the crying," he finally said to Morty. "I do that sometimes."

"Um." Morty had no clue how to answer that.

"Thank you for the bandage. That was very kind."

"Whatever. Let's get to work."

Paul did not move from the cart. He looked up into Morty's face. A thin sliver of snot was still dripping from his nose.

"Very kind," he said again.

"Yeah. I know."

Paul looked right into Morty's eyes. "I have a strange question."

"What?"

"Are... are you my friend now?"

"*What?*"

Morty was so seized with hysterical laughter that he could hardly keep his balance.

"Ha ha ha! Are you *serious*, kid?" he answered, propping himself on the cart.

But Paul was not laughing. He looked at the floor and blushed.

"I'm your *boss*, you gimp. Now just shut up and get the hell to work."

"Oh... okay. I'm sorry." Paul stepped down from the cart and slowly–very slowly, being extra careful with the knife–opened the first box of diapers and began filling the bottom shelf. Morty took another box and opened it too, sensing that this simple task was going to take a thousand years longer than it deserved. Watching Paul work so slowly and methodically, as if stocking shelves required the precision and planning of brain surgery, struck Morty as hilarious, and he had to force back more laughter to help Paul get the job done. *Well, this is going to be fun.*

"I had no idea what the deal was with this guy," Morty tells Jackie. "Did he have some kind of crush on me? Was he 'of the gay persuasion'? Or was he just *such* a loser that he had to ask his bosses to be his friends? Although, if he *did* have a crush on me, I couldn't blame him. Morty Bozzer can't help laying on the charm, even when he doesn't want to."

Jackie suppresses a snort.

"I didn't know much about the gays, or whatever he was, but I wanted to discourage this little weirdo from liking me too much. I got kind of mean for a while. Even meaner than I am with the other stock boys." He gives a proud smile. "I'd chew him out for not getting a job done right, even when he did. Or I'd walk past him when somebody else was around and go, 'Aw, man, did you get a whiff of that stink?' 'Cause of his B.O., right? And I kept telling him how fat he was. Whenever I saw him eating chips or pizza in the lunchroom–and man, he always seemed to be eating *something*–I'd say, 'With my cooking skills, I could help you eat better, Paul. No wonder you're so fat.'"

Jackie says nothing as her eyes wander to Morty's substantial gut.

"Sometimes I'd give him a job, but I'd leave something out or tell him one part wrong so he'd do the thing wrong and I'd chew him out for it. Once I had him build a vitamin display but told him the wrong aisle, and then I yelled at him for being stupid for doing it in the wrong spot!" He laughs.

Gaslighting an employee. How clever. She resists the urge to roll her eyes.

"But every time, Paul would just *take* it. He'd never argue, never defend himself. He'd just nod brainlessly, like he knew I was right. Even the vitamin thing, he went to the trouble of tearing the display down and rebuilding it in the right spot. I'd never seen a guy like this. That's when I started to feel a little sorry for him. Just a little, though."

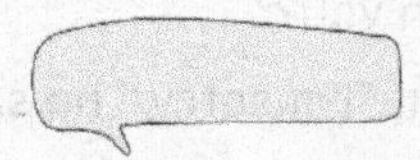

It was a week after Morty's first meeting with Paul, a quiet Tuesday morning in the store. Morty was cleaning up the seasonal aisle so it would be ready for the Back To School merch that would be arriving soon. He heard a sound. He could not place what it was. There was something familiar about the noise, but there was also something sick, gross and twisted about it. With a shudder, Morty realized that the noise seemed to be echoing, or mimicking, the tune of the background music overhead, which happened to be playing one of his favourite tunes, Sinatra's "My Way."

The strange sound was coming from the toilet-paper section. Morty left his cart and made his way to the end of the aisle as Greta, one of the cashiers, passed with a blend of a grimace and a smirk.

"What's going on?" Morty asked.

Greta just laughed. "It's Paul. Go see for yourself."

Morty was not sure he wanted to see. He definitely did not want to hear. But he went to the toilet-paper section out of managerial duty.

Paul was in the aisle by himself, stocking the new order of Royale tissues on the higher shelf. As he did, he was singing along to the music in a voice so off-key and grating that Morty wondered why Frankie himself was not rising from the dead to stop it. Paul warbled obliviously to himself about planning a cart and horse and then stepping along a highway.

"What are you doing, Paul?"

He turned to look at Morty. "Stocking the toilet paper. Like you asked."

"I mean, the *singing*. If you can call it that. Do you know how retarded you sound?"

Paul shrugged. "I like singing. It makes me feel good. Is that a problem?"

"Well, you're not here to sing, are you? You're here to do a job. You're gonna drive away customers who could be buying this stuff. What the hell's wrong with you?"

Paul looked at the floor. "I'm sorry," he said.

Morty laughed. "I'll give you credit for one thing though. Other than me, you're the only person working in this store who has any damn *taste*."

"What do you mean?"

"Ol' Blue Eyes."

Paul blinked. "My eyes are green."

"No–Sinatra! That was his nickname."

"Oh. Yes, I love Frank Sinatra. His voice was so nice."

"He's my *idol*, Paul. Him and the Duke, that is. I've worshipped that voice since I was a kid. Nobody could make a tune sound sincere like The Chairman did."

"Which chairman? Gary?"

Morty laughed again. "You may have good taste in music, but I've got a lot to teach you."

Paul stared at Morty as if waiting for him to start the lesson.

Morty lowered his voice, hoping none of the other employees would hear him. "So you want to be my *friend*, Paul? Like you said before?"

Paul shrugged. "I guess," he said.

"And you just mean *friend*, right? You're not a gay or anything like that?"

"I don't think so."

"Seems like something you *ought* to know by now."

"I guess I'm not. But I don't have any friends, and it was really nice how you put the bandage on my hand. I appreciated that."

"I'd have to do that for any worker here. And I don't usually hang out with co-workers, although I wouldn't want to with most of 'em anyway."

"Oh."

"But to be honest," Morty said, with a self-pitying sigh, "I don't have a lot of friends either. Well, I *do*, but they're all my parents' friends. And most of them live abroad."

"Really?"

"Tell you what. If you can keep it as our little secret–" Morty spun his head around quickly to make sure nobody else was nearby, "–and if you've got nothing after work tomorrow, let's go out for beer and wings. On me. That pub down the street. Twenty-five-cent wings on Wednesdays."

"You mean chicken wings?"

"No, ostrich ones. What else would they be?"

Paul thought about it, then nodded. "I'd love to."

"On one condition, though: Don't *ever* sing in this store again. Especially not Sinatra. Or Ella. Because you have no voice. Deal?"

Thus began the second attempted friendship of Paul Shoreditch's life.

"This guy was a real mess," Morty tells Jackie. "A total loser. But anybody who appreciates Frankie has the potential to be better. And who was the right guy to bring out the best in him? Who had the charm and the class to set him right?"

Morty gestures to himself with a grin.

"I don't know. Who?" asks Jackie.

Morty frowns. "Anyway, I wanted to turn him on to the pleasures of beer and wings. You know I'm an expert in cuisine–you've just had the perfect sample of Morty Bozzer craft–but I love to go out for beer and wings once in a while. I don't usually get to do it with other people, though. And I have high standards, like I do for everything. The wings ought to be big, yet still affordable, and the beer has to be good craft beer, none of that Labatt or Molson garbage. Fortunately, Los Tres Cerveceros down the street fills the bill."

Morty's beer-and-wings jaunt with Paul Shoreditch at Los Tres Cerveceros was not the height of wild partying. Morty had a good laugh at Paul's surprise that the wings were not from ostriches after all, but that laughter turned to disgust at Paul's habit of chewing noisily with his mouth wide open, and more so at the way Paul could not eat the wings without getting the sauce all over his face. Morty made sure to order extra wet naps, and the server complied with a pitying look. It became worse when Paul was reluctant to try the wheat beer that Morty had ordered for him; when Paul finally relented to Morty's pressure and took in a mouthful, the taste grossed him out so much that he spat it up all over his remaining wings. Morty ordered a Coke for him after that.

The chat also looked as if it would be a bust because Paul said almost nothing at first.

"Don't you *talk*?" said Morty. "I mean, holy cow."

Paul sipped his Coke again. "Yes," he said. "Of course I do. I'm sorry, but I'm not very good at conversation. I'm not in the habit much." He paused. "What do you want to talk about?"

It's a start, I suppose. "So... what do you like to *do*, Paul?"

Paul did his by-now familiar shrug.

"I like to sing," he replied.

"I figured that one out. What else?"

Paul thought for a moment, then shook his head with a blank expression.

"Do you have any other hobbies?" Another headshake. "Sports? Reading? Cooking, like me? Games? Camping? Politics? Anything?"

Same response.

"I've never seen such a blank slate. Do you even *have* a personality, Paul?"

Paul looked a little confused.

"What did you do for work before FunMart?"

Paul furrowed his brows as if he had to think about it. "A bunch of stuff," he said. "I was at McDonald's last, but I kept burning my hands on the grill."

Morty laughed. He could not help himself. "Lord!"

"And I delivered newspapers and flyers for a while, but I couldn't make a living at that. And I did some filing stuff at an office for a long time, but they fired me when I dropped ink all over some important documents. I didn't like it anyway because I kept getting paper cuts."

"And I thought *my* life was a dead end. You're a real loser, Paul. You're pathetic."

Paul nodded, accepting it as an incontrovertible fact.

"I was homeless for a long time, too."

Morty stopped laughing. He frowned. "You can't be serious."

"But I am. There were times when I couldn't get a job."

Morty took a breath to calm his inner rage. "I don't like derelicts, Paul. They're leeches. A drain on the economy. They take and take and take and never give anything back."

"That's what I hear a lot of people say about homelessness," said Paul with a half-shrug, "but that's not how I remember it."

"What do you mean?"

Paul thought about it. "Panhandling. A few people were generous, but most weren't."

"But you still *took* from them, Paul. You took money from society that you didn't earn."

"I didn't have much choice at the time."

Morty groaned. Then he lifted his beer glass with a bitter, "You're welcome, Paul."

Visibly confused, Paul nodded and lifted his glass too. "Uh. Thank you?"

Morty rubbed his eyes.

"Oh," said Paul. "You're being sarcastic. Sometimes I have trouble with that."

Morty decided to change the subject. "What about college? What did you major in?"

"I never went. They told me I was smart enough to go to university, maybe even smart enough to get a scholarship, but I was scared to go. High school was scary enough, and I didn't want any more school after that."

"Didn't your parents encourage you to go?"

Paul's face turned red, and his lips pursed a little. He looked almost angry.

"My m-mother," he stammered, "tried to talk me into the army."

"Oh yeah? Did you?"

"No. I tore up the application and I—" He cut himself off.

"What's wrong with the army? It's an honourable profession."

"If you don't get killed, I guess."

Morty laughed again. "Don't be stupid! That only happens when there's a war, and Canada's pretty chicken-shit when it comes to getting into wars. But the army would have been good for you. It would've taught you discipline, self-control, stoicism, responsibility, that kind of thing."

"I couldn't do it. It's all about fighting, and I had more than enough of that when I was a kid." Morty waited for Paul to elaborate, but Paul just asked, "Did *you* join the army?"

"Nah. Wasn't for me."

"But you say it's good and teaches you—"

"I already *knew* those things. Morty Bozzer's always been a real mature person, y'know. I didn't need those lessons. I'm saying it would've been perfect for *you*. The army is the perfect path for aimless young people who don't know what they want to do with their lives."

"But I *did* know. I wanted to sing. That's *all* I've ever wanted to do."

Morty looked at Paul's face. Every iota of it beamed sincerity.

"Come on!" he laughed. "I told you, you have no voice."

Paul looked down at the table, and Morty sighed to himself. *For the love of God, don't cry again, you wuss. You've embarrassed me enough tonight.*

"Look," Morty said more gently, "I get it. You wanted to be a singer. I wanted to be a chef. Life doesn't always work out like you want. But *I've* accepted it. Even though I have to work at this crappy store, I still cook on my own, just because I like it and want to do it. And even though you're terrible at singing, you can still do it. Just not at work. It's inappropriate."

Paul looked back up at Morty. He almost, but not quite, smiled.

"Hey," Morty continued, pointing to a chalkboard near the pub entrance, "I just remembered that this place has karaoke happening tonight. It starts early, too–eight o'clock."

"Carry... what?"

"Karaoke."

"What's that?"

"You honestly don't know?" Morty giggled again. "Where the hell did you *come* from, kid? Karaoke–when you get to sing songs in front of people. The DJ has a machine that plays the music part, and you sing along to it. You read the words off a screen. And–here's the important part about karaoke–you don't have to be any good."

Paul's face perked up. This was the first time Morty had seen a real flicker of joy in it.

"And," asked Paul, "what kind of songs do they let you sing?"

"Depends on the place, but the DJ here has a real good selection. They have lots of Sinatra and Satchmo and Ella. Mostly rock and pop standards, though."

"Do... do you think they have George Michaels?"

Morty looked at Paul and he laughed and cringed at once. "I must've been mistaken when I said you had taste," he said. "But yeah, they'd definitely have George Michael."

"What about Celine Dion?"

"You're gonna make me throw up, kid. But yeah, they'd have her too."

"Wow!" A broad, toothy smile took over Paul's face. "Can we stay for that?"

"Nobody's demanding permission. You stay for it if you want. I'm not."

"Don't you sing, Morty?"

"I do, but I'd rather jam a flaming pen knife through my tongue than hear *you* sing again. But go ahead. Knock yourself out."

Paul was visibly tired at work the next morning but unusually happy. He had stayed at Los Tres Cerveceros until two.

"Wow!" he told Morty, who was helping Paul face up the cough-medicine aisle. "They let me sing lots of stuff. I got to sing Frank Sinatra, and Barbara Streisand, and Mike Bolton, and Billie Holidays, and Maria Carey, and some other songs!" Paul stopped working and stared at nothing in particular. "I don't think I ever felt so *confident* before, Morty. They actually let me sing those wonderful songs in front of people! Like a real singer."

"Sounds like you went up a bunch of times," said Morty. "Normally, you're lucky if you get more than three songs a night. Wasn't the place packed?"

"It was at first," Paul remembered. "But people started leaving after I went up the first time. And then more after the next time. After one o'clock, there was hardly anybody there, and they just let me go up over and over."

Morty chuckled.

"I can't go back, though," Paul added.

"Why not?"

"The pub guys told me I was banned from the karaoke because they lost customers. They said it was my fault or something. They told me to go to other karaokes."

"Aren't you unhappy about that?"

"Why? There are *other* karaokes!"

Morty nodded. "Yeah, guess that makes sense. Just don't invite me along with you."

They were silent for a while, focusing on work. Then Morty had an idea.

"Hey Paul," he said, lowering his voice again, "are you busy on Saturday night?"

"No."

Stupid question. What the hell would this guy be doing? "I'd like to invite you to have dinner at my pad. As a friend, I'd like you to try my paella."

"Your what?"

"Paella. It's a Spanish dish with rice and chicken. Wings are great, but I want you to see what real classy cooking is like. And you might like wine better than beer. Maybe we'll watch a movie or two afterwards."

Paul looked puzzled for a moment, then nodded dutifully.

"Don't get so excited about it, kid! Your enthusiasm is boiling over."

Paul looked even more puzzled. "Do I look excited? What do you mean?"

"Don't worry about it, we'll have a good time. Just one thing–don't take this the wrong way, Paul, but don't go telling anybody here we hang out."

Morty expected Paul to react in a hurt way, but Paul just sighed and rolled his eyes a little, and then said, "Okay." *Guess he's heard that one before.*

The next morning was the health and safety workshop, in which Paul inadvertently became the star, and while it embarrassed him, it kept him happy for the rest of the day, although it distracted him from work. Morty did not like seeing FunMart employees distracted from their duties, and he definitely did not like Paul's weird, creepy little smile, which scared all customers away from his vicinity. *But what the hell. At least he's happy.*

Paul did enjoy Morty's paella, as well as the clafoutis Morty had made for dessert. He was less enthused by the glass of Sauvignon Blanc, but at least he did not spit it up.

"It's okay," he told Morty about the wine. "It kind of tastes like pop, but weird." Other than the impressive view of the downtown area, Morty's large, sprawling apartment did not make much of an impression on Paul either.

Morty dominated the conversation as Paul munched away noisily, explaining why Stephen Harper was the greatest Canadian Prime Minister in history, how Liberal politicians ruined the country by taxing and spending, how English teachers were overpaid fat cats whose jobs had virtually no purpose, why unions were the scum of the earth, why welfare and employment insurance needed to be eliminated from the Canadian system as soon as possible, why giant corporations should have had the right to do anything they wanted with no oversight or consequence, and why the previous day's training workshop had been a useless waste of time.

"Hippie bullshit," Morty told Paul. "That's all it is. I say we let the stupid workers kill themselves through accidents and thin out the ranks. Simple solution. No need to waste company time and money on those useless workshops."

"I liked it," Paul said, his mouth stuffed with clafoutis. "I liked learning the lifesaving stuff. It's something I might be able to use someday. We all might."

"Speak for yourself, kid."

"I didn't really like when the teacher kept telling them how good I was, though. That just made me feel strange. But I liked that I was *good* at it. I did something right." He swallowed. "It's only the second time in my life that I did something right."

Morty laughed. "Second time in your *life*? You say the weirdest things."

Paul put down his fork. "It's true," he said. "And since you're my friend, I wanted to show you the first."

"What do you mean?"

Paul pointed to the FunMart plastic bag he had brought lying on the floor by the door.

"What's in there?"

Paul got up and picked up the bag, then carried it back to Morty's dining table as carefully as if it were a wounded bird. Sitting down again, he slowly reached into the bag and pulled out a softball. An old softball, the whiteness long gone from twenty-eight years of dust and dirt and decay. Morty could see the letters "PS" carved into it.

"This," said Paul, displaying the ball in both hands over the table.

Morty looked at it, then laughed. "What? It's an old baseball."

"It's a softball. *My* softball."

"Great. What the hell's so special about an old softball?"

"I caught it."

Morty shrugged.

"I caught it when I was twelve. Practising with my friend Beef. It's so hard to catch a ball, isn't it? But I did it! And that's why I've kept it."

Morty looked at Paul's sincere face, then looked at the softball again, and then looked at Paul's face again. And he just shook his head and laughed.

"I'm sorry, Paul," he blurted between giggles, "but if catching a ball is the peak achievement of your life, then your life isn't worth very much, is it?"

Paul put the ball back in the bag. He closed his eyes as Morty went on laughing.

"Maybe I'll do something else sometime," Paul said.

"I certainly hope so."

Paul looked as if he were going to cry again and Morty winced, waiting for the waterfall to drown the meal he had so carefully prepared. But Paul got control of himself and said, "I'm sorry. I just thought you might want to see something that meant a lot to me."

"Oh, God." Morty slapped his forehead. "You *sure* you're not a queer, Paul? Because I kind of feel like we're on a date and nobody told me about it until now."

"I don't *think* I am."

"Well, do you like girls?"

Paul nodded. "I like them," he said. "I really do. But they don't like me much."

"Can't say I blame them."

Paul was silent for a minute.

"There's... one girl," he said softly, seemingly to himself more than Morty. "One girl I see at work. I like her a lot."

Morty looked at Paul, who did not look back. He was just staring down at his clafoutis and absentmindedly playing with his fork.

"Who is she?" asked Morty. "One of the cashiers?"

Paul nodded. "I don't know her. I don't even know her name. I just like looking at her and I want to talk to her sometimes, but I can't because I think she won't like me."

"Of course she won't. Not with that hair. Or those clothes. Or those squeaky shoes–you know how they echo through the store? Or that *smell*."

"Yes. You're right. That's why I don't even bother."

Morty laughed again, with less contempt. "So why don't you *change* all those things? Instead of being a pussy and accepting the way you are, like fate or something? Be proactive, kid. Buy new clothes and shoes. Get a better hairstyle. Shave better. And for the love of Pete, buy some deodorant."

"I already use deodorant. Deodorant is my friend."

"Whatever. So you have two friends."

"But I don't have enough money to get the new clothes and shoes."

"Hm. Well, maybe I can help you with that. My parents are pretty generous with money when they want to be. Maybe we can go shopping for new clothes together."

Paul looked up at Morty.

"Really?" he said, his face perking up. "You'd do that for me?"

"Well, that's what friends are for, huh?"

"I guess it is." Paul smiled a little. "I remember when my friend Beef once talked about how we'd go shopping for better clothes one day, but it never happened." He thought for a second. "You think we could get really cool clothes like the ones on the *Miami Vice* show?"

"What?" And Morty fell into uncontrollable giggling fits again. "Oh Lord. You're nothing if not entertaining, Paul."

The rest of the evening was spent watching Morty's DVDs of *Red River, Sands of Iwo Jima* and *Robin and the 7 Hoods.* Paul visibly flinched during the staged, phoney gunshot noises in the movies to Morty's mild amusement, but survived the evening, tired but happy.

"So you brought Paul to a mall to see what cool clothes were like," mumbles Jackie, more to herself than to Morty. *Fuck fuck fuck. This is just the Beef story all over again, isn't it? Hitting the same beat twice, as they say in the movie biz.*

Morty took Paul shopping at Scarborough Town Centre on the following Monday after work. "I don't really know much about what the young people are wearing these days," Morty said as they entered the mall, "but they've probably never heard of Don Johnson."

They went to Stars Men's Shop, where Morty had Paul fitted for a new suit, and then they went browsing at Bluenotes and the Gap and a few other places. Morty did not like the choices.

"The kids today," he said as they finished eating their A&W burgers and fries in the food court, "they're trying so hard to look hip that they've forgotten how to look classy. The suit'll work great for you, but you also want some casual duds that show you're a gentleman yet still know how to relax and have a good time."

"Where do we get those?"

"I'll show you right now," said Morty, pulling Paul out of his seat. "Bring your pop with you. We'll go where I always go."

"Where's that?" asked Paul as Morty led him in the direction of the mall exit.

"Bargain Jack's! It's open 'til midnight."

Bargain Jack's was a small second-hand clothing shop in the same plaza as FunMart, with an interior that resembled a warehouse more than a store. The place was nearly empty of people, save for a bored-looking clerk sitting behind the front counter and reading a *Toronto Sun*. The floor space was dominated by racks of clothes with hand-scrawled price signs tacked above them: "JEAN SHORT'S ONLY $5.37 EACH GOOD SUMMER WEAR!!!!!" one read, but Morty headed straight for the bins at the back of the store.

"They always have lots of good stuff in the discount bins," he told Paul. "And so cheap! You can get so many great things here for the price of just one thing at the mall."

Morty started rifling through the bins as Paul watched curiously, holding a Stars bag in one hand and an empty root beer cup in the other.

"Are you sure," Paul asked, gazing around the store in disbelief, "that this is a good place to get cool clothes?"

"How about this, huh?" said Morty, pulling a large green-and-white polo shirt out of the bin. "I think this would look great on you."

Paul looked at the shirt. "I saw a golf game on TV once," he said. "That looks like something a golfer would wear."

"It's great. It's full of class. It'll tell your girl you're a man who's sure of himself. And what about this?" Morty pulled a similar shirt out of the bin, a bright orange one with a purple horizontal stripe through the middle. "This'll get attention, huh?"

Paul nodded as Morty continued to pick out random duds from the bins—more polo shirts, a zig-zaggy wool sweater that looked about thirty years old, and several white pairs of athletic socks. He also grabbed two pairs of beige corduroy pants from the racks after taking a reasonable guess at Paul's waist size.

"You see?" Morty told Paul as the clerk rang the purchases. "It doesn't take a lot of effort to look like a classy guy, and it certainly doesn't cost much, either."

"I guess."

"Don't guess it—*know* it. Take it as impeccable advice from a friend."

"Right."

"And I'm a good friend, aren't I? Buying you all these clothes for you."

"Yes. I think you are."

"Damn straight."

"Thank you, Morty."

"And the next day, I took Paul out after work to get new shoes and a haircut," Morty tells Jackie, who has been torturing her belly with suppression of laughter. "Dress shoes and running shoes, he needed both. Did he look like a normal guy in the end? No. He looked like an ugly guy playing dress-up as a cool guy. But it was an improvement, I'll give him that."

Morty hoped to see a fast change, but even he—and everybody else—was shocked and confused to see Paul show up for work the next day wearing his new grey suit and shiny black dress shoes. The suit was a full three-piece job with a vest. Paul's forehead was bathed in sweat.

"What the hell, Paul?" said Morty, distracted from his task of checking a new shipment of laxatives in the back room. "Those clothes aren't for work. Well, not for a stock-boy job. Maybe if you were a business exec."

Paul did not reply. He just gave Morty a nervous smile.

"Aren't you hot? It's July."

Paul nodded. "Yes."

"Well, what's with the suit?"

Paul smiled awkwardly again. "I'm going to tell her," he said. "I'm going to tell her how much I like her, and I want to look classy when I do it."

Morty groaned. *What can I do? I set the weirdo up for this.*

"All right," he said. "I'm not supposed to encourage romance between staff, but fine. Go and talk to her. Just don't come on too strong."

"What do you mean?"

"Well, don't be all, 'I love you, I love you,' or anything. You know what I mean?"

Paul looked lost, as if that had been his entire plan.

"Just be calm and cool, and tell her casually that you'd like to get to know her, and would she like to go out for a coffee sometime after work. Okay?"

Paul thought about it, then nodded. "Right."

"And try not to make an ass of yourself when you're doing it."

"Okay."

"Oh–and Paul? Try to learn her *name* this time, all right?"

Paul went away, and Morty placed the laxative boxes on a cart and wheeled it out to the proper aisle in the store.

Not long after he started stocking the laxatives, he heard the sound of laughter from the direction of the front cash registers. Then he heard it again–louder. Definitely a group of women. Then he heard it again, even louder, and it was clear that the laughter had a contemptuous tone in it. *Yeah, he's making an ass of himself.*

Morty finished the job and began pushing his cart in the direction of the back room when he heard footsteps running behind him. *Here we go,* he thought as he turned around, expecting to see Paul sniffling and trailing a river of tears on the floor.

But Paul was grinning like a giddy college girl after too many drinks.

"She said yes!" said Paul, beaming.

"She *did*?"

"We're going out for a drink after work. Today."

"She... didn't *laugh* at you?"

"She did, a little." Paul shrugged with a lopsided grin. "And the other girls, they laughed a *lot*. But then she stopped laughing and she looked at me and said, 'You're weird, but you know what? You're also the first man who ever had the decency to dress up for me!' And she said we'd go out after work." Paul shrugged again in amazement. "The suit worked!"

"I guess it did."

"Thank you, Morty!"

"No problem. Now take off the jacket and tie and let's get to work."

Paul followed Morty to the back room and took off the jacket and tie as ordered. "I don't like wearing the tie, anyway. I feel like I'm going to choke to death."

Morty ignored him as he checked his clipboard for the next job for Paul.

"But I have to put it back on later," Paul added. "She *really* liked the tie. She said, 'I'll go out with you only if you promise to wear that cool tie,' and I said, 'I will, Kathy.'"

Morty dropped his pen.

He jerked his head in Paul's direction.

"Not *Kathy*?"

"Yes. That's her name."

"Kathy *McDougal*?"

"I forgot to ask her last name."

"She's the only Kathy who works here." Morty turned around and looked at Paul with his arms crossed. "*That's* the girl you've been crushing on?"

Paul looked at the floor, blushing.

"But she's such a bitch. Why do you like her?"

Paul shrugged. "I don't know. I just do."

Morty contemplated. "I don't get it," he said, half to himself. "I lay all my charms on her, and she reports me. But you..."

"Excuse me," Jackie interrupts the story. "These *charms* that you laid upon Kathy. I'm just curious... what are your techniques for charming a woman?"

Morty cocks one eyebrow and gives her a grin that attempts, but fails spectacularly, to look suave and dashing.

"Well?"

Morty coughs. "Well, I know all the old foolproof lines. 'Hey, doll, are you from Tennessee? 'Cause you're the only—'"

"'Ten I see.'"

"Yeah. Or the classic, 'If I told you you had a great body—'"

"'Would you hold it against me.'"

"You've heard that one too."

"And this failed to charm Kathy, somehow."

"I swear, I just *talked* to her! Bitch couldn't be charmed."

Jackie nods. "Continue."

"Anyway," Morty went on to Paul, "I don't know what you see in her. She's a bit fat, isn't she?"

"I think she's beautiful."

"Well. Good luck on that one, Paul. I don't think you're gonna get far." Morty turned back to the clipboard. "Now stop distracting me from work."

But Paul went much further with Kathy than anyone had reason to expect. He was tight-lipped about it but seemed happy for the next several weeks. That childlike yet creepy smile baffled and frightened the few store customers and staff members who dared to approach him. Morty was fine with Paul's silence as he did not want to know anything.

The only downside was that the singing had started again. When U2's "Pride (In the Name of Love)" was playing in the background music one afternoon, Morty overheard Paul in another aisle, wheezing and mangling the lyrics in his own special way. He sang about a shuddering eye in the Memphis sky that freed the last days of somebody's life, or something.

"Paul!" snapped Morty as he came around the corner. "What the hell did I tell you about singing on the job?"

Paul looked up and blushed a little.

"Sorry, Morty," he said. "I forgot. I'm just so happy these days, sometimes I can't help it."

"Sing at karaoke, then. Work is no place to be happy."

Paul turned back to his task.

"Has *Kathy* heard you sing like that?" Morty asked, his voice lower.

"Not that I remember."

"Good."

Morty watched Paul's mouth curl into an involuntary smile as he worked. *Clearly, he's gotten laid. At least once.* He almost gagged. The mental image of those two getting it on was as repulsive to Morty as a close-up video of a monkey's birth.

One morning in September, Morty noticed that no work was getting done in the seasonal aisle where Paul was supposed to be taking down the unsold Back To School merch and replacing it with a shipment of Halloween stock. Morty furiously marched around the store looking for the soldier gone AWOL, then made for the back room. He found Paul sitting on a table in a corner by the receiving area scrolling intensely down the screen of a Samsung cell phone.

"Paul!"

The little man let out a soft yelp and leaped off the table.

"What the hell are you doing? Get back to work!"

Paul stood at attention, almost as if he really were a soldier. "Sorry. I'm sorry." He slipped the phone into his shirt pocket and followed Morty back into the store.

Half an hour later, Morty returned to the seasonal aisle to check up on Paul again. He was there, but only a few of the racks were filled. Paul was engrossed with the phone again.

"Come on, Paul! What are you doing?"

Again, Paul emitted a soft, startled cry and looked up. He dropped the phone on the floor, but the Otter case encompassing it prevented breakage.

"Sorry, Morty," he said, bending down to pick up the phone. "This thing is so distracting."

"I know. You shouldn't bring your cell phone to work. At least turn it off and put it away."

"Okay." He turned the phone off.

Morty turned around to return to the back room, then turned back to face Paul again. "Since when do you use a mobile phone, anyway?"

"Since the weekend. Kathy gave it to me."

"Kathy actually bought you a cell phone?"

"Oh, no. She gave me her old one because she just bought a new one. She got a Samsung S3. This one's a Samsung SI."

"Ah."

"She was showing me some other stuff, too. She showed me all around the Internet, on her computer at home and on the phone. It's amazing! I've never seen anything like it. So much information, and you can talk with people all over the world..."

Morty gaped. "You've *never* been on the Internet before?"

"No."

"Never ever? You're saying you've had twenty years or so to use the Internet and you *still* never got around to it?"

"I never felt like I had much use for it, until now." Paul smiled. "I love using the computer mouse! It's so easy and fun. I wish my phone had a mouse too."

Morty nodded, unsure how to respond.

"And Spitter–I like Spitter a lot."

"What the hell is Spitter?"

"It's a website where you can write things and put them on the Internet, and then everyone can read them. Let me show you." Paul picked up the phone. "Wait. I have to turn it back on."

"Don't bother. I don't care."

"I like to write about my favourite singers. Oh–and Kathy showed me this big website she made up. It's called 'Kitty Corner', I think. There's lots of cats on it. Really cute."

"I'm sure."

"And she has real cats too–three of them. But they don't like me very much. One of them tried to scratch me when I petted it."

Morty did not reply.

"She had four cats, but one just died." Paul made a strange face. "Kathy wouldn't tell me how it died. I don't know why." Then he smiled again. "I liked the cell phone so much, you know what I did? I gave Kathy my softball."

"Your what? Oh, *that* thing."

"Yes. I wanted her to have something that meant a lot to me."

"Oh, Lord." Morty sighed and shook his head. "What do you *see* in her, anyway?"

Paul did not answer. He just blushed and smiled.

"And don't take this the wrong way," Morty added, "but... what in the name of God Almighty does that chick see in *you*?"

Paul shrugged. "She says I'm not like the other men she meets. She hates most people, but especially men because they're so bad and abusive."

"Yeah, that doesn't surprise me."

"She talks about *you* a lot." Paul smiled in a way that looked as if he were about to laugh, but no laughter emerged. "She hates all the clothes you bought me, except the suit. And she thinks you're really creepy. She calls you the Jack the Ripper of FunMart."

"I'll bet she does." *Bitch.*

"But she says I'm different. Weird, but different."

Morty thought for a moment, then nodded with a chuckle.

"You sure are, Paul. You sure the hell are. Now get back to work."

"He was so happy," Morty tells Jackie. "He told me he was happier than he'd ever been. Don't ask me how anybody could be even a little content when working in a scuzzy place like this and spending so much of your time with that bitch. Or when you looked like such a freak. But he was. I asked him why, and he said something like, 'This is the first time everything has worked out for me! I have a job, I have a good friend like you, I have a girlfriend, I know how to dress nice, I get to sing for people at the karaoke, and this Spitter thing is so much fun. I have it all!' I guess when you have low expectations in life, anything can look like luxury, eh?"

"I guess," Jackie replies.

"Not like with me." Morty frowns and gives Jackie a touch of the puppy-dog eyes. "I was gonna be so much better than this. Morty Bozzer was gonna be a famous chef. And look where I am. Stuck here in a dead end. Maybe I need to lower my expectations too."

"Good idea."

"I deserve so much better, though. Believe me. Sometimes you just know you were meant for better things. My mother used to tell me—"

"ANYWAY. What happened with Paul?"

Paul was happy, but Morty was miffed that Paul was getting so little work done, even less than usual. That Samsung phone was distracting him all the time. Morty lectured Paul over and over about the importance of staying focused and being productive.

"For Christ's sake, kid," Morty once told him in a back-room chat, "do you even *phone* anybody with that thing?"

Paul shook his head. "I hate talking on the phone. I'm too shy for it, I guess. I just like using the Internet on it."

"As your boss, I bet I'd be completely within my rights if I confiscated that damn thing and locked it away."

Paul looked horrified. "No! Please don't. I love this phone."

"But as your *friend*, I'm willing to go easy on you. Still, that doesn't mean you can take advantage of our friendship. I need you to put the phone away once in a while."

Paul sighed and nodded. "Okay. You're right, Morty." He turned the Samsung phone off and stuck it into his shirt pocket.

"Besides, you have plenty of time outside work hours to surf the silly Internet all you want." Morty turned to his clipboard to assign Paul his next task, then paused. "What the hell do you find so fascinating online today, anyway? Is it that Spitter thing?"

"I was looking up advice on how to behave at a party."

"A party?"

"Yes. Kathy has a birthday next month. She's turning thirty-two. And she's having a big birthday party at her apartment. I've never been invited to a party before."

"Oh."

"She's going to invite a bunch of people. So I'll get to meet her friends."

"She *has* friends?!"

"A few, she says. Mostly other writers and bloggers she knows. She wants them to write for her new website. And also a few musicians from back when she used to play guitar in cafés in Vancouver. Did you know she can play guitar?"

"No. Nor do I care."

"That's why I want to know how to behave at a party, so her

friends will like me too." Paul shrugged. "What about you? You've probably been to a lot of parties. Do you have any advice on what I should do?"

Morty doubled over in laughter.

"Oh, Paul," he said. "Paul, Paul, Paul. You're so precious, you know that? My best advice to you: do as little as possible."

"What do you mean?"

"Maybe you should just sit and drink wine and eat snacks and keep your mouth shut. Don't talk to anybody unless they talk to you first."

"Okay. She said there'd be wine, so I'll have some." Paul had grown to like Morty's white wine a lot. "And when they talk to me? What then?"

"What do you think? Have a normal conversation. Answer their questions, continue the discussion. But don't do anything weird."

"What do you mean by weird?"

Morty tried to think of how to explain in a way that did not imply or say *everything you already do*. He gave up.

"Never mind," he told Paul. "We're wasting time. Here's your next job."

That was the last that Paul or Morty mentioned Kathy's birthday party until a few weeks later after Paul failed to show up to work on a Monday. And the following day.

Morty phoned Paul's cell number several times over those two days. No answer every time. Morty was more annoyed than anything else, as picking up the (minimal) slack from Paul's absence was keeping him busier than he wanted to be. But underneath his annoyance was a speck of concern. Was Paul okay? Had he gotten into trouble?

Paul was absent on Wednesday too, but Morty saw him when he arrived home from work. When he stepped off the elevator, he saw

Paul's familiar form sitting by the entrance to his penthouse apartment, head in hands.

"Where the hell have you been?" Morty griped as he charged down the hall. "Gary's just gunning to fire you."

Paul let out a long, loud, childish sob. Morty realized that Paul had been sitting there crying for a while. *Oh, Lord. Here we go.*

"What's wrong, Paul?"

"It's horrible," Paul sobbed. "Terrible things are happening."

"Calm down, kid. Let's get inside before the neighbours complain."

Morty let Paul in, and the latter flopped onto the couch in despair. There were still tears on his face, and the area around his eyes was red from rubbing them with his hands.

"I'm sorry," said Paul. "I know. I've been making that noise again."

"Huh?"

Paul did not explain. He sat and sniffled.

"Do you want a drink or something? Some wine?"

Paul shook his head. "No. *Anything* but wine."

"Fine. Just tell me what's been going on."

"It's terrible, Morty. They're saying I did these awful things."

"Who? Where?"

"On the Internet!"

After a brief silence, Morty snickered and laughed.

"Come on, Paul. It's just the stupid Internet. Nobody cares what anybody says there."

"But they *do*! Somebody made this website all about me, and it's saying all these mean things that don't make any sense. And I've been getting these nasty e-mails, too. People are saying..."

"What?"

"They're accusing me of..." Paul trailed off and started sobbing again.

Morty rolled his eyes. "Look, I'm sure it's nothing. The Internet is just a bunch of immature people spreading gossip. It'll pass."

Paul shook his head. "I don't think so."

Morty just stared out the window at the Toronto skyline for a long moment. He did not know what to say.

"Morty?" said Paul, his sobbing and sniffling having stopped for the moment. "Do you think I could stay here for a while?"

Morty stiffened. "Stay... here?"

"Yes. Your apartment is so big, and I need a place to hide out."

"I don't know about that. How long?"

Paul let out one of his rare chuckles, although it was coloured with ironic melancholy.

"Forever, maybe," he said.

"Forever?"

"I don't know if I can go back out into that world again. I never felt right there in the first place, but now it's too much."

"Why can't you just go back to your own place?" Morty realized that he knew absolutely nothing about where Paul lived.

Paul shook his head again. "I can't. My landlord kicked me out. He never liked me anyway, but now he's kicked me out. Wouldn't even let me get my belongings, except my phone and my jacket. Somebody e-mailed him and he believed it. He thinks I'm a..."

Paul looked as if he were about to explode in tears again. Morty tried to distract him with an interjection: "What about Kathy? Why not hide out at her place?"

The move backfired. Paul cried more fiercely.

"I felt bad about it," Morty tells Jackie, "but I couldn't let the guy stay with me. The last time I'd had a house guest, the guy had stayed for four months after telling me three days. And think about it, I was running a classy penthouse condo. I couldn't let Paul cramp my style."

"You have a *style*?" blurts Jackie.

Morty sat down next to Paul and said gently, "I'm sorry, kid. I know the place looks big, but it's not built to house two people—even two good friends like us."

He expected Paul to start bawling again, but he did not. Paul nodded, paused, and then stood up and approached the door to Morty's apartment.

"Where are you going?"

Paul turned and looked at Morty.

"There's only one place I can think of to go now," he said.

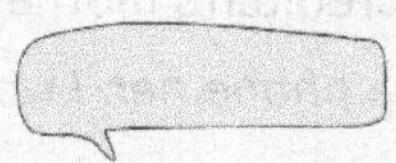

"And he left," Morty tells Jackie. "And I never saw him again–not alive."

"I see."

"I never found out where he went."

"His parents." Jackie has been connecting the dots in her head. "That must've been when he went to live with his parents in Cambridge."

"Ah. I guess he would've been treated better there?"

"I highly doubt that."

Jackie flicks off the Olympus recorder and puts it in her purse.

"You're... not leaving already, are you?" whines Morty.

"Afraid so."

"You haven't finished my Beef Wellington. Isn't it great?"

"It's like a dream. I have to go."

"Are you sure you don't want to just, I don't know, stick around for a while? Just to talk. My job is boring sometimes. I get lonely."

Jackie gets up from her seat. "Thanks for your time today, Mr. Bozzer. You've cleared up a few things for me."

"No problem!" Morty stands up and holds out his hand for a handshake. Jackie shakes it with the minimum enthusiasm required. "And let me know if you need more info. Maybe I'll cook another fancy dish for you. Or if you just want to shoot the br—"

Jackie is out the office door before Morty can finish.

She exits FunMart briskly, as if eager to avoid contamination by the atmosphere. She cannot decide which she wants more—a cup of coffee, or a drink. *Too early in the day for a drink.* And she is still exhausted from the lack of sleep.

As she gets a cappuccino from the Second Cup across the street, Jackie basks in a feeling of freedom. But it is temporary. She is out of that awful store, but she has to steel herself for another conversation with Paul Shoreditch's mother.

This time, I'm just gonna phone her. I won't be stupid.

TWELVE

Jackie stops by a McDonald's after she leaves the downtown subway station, just before heading to work. She orders a Big Mac with Super Size fries and a large coffee, forgetting she already had a Second Cup latte after her interview with Morty Bozzer. She wants comfort calories in her face right now, and she hopes the coffee will keep her alert at the call centre after her inability to sleep. On the walk to work after the meal, the chilly fall air makes her shiver, and she yearns for a cigarette.

Seventeen years since I've had a Gauloise, and I crave it more than ever now. What the hell is wrong with me lately?

All through the workday, the thought of her next assignment in the ostensibly aborted Paul Shoreditch story nags her. She feels Brain tugging at her elbow as if to warn her she is going to find out something awful.

I've got a bad feeling about this, Han Solo drawls in her mind.

Shut the fuck up, Flyboy.

When she gets home, she looks over her DVD collection for something to lift her spirits. Nothing jumps out at her. Not even Chaplin or Keaton or Tati, not even classic Looney Tunes or Monty Python or *Simpsons* or *Arrested Development*. For the first time she can remember, her collection of movies and TV shows look like an empty wasteland. Some she has watched so many times she could probably play every shot back in her head perfectly. There are a few she keeps meaning to watch a second time and likely never will. Why has she spent so much money on this over the years when she could have gone back to school, or travelled, or rented a better apartment? Why has she spent so much of her life watching movies by herself when she could have been watching them with others—or done *anything* with others? She could have made more friends. She could have *lived* more.

When did I get this morbid and depressing? Maybe this happens when you investigate a story as dark as Paul Shoreditch's—even on your own, with no expectation of compensation or glory. *Is this what real journalists feel like? When they do stories about murders or suicides, or even workplace accidents? Or does desensitization happen early?*

Jackie gives up and goes to bed.

She lies awake for hours. She wants to blame her anxiety over the planned phone call but suspects her insomnia is a direct result of all that damn coffee she drank and all the junk food she ate today. *Yeah. I deserve this.*

She makes the return trip to dreamland. The image is fuzzy, but there is a sense of tired familiarity. When the fuzziness clears, she can see the beagle puppy staring at her again. No change in expression, no joy, no sadness, no threatening behaviour.

What is it? Do you have something to tell me?

No reply.

Maybe I've done mean things in my life, puppy. Maybe I've done some bad things without realizing how bad they were. But haven't we all?

Again, nothing.

I shouldn't have written that terrible thing to you. I know that. I even knew it at the time. I want your forgiveness, but I don't know if I have the right to ask for it. Or the courage.

Still no change, but Jackie senses something. She gets the impression the puppy *does* want to tell her something, but not in words.

Maybe I have to forgive others, too? If I expect forgiveness, then I have to give it to others? Is that what it's all about? Is that how you stop the cycle? Please tell me.

The puppy fades away and the scene morphs into a schoolyard. A familiar one. She stands on the top rung of a slide. In front of her is a ginger girl from her class wearing a pink *Little Mermaid* spring jacket, sitting at the top of the slide. The girl does not move, though. She has never slid down a slide before, and she is scared.

And Jackie remembers. First grade. Recess. She was a little too impatient, and the girl just sat there, and little Jackie got angry. The only way she would ever get her turn would be to give the other girl a push.

But the other girl toppled over the side and landed on the grass below. Just a few bruises, but how she screamed and cried. And how the other kids hated Jackie that day–really *hated* her–calling her a bully and a meanie. And how the principal scolded her, and how her parents lectured her.

She relives it all in the dream and then wakes up.

Staring up at the ceiling in the nighttime darkness, she thinks about it. *I forgot all about that. That was almost thirty years ago.* And yet... life moved on. Neither her parents nor her teacher or principal ever mentioned the incident again; they granted that the lesson was learned. The other kids probably forgot about it after the next big schoolyard scandal. Even the ginger girl, whose name Jackie cannot remember, never held any lasting grudge as far as she can recall. Life moved on, and everybody forgot about it. As if it were erased from time.

Sometimes you do things, and then they're gone. Sometimes other people do things to you, and then they're gone too. They don't change everything if nobody lets them. If you let something go, life can move on and nobody gets more hurt. We're all doing the best we can with the limited information we've been given.

But how far can it go? Can everything be forgiven? Jackie wants to think so, not so much for her own sake but for Paul Shoreditch's. Even if he did anything as bad as Kathy McDougal has insinuated, as so many people believe, is he entitled to forgiveness, too?

She wishes the beagle were still there to hear her questions. But she suspects, even knows, that the puppy would expect her to find the answers herself.

She cannot remember any more dreams when she wakes up at nine.

After two cups of Maxwell House, she sits in front of her desktop, Sam Spade staring at her from the screen, her phone on the desk.

"I fucking hate this woman so much, Bogie," she tells him. "I don't want to talk to her again. But there's something missing here. It's a story without an ending, like you once said. Can I have some courage? You always showed lots of it, and I need it now."

No answer, of course.

Jackie searches for Rick's old e-mail with Lydia Shoreditch's contact info. The abusive messages responding to the bus incident are still coming in, but not as frequently. Taking a deep breath, she dials the number. No answer after seven rings. Jackie is about to hang up when that nicotine-mangled croak answers. Jackie reminds Mrs. Shoreditch who she is; this is followed by a silence, during which she imagines Mrs. Shoreditch straining her pitiful little brain for a hint.

"Oh," she answers. "You again."

"I wanted to ask you a few more questions."

"You picked a lousy time for it, young lady. Harvey and me are packing the car."

"Going away?"

"Heading to our trailer in Texas. You don't think we stick around up here in *Canada* when the goddamn weather starts getting cold, do you?"

Jackie thinks she detects an underlying contempt in "Canada," similar to the one Mrs. Shoreditch had previously imbued into "Toe-Ron-Toe."

"If it's a bad time," she replies, "I can call your cell while you're on your way down."

Mrs. Shoreditch scoffs. "Don't be stupid. We don't have a cellular phone. Those things can give you cancer."

"Maybe I can call you in Texas? If you have a landline there."

Jackie hears a long sigh. "All right. Ask your questions but make it quick."

"It's really one big question. What happened after Paul came back to stay with you? From 2013 until his... until this year."

Mrs. Shoreditch lets out another long, bitter sigh.

Then she yells, "Hey! Be careful, stupid!"

"What?"

"Not you. My moron of a husband almost dropped something." Her voice becomes distant as Jackie hears her yell, "Why the hell are you carrying all those bags at once? Even a goddamn two-year-old's got the sense to take one at a time!"

Jackie hears a faint "Yes, m'love," in the background.

"What an idiot," Mrs. Shoreditch says to Jackie. "So Paul came back to us after he got in trouble on the computers. I gave him what for for a while–never letting him forget about the time he struck down his own mother!–but he said he was sorry for that, he'd changed, and I just didn't have the heart to turn him away. I always wanted to do right by the boy. You know that, right?"

"Sure."

"We let him stay in our guest room. And he hardly ever left it. He just wanted to stay up there and play on his cellular phone."

"Play?"

"Whatever you do with the computers now. The cellular phones today–they're all just little computers, aren't they?"

"You could say that."

"So he was using it like the computers. But something was making him cry all the goddamn time. After a few days of that, I march right into his room and I scream, 'Stop that!' and give him a hard smack in the face. A tough-love smack, like always. You got to be cruel to be kind sometimes."

Jackie fights the urge to punch a wall.

"So I say to him, 'You're a bigger idiot than your father. You're forty now, and a forty-year-old man does not sit in a room all day and cry and play games on a phone. You're gonna get cancer from that phone, you know. But if you're gonna stay with us, you're not gonna be a mooch. You're gonna Earn Your Salt like you never have before. You're gonna get a job and pay us rent, and if you can't get a job right away, then *we're* gonna have to put you to work until you do.' And I did. Just like when he was a boy, I worked him good. In no time, he got the house clean as it ever was, and that left Harvey and me plenty of time to do what we wanted.

"Soon, it was time for me and Harvey to go to Texas, like every year. We wanted to take him with us–'cause Texas is full of real men, men who know how to stand up for themselves and treat people like they deserve, so they'd be a good influence on him–but he didn't wanna go. He said he'd stay in Cambridge and look after the house. And me and Harvey, we said, that's a good deal. So we left him here for the winter and had a good time in Corpus Christi. When we got back in April, my word! The house looked great and so did the lawn. I was proud of him.

"I tried to make him feel good about the great work he'd done for us, but it didn't get through his skull. He was still sad, still crying in his room sometimes. So I just point-blank asked him: 'What is it? What the hell is wrong with you, anyways?' And he says, 'You wouldn't understand.' And I say, 'No, I bet I won't, but you ought to tell me anyway.'

"He tells us all about this girlfriend of his in Toe-Ron-Toe and how she's mad at him. I was shocked as hell, in a good way. He had a *girlfriend*? Harvey and me always thought he was a queen-size fag, and now he had a girlfriend! So he goes on about how she keeps sending him computer mail messages over the phone about how bad he treated her. And I want him to get back together with the girlfriend because that might be what saves him; finally, he gets a girlfriend and even a wife, like a normal man. So I tell him, 'Look. As a man, you got a duty and a responsibility to make things right again. Go stake your claim. Tell her you're sorry for whatever you did. Send her flowers. Take her out for a malted. Do what you can to win her back.' He said he'd give it a whirl."

"And that didn't work?" says Jackie, trying to hide the sarcasm in her tone.

"Of course not. 'Cause he still wouldn't leave the goddamn house! I was hoping he'd get up off his butt and go back to the city to court her again, no matter how good the house looked, but he wouldn't go. 'People hate me there. They think I did some terrible things,' he'd say. So all he did was send the girl electric mails on the cellular phone, and sent her roses through the computers. But every time he did, the girl just sent nastier mails back to him."

Jackie recoils as she imagines the e-mail conversations. "And how long did this go on for?"

"Let me think..." Mrs. Shoreditch pauses as if doing complex calculus in her mind. "I'd say... another five-and-a-half years."

"Five-and-a-half *years*?"

"Yeah. Right up to the time he died."

"Your son tried to woo back his ex-girlfriend over the Internet continuously over five-and-a-half years? And she kept on sending nasty replies over that whole period?"

"Yeah. And I told him, 'I guess I was right about you in the first place. You *are* as queer as a three-headed calf. Any normal man would've given up years ago and found another girl, but you clearly don't like girls much anyways if you're stuck on just the one."

Jackie does not try to make sense of Mrs. Shoreditch's logic. She fumes and ponders. She has little trouble imagining Kathy McDougal constantly sending verbally and emotionally abusive e-mails to a man over a period of years. But Paul's response? *The man was either hopelessly, chronically in love with her, or some kind of sadomasochistic freak, desperate for more pain and suffering. Maybe he had to be, to live the life he did.*

"Well, if you're done," adds Mrs. Shoreditch, "me and Harvey want to get moving soon before the traffic's bad."

"Mrs. Shoreditch," says Jackie with a confidence she rarely reaches without the aid of a keyboard, "tell me what happened on October 15."

"You said it was gonna be *one* question."

"The last time we spoke, you said that he went back to Toronto on the 15th. Why?"

"How the hell would I remember that?"

"Because you do. It was the day your son died. WHAT. HAPPENED?"

Jackie stuns herself with her bold, forceful assertiveness. It appears to have an effect on Mrs. Shoreditch too, as it takes her a weighty moment to reply.

"What I remember is, I was mad at him 'cause the dining room hadn't been dusted that morning. You can always tell these things. So I go up to his room and there he is again, lying on his bed and crying, harder than ever. The cellular phone is sitting on the bed.

"'What is it? What the hell is wrong with you today?' I yell at him. He just keeps on crying, and he points to the phone. I didn't want to pick it up 'cause I don't know anything about the cellular phones and how dangerous they are, but I didn't know what else to do. So I picked it up and saw writing on the screen. Had to go get my reading glasses. It was a big, long letter from the girl. Her name was MacDouglas or something–don't ask me why he was hung up on a Scotch girl. I don't remember the whole thing, but it was a real mad letter.

"Part of it went like this: 'You are an abuser, Paul. I've told you so many times. You're one of the most abusive and hurtful men I've ever known. I will never forgive what you've done to me. Since I've known you, my life has been hell. The way you treat women is a disgrace. If there were any justice in the world, you'd be rotting in jail.' And it goes on like that. I don't remember the exact words, and there was a lot more bad language than I'm letting on, and also lots of stuff about 'accountability' and 'consequences' that I didn't understand, but that was the gist.

"So I say to him, 'What've you been doing to this girl? What's all this about abuse?' And he says, 'I don't even *know*.' I ask him how he can't know something like that, and he says, 'She's been telling me I'm an abuser for years, but when I ask her how, she just says, "You *know* how." But I swear I don't. I just keep telling her I'm sorry, and she gets even more angry.'

"I just stood there and sighed. Couldn't believe I'd failed so bad as a mother. Who'd've thought my only boy would turn out to be a stupid wimp *and* a mistreater of girls? So I sit down on the bed with him, and I say, in this real nice voice, 'Look. It sounds like you've done some bad things. We've all done bad things, but maybe you've done more than most people. It's not enough to say you're sorry. You got to make amends for what you've done. You got to go back to the city right now and see the Scotch girl. No holds barred. Whatever it takes for her to take you back.'

"He looks at me and he says, 'And what if she still doesn't?'

"I answer him, 'Then there's no hope for you, I guess. No hope left at all.'

"He looks at me kind of strange. And he repeats what I said last–'No hope left at all,' in a strange kind of tone, like he meant it in a completely different way than what I said. And then he nods, and he stands up and goes to the bedroom door, and he says to me, 'Goodbye, Mother.' And he leaves for the city, and I never saw him again. Until he was dead."

There is a long silence on both ends of the line. Jackie's chest and stomach are a simmering cauldron of rage.

"Mrs. Shoreditch," she says, in a low, steady voice, "do you know what you did?"

"I haven't the foggiest idea what you mean."

"Your son committed suicide that day. After he visited his ex-girlfriend. I'm pretty sure he did. And it was because of what you said."

Jackie hears a contemptuous cackle on the other end.

"Suicide?" laughs Mrs. Shoreditch. "What the hell put *that* idea in your head, young lady? He fell from a building, by accident. He never would've had to guts to kill himself."

"How can you be so *callous*?" Jackie barely realizes that a tear is hanging on the edge of her left eye. "This was your only son. What the fuck is *wrong* with you?"

Mrs. Shoreditch responds with a tut-tutting sound. "There's no need for that kind of language," she adds. "You know how sad I feel he's gone, but I'm not to blame."

"You feel *nothing at all*, you worthless hag." Jackie's voice gets louder. "I'm sure that Paul Shoreditch was not a perfect person. But he was your *son*! And how did you treat him? Like a *slave*. Like a fucking *slave*. You're a worse mother than Joan Crawford."

"Crawford? What the hell does *she*—"

"Go fuck yourself. You deserve to rot in hell. I hope that when you croak, it's horrible and painful. And I hope that next spring, somebody pours salt and vinegar and herbicides all over your fucking lawn, you crusty little maggot-faced old shitbag!"

Jackie disconnects.

She puts the phone down, closes her eyes and takes several deep breaths to calm herself.

She opens her eyes.

Wow. That felt good. That felt really, really good.

She looks at Sam Spade's face on the computer monitor.

"How was that?" she asks him. "Not very eloquent, but do I pass?"

THIRTEEN

A week or so goes by.

Jackie is eating a late breakfast while listening to Bernard Herrmann's score from *Marnie* when the tinny *Midnight Cowboy* theme sounds from her purse. It has been a while since she heard it; nobody phones her these days except for her parents.

The call is coming from the intercom at the front entrance of the building.

"Hey, Jackie. I thought you'd be home."

What the hell? Natalie's voice.

Ten minutes later, they sit with drinks at a quiet brunch café around the corner from her building.

Natalie's hair looks unwashed. She is dressed in an old, faded blue T-shirt and jeans and seems strangely solemn. After a minute or two of sipping, Jackie asks, "How are you, anyway?"

"Okay. All things considered."

Oh–the unemployment thing. "How's the job hunt going?"

"Not well. But something'll turn up." Natalie smiles with a small shrug.

"Hope so. Fingers crossed."

"Thanks."

"So..." Jackie breathes a few times and raises her eyebrows.

"How've *you* been, Jackie?"

"Fine. I... was thinking of calling you, actually," she lies.

"Mm-hm?"

"Just to say I'm sorry about that last time at the Knoll. Guess I was kind of a dick."

Natalie puts down her hot chocolate and leans back in her seat. "I want to apologize too."

Jackie blinks. "Really? For what?"

"I don't know what. Maybe for walking out like that. Maybe for overreacting." She clasps her hands and squints as if struggling to remember some important puzzle solution. "I just feel like I should apologize for *something*."

"I don't get it."

Natalie coughs. "I just found out what happened. The thing on the bus, the video, all that." She leans forward again and looks at Jackie. "Seriously, how *are* you?"

"Same as you... okay, all things considered."

"I checked that website you write for. Also your own site. No new reviews or essays. Sure you're okay?"

"Yeah. They don't want me writing for the *Voice* anymore."

"I'm sorry."

"Don't worry about it. My editor was a dumbass. And maybe I'm not cut out to be a film critic or journalist after all."

"Sure you are. Just keep looking for something better."

"Still got the HPO job at any rate."

Natalie clears her throat and looks at the wall. "I guess what I wanna say is, being unemployed is really shitty, but being mobbed on the Internet is also really shitty. It was wrong and presumptuous of me to think you wouldn't be able to sympathize, or that something couldn't happen to you." She looks at Jackie again. "And I shouldn't have criticized your movie references. No matter how annoying they are," she adds with a chortle.

"No worries."

"Well, I want to apologize. For both of us. It was a bad note to end on."

"Accepted. If you accept mine."

They are quiet for a long moment. Jackie hesitates to say what she wants to say.

"I really am glad you came, Natalie. I don't have anybody to talk to these days. I don't even know if I have any friends anymore, or any purpose. Before, I didn't really care if I had a lot of friends, because I could always reach people by writing about movies. Now nobody wants to read my writing anymore, and I feel like my purpose is gone, and I'm just alone with nothing but my movies and useless dreams." A beat. "Is that anything like you've been feeling since you lost your job?"

"Sometimes. But I get over it quickly. I just keep moving."

"Maybe that's all I can do. Maybe that's the only reason I went on with this Shoreditch thing when I didn't have to. Just to keep moving."

"Shoreditch thing?"

"Never mind. Long story."

Another heavy silence. Jackie's phone whistles. "New message," it reads.

Is this Jackie Roberts? the text says. **My name is Megan Baker. Please call me ASAP.** The number has a (604) area code. Jackie feels a small stab of *déjà vu*.

"Jackie?" says Natalie.

Jackie looks up with a jerk. "Sorry. Got distracted."

"Remember when we took that trip to Montreal? That long weekend?"

"Yes."

"And you dragged me to that little deli place, the one where they served the sausage on the bun, or whatever it was?"

"Wilensky. The Special."

"Right. And we went down that street nearby and you were all excited, going, 'Mordecai Richler grew up here!' And then we stopped by Pierre Trudeau's house and stared at it, and then you were going on and on about how we should look for the subway station where they filmed *Last Temptation of Christ* or something?"

"*Jesus of Montreal*. Yeah, I remember."

"Right."

Jackie half-smiles in embarrassment. "You were pissed off, weren't you, Nat?"

Natalie shakes her head. "More bored than pissed. All I wanted to do was go back to those poutine and smoked meat places. And back to the hostel room for some, y'know, alone time."

"I'm sorry. I should've been more considerate of what you wanted to do."

"Don't be sorry. I kind of miss that trip now. I don't know why. Sometimes you miss things you didn't like at the time."

The way Holden Caulfield did. Jackie stops herself from saying it out loud.

"So I don't really know what my point was supposed to be," Natalie goes on. "Maybe that sometimes things aren't as bad as we think they are. Or that they don't seem so bad after time passes, or that we look at things the wrong way and react badly. You know?"

"I think so."

Another silence, but a nice one.

"So," says Natalie, "do you want to keep meeting at the Knoll?"

"Not really."

"Me neither."

They both laugh.

"That was easy," Jackie says.

Another text whistle. **I hope I have the right number. Please get back to me today.**

Who is this person? Jackie is sure she does not know a Megan Baker, either personally or through the *Indie Voice*, and she has never been to Vancouver. She wonders if this is another troll–a latecomer to the Bash Jackie For Screaming At Kids party, but one who somehow got her cell number. *Maybe I'll call her back this afternoon. Or maybe I'll forget. Who cares?*

"By the way," Natalie suddenly asks, "what happened with that thing you said you were writing? About the asshole."

"That's what I meant by the Shoreditch thing."

"Did you ever finish it?"

"Yes and no."

"I don't get it."

"Still a couple of loose ends." Jackie forces an unconvincing laugh. "What can I say? The asshole may have been falsely accused of sexual assault."

Natalie frowns. "What the fuck are you saying? That's impossible."

"Is it?"

"A false accusation? Come on! *Nobody* would make up that kind of thing. Ever."

Jackie shrugs. A big part of her wants to smack her down with a lecture, but she cannot. *Who am I to preach?* Not long ago, she might have caught herself saying something like that.

"Well," she tells Natalie, "I guess that makes this the first time, doesn't it?"

Busy day on the phones at the call centre. Lots of chatter

throughout the office, none sociable. Jackie is on her second cup of coffee from the Tim Hortons across the street. The conversation with Natalie has left her feeling refreshed in the way only a good reconciliation can. And she has been on a high since her phone confrontation with Lydia Shoreditch. *If I can tell that old bat off,* she thinks, *who knows what else I can do.* Maybe real-world confrontation will become her new hobby. There must be other people in her life she can start standing up to. Rick Pevere? *I'm going to march into his stupid basement office one day and rip whatever he's eating right out of his hands and call him a moron to his face. And an asshole for kicking me off the website.* Her parents? *No, they're not bad or anything. Just annoying and needy.* Sam? *Wait until I get a better job first, then tell her where to stick this one.* How about the tattletalers in the office? *Absolutely. As soon as I find out who it is, they're gonna get a mouthful of Jackie. Fuck him, or her, or them.*

About three o'clock. She has just sold a pair of tickets to a Mozart Requiem concert in January. "Thank you!" says the lady on the other end, who Jackie guesses is in her sixties. "It's been so nice chatting with somebody so polite and knowledgeable about music."

"You're very welcome. Give us a call if you have any questions."

Jackie records another sale on the computer screen. She is on a minor roll. *Maybe this is what I'm meant to do? Maybe I never was a writer or journalist or anything. Maybe I should learn to love this job. Or at least, selling stuff...*

The next lead is a man in Oshawa. He takes a while to pick up, and Jackie uses the delay to check inside her purse. Just as she thought: the Olympus is still there, next to her cell, which she keeps turned off at work. She has kept meaning and forgetting to put the recorder away at home since the Morty interview. On a whim, she deletes the interview, clearing up the storage space. *I was never going to use it anyway. I'm not gonna write this story, even for myself. Stop dreaming.*

The Oshawa man interrupts Jackie's opening spiel. "Why do you guys keep calling us?" the man whines in a gruff voice. "We're not interested."

"Would you like me to take you off our calling list?"

"You should've taken us off a couple years ago. You call us two or three times a year and we always say we're not interested, and you never get the point."

"I'll make sure we take you off this time, sir."

That should be the end of it, but this guy has a piece to speak.

"What is it with you people, anyways?" he says. "Do you really enjoy harassing people all the time? Don't you have anything better to do?"

"Sir, this is just my job—"

"Then get another job. What kind of a person are you, anyways, getting some sick pleasure out of calling people at weird times to nag them into buying stuff they don't want or need? Don't you have any conscience, any morals? What the hell is wrong with you?"

Hang up. Hang up. Or at least answer him back. Tell him what an asshole he's being. But nothing comes out. Of course, she could be fired for being rude to a potential customer if somebody is listening or tracking the call. But even then, she feels voiceless. If only this were some trolling punk online. She feels a momentary wave of nostalgia for the way she, until very recently, used to pick fights with morons on the web.

"Just go fuck yourself," the man says, and he hangs up.

"Wow. What a piece of sh—" Jackie says out loud, cutting herself off. *Damn. Close.*

She takes the customer off the calling list and records the call as no sale.

INCOMING CALL, the computer screen suddenly reads. None of the usual listed customer info except for a familiar phone number with a (604) area code.

What the...? This has never happened before. *I didn't even know we got incoming calls.*

"Uh... hello?" she stammers.

"Is this Jackie Roberts?" A female voice, probably around Jackie's age, with an urgent tone.

"Yes."

"Oh my God. I've been trying to reach you all day." The voice takes a few long, deep breaths as if trying to relax. "I got in touch with that web mag you write for, and the guy there gave me your cell number. Been texting and calling, but no answer. Then I called him back, and he told me you worked for the HPO, so I called them, and then they transferred me here..." Another breath. "Thank God I've found you!"

"Calm down. Who is this?"

"My name's Megan. I saw your post on that website yesterday and I wanted to reply, but my laptop won't let me–some glitch or something. But your account page on the site showed an IP address, and my brother–he works for IBM in Markham, major tech geek–I got him to do some digging from there. He found your real identity." Pause. "I need you to meet somebody. Now."

"Now?"

"We're here from Vancouver, seeing friends. Our plane home leaves tonight."

"Hold on–what the hell are you talking about? My posts on what website?"

"The one about Paul Shoreditch."

"Fuck Paul Shoreditch dot com?"

Oh, SHIT. The other callers have heard her, and she knows it.

"Yes!" the voice says.

Jackie thinks. "Uh," she says, "I'm not really working on that story anymore."

"No?"

"I've kind of abandoned it."

"But you have to do the story." The voice sounds desperate. "Somebody has to tell the truth about that guy and what he's done."

Jackie groans.

"I don't believe you," she says. "After what I've heard, I've concluded that he didn't do it."

"Didn't do what?"

"He didn't rape anybody!"

Oh, SHIT again.

"Jackie," says a voice behind her, "what's going on?"

Jackie spins around in her seat.

Sam and Patty stand there, glaring down at her. Sam has her arms crossed. Patty is holding her clipboard like a loaded weapon. Many other employees are looking at her from their cubicles in morbid curiosity.

"Well," Megan continues, "I've got something else for you to hear. We're at the Icon hotel on Wellington West–checked out this morning. I think that's not far from the HPO?"

Jackie turns back around. "It's close," she squeaks.

"Do you know a good pub or whatever nearby where we could meet?"

"I'm at work, Megan. I can't come right now."

"But we have to get to the airport soon. You have to meet my friend."

"And who's your friend?"

Megan tells her.

Oh, fuck.

"So," says Megan, "you know a spot?"

"Um." Jackie can only throw out the first place that comes to mind. "Um. There's that JFK diner place–the Greasy Knoll. It's close to both of us. You've seen it?"

Megan has. Jackie says she can be there in a few minutes.

"Jackie!" Sam snaps as soon as Jackie disconnects. "*What* was that conversation about?"

She takes off her headset and turns in her seat. Everybody is staring at her now.

"Um," she says. "I have to go."

"You have to go?"

"My mother just died."

Jackie does not look at Sam or Patty, or any of the others. She stands up and grabs her purse with one hand, her jacket with the other.

"But Jackie," Sam says, "your mother died last year."

Crap. I must've used that one before.

"Um," she replies, "yeah. That was... my *other* mother."

And she walks past them, right out of the office.

She keeps going until she gets to the Knoll. The place is packed this time, apparently with regulars and tourists, but she spots two young women sitting by the large Badge Man poster not far from the entrance, with big check-in luggage bags and smaller backpacks on the floor beside them. One of the women is a voluptuous redhead in a pink turtleneck. The other is a thin, perky-looking brunette in a white sweater who appears to be about thirty.

"Jackie," says the redhead as she approaches the table, "I'm Megan."

"Hi."

"And *this,*" she adds, indicating the other woman, "is Fiona."

FOURTEEN

"This... is the *weirdest* theme restaurant I've ever seen." Fiona says this after a long, uncomfortable pause, the first words anybody has said since Jackie sat down with the pair.

"The food's great," Jackie says. "I used to come here now and then with a friend. Never thought I'd come back."

"Why?"

"No reason."

A server in one of those cheap Jacqueline Kennedy knockoff pink uniforms drops by the table to take drink orders. Megan and Fiona each order a Coke. Jackie asks for a glass of water.

"So," says Jackie, "you two've been here visiting friends?"

Megan nods quickly. "I did my degree at York University. Business admin. I still come back every year or so to see old friends. Fiona's come with me a couple of times, too, though I had to talk her into it this time. She didn't want to. Bad memories."

Jackie looks at Fiona, who stares at the table with a dejected frown.

Here we go. She takes the Olympus out of her purse and flicks it on, a little worried that the chatting customers in the place will drown out some of the interview.

"Fiona," she asks, "can you tell me what happened when you were visiting Toronto with Megan in October 2013?"

Fiona closes her eyes and shakes her head in a bemused fashion. "God," she says, close to a whisper. "I almost *died* that night."

"That night?"

"A birthday party at Kathy McDougal's place," Megan interjects. "She's an old fr—uh, *former* friend of mine. I assume you've talked to her, too? Editor of *Kat's Korner*?"

"Yes."

"Have you seen that private blog post of hers? On BBB?"

"Yes."

Fiona sighs. "That fucking Internet," she says, her face tightening. "I hate it so much sometimes. I rarely go on it anymore."

"What can you tell me about that party, Fiona?" asks Jackie.

Fiona hesitates. "I don't like talking about it. Oh, not because I almost died. Because of all the crazy shit that went down afterwards."

Jackie nods. "Fiona," she says, her voice gentle, "I hope I'm not being too blunt when I ask this, but I have to get it out of the way: Did Paul Shoreditch assault you?"

Fiona and Megan look at her with a strange expression.

Both look as if they want to laugh, but their anger is stopping them.

"*Assault* me?" Fiona replies, her tone low but full of subdued rage.

She is about to elaborate when Mrs. Kennedy returns with their drinks. After they thank the server and she leaves, Jackie asks, "Well?"

Fiona and Megan give each other a knowing look, then look at Jackie again.

"No," says Fiona. "I can confirm to you unequivocally that Paul Shoreditch did *not* assault me in any way, shape, or form."

Jackie lets out a breath. She did not know she was holding it.

"I suppose Kathy McDougal told you he did?" Fiona adds.

"She did. So it's not true?" Jackie takes a sip of her water.

"Paul Shoreditch saved my life!"

And just like somebody in a terrible TV sitcom, Jackie pulls a spit take, spraying her water on the table in front of her.

"Sorry," she says, collecting herself as she wipes off the recorder and her area of the table with her November 22 Napkins. "Sorry. What the *fuck* did you just say?"

"He saved my life. I was choking on one of Kathy's *hors d'oeuvres*, and he gave me the Heimlich manoeuvre."

Jackie's brain feels as if it has switched to overload.

"I posted about it once on... that awful website," Fiona goes on. "I just used my last name, 'Wright.' But nobody took it seriously."

"So... let me see if I've got this right," says Jackie. "It was all a huge misunderstanding? Kathy saw him giving you the Heimlich... but she didn't see it very clearly and thought he was assaulting you or something? Is that it?"

Fiona laughs bitterly.

"Oh, *please*," Megan snaps. "Kathy knew exactly what was going on. And still does."

"She knew what happened?"

"Of course she did."

"For fuck's sake. You're telling me she *knew* Fiona was choking. That he was saving her life."

"She's the one who called the ambulance." Pause. "Eventually."

"Then why would she—"

"Because she's a fucking *psycho*!" Megan is almost yelling now, but the Knoll is busy enough that she does not stand out. "I think she's a pathological liar too! Everything that comes out of that woman's mouth is either a lie or some disingenuous half-truth. Isn't that obvious?"

Yes. Of course it is.

"Megan had to cut herself off completely from Kathy after she started telling people Paul had done something nasty to me," Fiona says. "The blog post, the website... It was all too much."

"Oh my God," groans Megan. "She was always a bit weird, but she *totally* went off the deep end after that. Holy fuck."

"I feel so sorry for Paul," says Fiona. "Poor guy. I never got a chance to thank him. And all the stuff that's been said about him. I always wondered if there was something I could do to stop it all, but I don't know how to deal with mobs."

Megan shakes her head with a frown as if to say, *Neither do I.*

"So do you know Paul, too?" Fiona asks Jackie.

"Know... Paul?"

"Yes. What's he up to these days?"

"Paul?" says Jackie, her voice weak. "You haven't heard?"

"Heard what? Is he okay?"

Jackie's jaw drops. "But..." She turns to Megan. "You said you were looking at that website. That's how you saw my posts?"

"Right," says Megan.

"Didn't you see anything *else*?"

Megan winces. "I don't look at that site any more than necessary. I can't bear it. Certainly not those 'Avenger' posts–too ugly and awful."

"Oh."

"We were talking about Kathy and Paul at the hotel yesterday; I just called up the website to show Fiona one of the more fucked-up rants I remembered, and I stumbled on your 'Looking for information' post, but that's it."

"Oh."

"Where *is* Paul now?" asks Fiona. "Is he hiding out somewhere safe?"

Jackie swallows hard. *I can't. I can't tell them.*

"You could say that," she lets out as she looks randomly at Badge Man shooting at her with his nonexistent rifle. "He's somewhere no one can hurt him anymore."

Before either can reply, Jackie stands up, flicks off the recorder and puts it back in her purse. She grabs her jacket.

"You're leaving already?" asks Megan.

"Apparently."

"But you just got here."

"I got what I needed. Sorry–not to be rude, but I've gotta go."

They stare at her as she puts her jacket on.

"Well... nice meeting you, I guess," says Fiona.

"Have a good flight. As it happens, I've got to take a trip west too."

She turns, leaves the Knoll for the last time, and makes for the subway.

FIFTEEN

Jackie does not know what she will do when she gets to Kathy McDougal's apartment. *Do I accuse her directly? Do I ask questions to lead her into a confession, like a lawyer or a tricky private investigator in a TV show?* But Jackie never comes up with an answer. All through the long subway ride, all through the bus ride, she hopes for another pointless delay but for once, the transit system is reliable.

It is starting to get dark when Jackie arrives at the apartment building. As she walks through the front visitors' parking lot, it hits her that this may have been the location of Paul Shoreditch's death. *An apartment building in Etobicoke, right? A twenty-something-storey fall, the reports said?* She shudders as if she expects to see a ghost. It could have been anywhere on the pavement, on the grass, on the curb, anywhere along the front façade she is looking at now. It could have been behind the building. She has a vivid mental image of yellow police tape, a police car or two, maybe an ambulance, maybe men and women in uniforms and with cold, indifferent expressions. Every tragedy is another day on a dirty job for them. And blood–definitely blood, and lots of it. And a body...

Jackie tries to think of anything else. A movie, a song, a poem...

She dials Kathy's buzz code on the intercom.

No answer.

She disconnects and hesitates, wondering if this is a mistake. *What am I going to say?* Kathy might not even be home, though Jackie has trouble imagining her going out anywhere. She has a few friends, but they come to her.

Jackie could leave. She could go back to work and admit she was lying and take whatever consequences Sam sees fit. She could stop caring about this bizarre, horrible story and go back to living her life, whatever is left of it to live.

A curly-haired, middle-aged woman in a blue fall coat enters walking a hyper, brown dachshund. Jackie is grateful it is not a beagle puppy.

The woman pulls an electronic key from her purse and beeps it against the black gadget next to the door. She opens the door, sees Jackie and stops, looking at her expectantly.

Jackie feigns an embarrassed smile. "I forgot my key."

They both enter and head to the elevator.

She gets no answer when she knocks. Then she turns the doorknob and finds it unlocked. She pushes the door open slowly and steps inside.

The first thing she notices is the dimness. All of the lights appear to be turned off; the only light comes through the large main window over the balcony, which has no drapes or curtains over it.

The second thing is the smell.

Not just cat litter this time. A different smell. She has never smelled anything like this before–a cold, heavy, sick, putrid stink that seems to grab the back of the throat. There is something fecal about the smell, but also the sense of rotting meat mixed with a revolting sweetness and maybe a touch of cheap perfume. Jackie's stomach feels queasy.

She spots the room down the hall, the one that she is pretty sure she remembers as the bedroom. The door is wide open.

She takes a hesitant step towards the bedroom, then another, and another. The stink becomes more intense as she approaches the doorway, and she catches a strange, faint buzzing sound.

She moves to call out, "Kathy?" But it gets stuck in her mouth.

Then she closes her eyes and takes one last step into the doorway.

At first, she has no idea what she is looking at. The only apparent light source in the room, apart from another window to the dusky outdoors, is a small desk lamp beside Kathy's computer, which appears to be shut off or in sleep mode. The air seems to be–*shaking?*–in front of Jackie's eyes, mostly near the floor around a few oddly shaped objects lying in the centre of the room. A figure is sitting still in the desk chair.

"Hey, stranger," a voice slurs from the sitting figure. Kathy's voice, but with the shrieking energy toned down to a murmur. "Come to join the fun, huh?"

"What's going on?"

No answer.

Jackie feels around the wall by the door, finds a light switch and flicks it on.

The shaking air is a swarm of flies.

They are buzzing around Garfield, the orange Exotic Shorthair, lying on the floor. His head is mashed flat into a mess of dried blood and brain tissue. Kathy's large, white computer–not the monitor, but the computer tower itself–lies on its side near the cat's body, one corner caked in dried blood. Kathy sits back in the chair in a plain white T-shirt and grey jogging pants, her outie belly button bulging out atop her large belly under the too-small shirt. A few long, red scratches line the left side of Kathy's face, and there are small streaks of darkened blood on her arms, too. There are three liquor bottles on the desk, probably whiskey, two empty and one near-empty.

Jackie takes several seconds to gather all these details in front of her.

"The little shit jumped on my keyboard while I was trying to write!" Kathy suddenly squeals. "So I grabbed him and whipped him onto the floor, and then I whacked him hard with the computer." She laughs, casually and sardonically, as if somebody has just told her a dirty joke. "Then Robert Smith attacked me, and I smacked him around a bit too. Now he's hiding from me. Hiding for almost two days now. He's gonna have to come out sometime, though, if he ever wants to eat again." She laughs again, longer. "Good thing I've still got web access on my phone.

"Poor little Garfy!" Kathy says to the dead cat. "*Why* did you make me do that?"

Jackie turns the light back off. And she pukes on the floor.

"Watch it! I have so much to clean up already," Kathy says.

Minutes have passed. The smell of Jackie's fresh vomit fights to overtake that of the kitty corpse, but the latter has too much of a head start. Jackie and Kathy have barely moved. They have been staring at each other in the dim light, now closer to darkness, as the late afternoon is giving way to the early November evening.

Kathy ends the barren silence.

"So why the fuck are you here, anyway?" she snaps.

Jackie has forgotten why. She pauses to collect herself.

"I want to find out the truth," she croaks.

"Truth?"

"You've lied to me. And to a lot of people."

"About what?"

"Everything." Jackie takes a slow breath. Her heart pounds as if it wants to escape. She wonders if Kathy has another computer tower hidden in the room ready to whip at Jackie's head. But she swallows these fears as she reaches into her purse and taps something inside, then keeps the purse open. "You lied to me about Paul Shoreditch, about your relationship with him, about your birthday party, about that fucked-up BBB post. You wrote that and it was nothing but lies, too."

She expects Kathy to leap into denial. *I didn't do nuttin', copper.* But Kathy giggles. Her drunk giggling is more frightening than anything else about the scene.

"Wasn't it *beautiful*?" Kathy says in a near-whisper.

"What?"

"That blog post. Wasn't it beautiful the way people just *believed* it? So many people! I didn't have to do anything. They just took it as truth! They didn't question or challenge it, they didn't try to find out any more, they didn't ask anybody else. They just believed it!" Kathy's voice raises a touch, and Jackie thinks she hears two hands clasp together in restrained excitement. "It was a real work of art, wasn't it? It really was! The things you can do in this digital world. The power it gives you. You can make your own reality. You can even be another *person*!"

"Like you did? The way you posed as Avenger of the Weak? And fuck knows who else?"

Kathy does not answer. She just giggles again. "The things you can do!"

"Just tell me the truth about *something*, Kathy."

Kathy giggles again, and Jackie fears the laughter will climb into a crescendo until it turns into the deranged cackle of the Wicked Witch of the West, or the standard madman laugh out of old cartoons. This whole setup feels like a cheesy movie climax: Jackie is the hero who has just tracked down the villain to his secret lair and is about to find out all of his most deranged plans in a final cackling monologue. But Kathy keeps giggling at the same level, like a brace-toothed little girl chortling at a swear word.

"Truth? Who the fuck cares about *truth*?" Kathy shrieks. "If you can ruin somebody, some shitface who deserves to be ruined, the truth is an obstacle! Fuck the truth!"

"Did Paul Shoreditch deserve to be ruined? Did he *do* anything to deserve it?"

"Did he do anything *not* to?"

"Yes. Once." Jackie feels a crack in her voice but tries to control it. "He did *one* good thing. That I know of. At least one good thing in his whole life. And how did you reward him for that? By spreading lies. Hundreds of people, who knew absolutely nothing about the guy, believed your lies. Maybe far more."

Kathy does not respond. She wavers in the dark.

This isn't just any movie climax. It's Apocalypse Now. *I'm Willard, at the end of the mission, and she's Kurtz-psychotic, drunk with power, hiding in the shadows of his bedroom and waiting for one of us to destroy the other while the body of his latest victim rots. The horror.*

"I don't get it, Kathy. I don't know what the hell life has done to you to make you like this. I don't *want* to judge you. But there has to be a reason. What did he *do*? What could Paul have possibly done to make you go to all this trouble?"

She hears Kathy breathing deeply, and although they cannot see each other's faces in the dim light, Jackie imagines Kathy glaring back at her with an expression that reads, *How can you be so stupid? What else could it be?*

"What did he do?" Kathy says. Then louder, "What did he *do*?"

And in a scream that seems to split the whole building apart, that seems to tear the whole sky into pieces with violence and fury, she erupts with four simple words:

"HE! RUINED! MY! PARTY!!!!!!"

The ensuing silence echoes through the apartment more than the screaming does. Jackie hears Kathy's breath heaving with righteous anger.

"What party?" Jackie asks, her low, shaky voice sounding to her like a pipsqueak after the blast. "The... *birthday* party? Here?"

No reply. Just breathing.

"But how?"

"That *fucking singing*!" Kathy screams, and she punches one of the empty bottles on the desk. The bottle flies into the wall and shatters into pieces, which land on the desk and the floor underneath. A second later comes a thump on the ceiling, presumably from a neighbour.

"He drank, like, a full bottle of Chardonnay," she goes on. "Some creep manager at work got him hooked on white wine, so he gobbles that up, *way* more than he can handle, and then that retard Fiona... she starts *talking* to the little fucker, trying to make conversation with him. Why? Why the shit would anybody wanna talk to him? Who knows. He doesn't say much, and she asks him what he does, and he goes, 'I like to sing. I'm a singer.' So she takes him literally like he's a fucking professional or something, and asks him to sing something. 'Sing "Moon River". That's my favourite song.' And you know what the little piece of shit goes and does?"

Jackie assumes the question is rhetorical, but Kathy does not continue, so she clears her throat and replies, "Uh... he sings it?"

"Did he ever!" Kathy smacks her fist down on her desk in fury and loathing so hard that Jackie is surprised the desk does not split in half. "The drunken creep steps up on the fucking table like it's a fucking karaoke stage, and he sings it *for the whole fucking room*!

"You should've seen the way my friends' faces just *dropped*. The way it killed the whole buzz of the party. They couldn't believe what they were hearing! Even the *cats* couldn't take it! No one could believe anything in the world could sound so horrible."

Jackie does not know how to respond, or if responding is a good idea.

"Thank God Fiona choked on that chicken nugget!" Kathy adds.

Jackie blinks. *What?*

"Sorry," she says. "Did I just hear you say, 'Thank God Fiona choked—'"

"Thank *somebody* for it. Something or somebody must have made her choke! Or it was her reaction to his voice. Who knows?"

"But why—"

"It *stopped* him! When she fell and smacked her head on the floor, he stopped the singing and jumped down to do the Heimlich thing on her. If it wasn't for that, he'd have gone on and on and on! We'd probably *still* be listening to him right now!"

Jackie looks at the floor, struggling to believe what she has just heard.

"That's it, then?" she says. "Seriously? You wrote that BBB thing, you told those lies, you made him hide away from everybody for years–because of *singing*?"

Kathy laughs again, that same childish giggle.

"That's *it*? That's *all*?"

More giggling. "Did you ever hear him sing?"

"No."

"Trust me. If you did, you might've done some sick shit too!"

"I seriously doubt that."

"Think about it. Are you so perfect? Haven't *you* ever been driven to do anything mean?"

Jackie winces. The nasty Spitter post to the beagle puppy castigates her like an accusing finger from a cross-examining defence lawyer.

"Yes," she answers. "Very recently."

"So you're human, then. Just like me."

"Yes. I'm human. But I still can't imagine that a bit of *singing*–"

Jackie cuts herself off. Kathy giggles again.

"*The song that never ends!*" Kathy warbles. "Remember?"

Jackie hangs her head as Kathy continues to laugh. *Change the subject, for fuck's sake. Get her to admit more.*

"That wasn't the last time you saw Paul Shoreditch, though, was it?" Jackie says. She cringes as she hears herself as a bad actor playing detective. "You saw him just before he died, didn't you?" She gulps. "You–you saw him *here*."

For the first time, Kathy seems taken aback. "How did you know that?"

"I talked to his mom. She said you kept sending nasty e-mails to him during the last several years of his life. And that's why he came *here*, isn't it? And killed himself–*here*."

Another long pause. Kathy breathes deeply, and Jackie trembles, wondering if the woman is about to turn violent. But when Kathy speaks, her voice is low, slow, even measured.

"He came," she says, "because he thought he'd been abusing me. Maybe because I'd been telling him that over and over in years of e-mails." A small laugh. "He came to *apologize*. Because he actually believed it. I'd brainwashed him or maybe broken his brain. So he comes, and I let him in, and he comes up to me, and I could see from his face that he'd been crying on the way. And he *kneels*. He fucking *kneels* before me like a knight in a fairy tale or something, and he says to me, still half-crying, 'I'm so sorry. I don't know how to treat women. I'm so sorry. I want to do better, Kathy. Please take me back.' I don't remember the exact words, but it was like that, over and over. 'Please let me be your boyfriend again. I want to learn to be better.' And he really meant it." Kathy's voice has steadily grown louder but stays evenly paced. "It was so *funny* how he meant it! So sick and so funny that I almost had to swallow my tongue not to laugh my ass off. Grovelling there in front of me, no dignity or shame, and saying stuff like, 'What can I do to make everything better? Please tell me what I can do.' You wanna know what I did then?"

Jackie does not answer. She feels nauseous again and not from the smells in the room.

"I kicked him in the temple!"

She still cannot see Kathy's face, but she knows, without any possible doubt, that her expression sports a proud and boastful grin, the same one she wore when she was showing off *Kat's Korner* on the computer monitor not long ago.

"I sure did! I booted him on the side of the face, and he cried out like a stupid little kid. And then he rolled over on the floor, and I stomped on his big belly and his balls and his tiny little dick, and he just kept crying! Yelping from the pain and crying for me to stop and to forgive him."

Why couldn't you get back up and deck her, Paul? Like you did to your mom? But forty-six years old is a long way from nineteen, Jackie thinks. And love–or the misguided perception of it–makes everybody do foolish things.

"And I looked at him in the eyes, and I said, 'Paul, I can never forgive what you did to me. I can never forgive what you've done to everybody in your life. You're shit, Paul! You are a disease! You should be wiped off the earth like snot from a baby's dripping nose.' And I could tell from the way he looked back at me that he believed me, that he knew it was true. And I kicked him one last time, and I said, 'The only thing you can do right now to make everything better is to crawl to that door there, go onto the balcony and throw yourself off it!'"

The giggle returns–that childish, sadistic giggle, the kind that adolescent boys emit when they torture bugs and mice for kicks–so intense that Kathy can barely get out her punchline.

"Who'd have thought..." she says, interrupting herself with more laughter, "who'd have thought... that the little shithead... would actually go and *do* it?"

It is dark in Kathy's apartment. Jackie does not know if an hour has gone by or a minute since Kathy spoke. She sits on the floor and leans against the wall near the open bedroom door, as far as she can be from the dead cat and her own puke. Kathy has not moved from the chair.

Kathy breaks the long silence again. "I went out onto the balcony right after he fell. Didn't stay long–I was worried about witnesses, maybe somebody might think I pushed him off or something. He'd left something on the floor of the balcony. Know what?"

No answer from Jackie.

"His fucking cell phone! Technically, *mine*, the one *I* gave him six years ago. Can you believe it? Turned out he decided to make one last post on Spitter before he snuffed it. The nerve! I was scared he'd mentioned me or something. But it was all good! Just some self-pitying bullshit about how we all wanted this to happen." A quick snorty laugh. "Well, he wasn't wrong! I made sure to destroy the phone right away, just to be safe. I don't think he ever phoned anybody with it–certainly not me–but you never know what could be traced to me."

"What about the cops? Didn't they question you?"

Kathy giggles again. "Stupid cops! Of *course* they did. A couple of men. I think they questioned a lot of people in the building. Thank fuck they weren't the same cops who investigated the party six years ago–*that* would've been messy!"

"And... ?"

"I played dumb. They always think we women are dumb anyway, and I didn't disappoint them! They showed me a picture, and I was all, 'Yecccch! I think I'd remember a face like *that*!' They said a few people in the building said he looked a bit familiar–people who've been here a while, I guess–but I looked the cops in the eyes and shrugged. 'No, sir. Never seen him.'

"I only got nervous when they told me he landed below where my balcony is. I don't know shit about forensics or whatever, but I was worried they could figure out where he fell from. But then I remembered something." Kathy jerks a thumb to her left. "The apartment next door!"

"What about it?"

"Empty! I think there was a family or something there, but they moved out at the beginning of October, and nobody's rented it yet. I'm pretty sure it's unlocked and unoccupied. And it shares the same balcony with me! Just a cement wall dividing it. So I told the cops I'd heard a few strange noises coming from next door but didn't think anything of it at the time. 'Maybe he lives there? Or he was visiting somebody?' Didn't let on I knew it was empty. I'd let them find that out on their own, if they didn't already know.

"I wasn't sure they bought it. Even to *me* it sounded kinda flimsy, and I'm the best liar I know. But they took it down and left. And lo and behold!" Jackie hears a noise that sounds like Kathy rubbing her hands together. "Next thing I heard, they were calling it an apparent accident. As if they'd just given up on the case or something. I was in the clear!"

"They actually believed you?"

"People *always* believe me." Kathy laughs softly. "And

besides–what do I always say? The police are useless!"

Both are quiet again for several long, pensive minutes. Then Jackie speaks. "I don't understand," she says quietly. "I just don't understand. I don't understand it at all."

Where has she heard those words before? *Oh–right. The woodcutter from* Rashomon.

Even in the depths of hell, the useless movie references keep coming.

"What?" snaps Kathy. "What don't you understand?"

Jackie struggles to explain, but the words she wants do not come. "I... all this. All that you've done. All you continue to do. All out of pure anger and hate." She leans her head back against the wall. "How can you live like that?"

"Live like what?"

"Just... living on *hate.*"

Kathy laughs again, but differently. A quiet, whispering chuckle with a small yet perceptible dose of condescension.

"Living on hate is all people *ever* do, Jackie."

"I can't believe that."

"Well, you better start!" The whisper-chuckle again. "If you're ever going to get anywhere in this world, to make your mark among the powerful and steal your rightful place from them, you better realize that there is nothing more powerful in this life than hate. Hate is the currency we exchange. It's the energy we run on! It's what keeps the blood coursing through our veins and the ideas pumping out of our minds."

Jackie cannot wrap her head around what she is hearing. Is this the booze talking, or is it the crazy? *Maybe a bit of both.*

"Without hate, we'd have nothing to strive for, nothing to yearn for. Hate is the only thing that spurs us to get our fair share, to hold oppressors accountable, to make a mark and change things. That's the way it's always been, right through history. Look it up!"

"Look *what* up?"

"History!" Kathy rises out of her seat. "Every war that's ever been waged, every revolution that's ever been launched, every assassination, every social upheaval–it's always because somebody hated somebody or something!"

"I think your notion of history may be a little... oversimplified."

Kathy takes a few steps towards Jackie, who trembles as she nears.

"Look it up!" she spouts again. "It's always a struggle to topple kings and dictators. Only a strong, collective hate from everybody else can do it. That's why I love *this* so much!" On the word "this", she points with gleeful ferocity at the space under her desk where her computer should be, then sighs angrily and points at it on the floor. "*This,*" she repeats. "This is what connects us. This brings our hate together so fast, so easy. Think of it, Jackie! Think what we can do, how we can change the world! Imagine harnessing all this collective power! It's already doing so, bringing down the privileged, one by one!"

"*Privileged*?" Jackie is nervous, but that does not stop her from snapping back. "Come on. Come on! Was Paul Shoreditch your idea of *privileged*?"

"Of course."

"Do you even know *anything* about the guy? Did you know he was homeless once? Do you understand what a fucking *lunatic* he had for a mother? Do you know about the bullying he went through as a kid? How alone he was? Because if you want to know the truth, Paul Shoreditch's life kind of sucked."

Jackie means to go on, but her last statement catches her off guard. *Paul Shoreditch's life kind of sucked.* This may be the first time she has honestly admitted it to herself.

Kathy laughs again–less childishly and more contemptuously. "Boo fucking hoo," she says, taking another two steps in Jackie's direction. "Meanwhile, women are being raped. Black people are being shot by cops. Trans people are being murdered. North Koreans are being starved. Africans are dying from famine. Australia's burning into a crisp. So's California. The ice caps are melting, and animals are going extinct. And on and on. So much *real* suffering in this shithole of a world, Jackie! You know how naïve and out of touch you sound? Why should *anybody* care if Paul's life sucked? One more white, male, straight asshole gets your pity! Fuck that!"

"You're... not wrong, I guess," Jackie stammers, her hands shaking. Kathy is standing right over her, glaring at her, and even in the near-total lack of light, Jackie can barely look at those eyes of hers, which seem to blaze with absolute nuttery. Her breath reeks of booze. "Not totally. I know there's a lot of meaningless suffering out there. A lot of inequality. I know I've said those same kinds of things myself, or at least written them." She feels herself cowering back into the wall. "But... that's no excuse to cause *more* suffering."

Kathy's mouth cringes in fury and her hands curl into fists, and Jackie is terrified Kathy is going to beat her half to death.

But nothing happens. Kathy just sways a little.

Jackie swallows. "This... power you mentioned," she says, her voice cracking. "This collective power you want to harness. Did it ever occur to you, just once, to do it with *love*? Not with hate, but love? Kindness, at least?"

Who am I, that I should be kind? is what Jackie imagines her answering, right out of Miss Havisham in *Great Expectations*. But Kathy says nothing, and her expression goes blank. An instant drop from rage to dead nothingness.

And she sways more, and Jackie wonders if she is going to fall on top of her.

Kathy does fall, but the other way. She lands right on her rear end and sits on the floor.

More silence. Then Kathy tips over and lies down.

Jesus. Even more wasted than I thought.

"Get the fuck out of here," Kathy mumbles.

Jackie puts her hand on the wall to manoeuvre herself into a standing position. She picks up her open purse and steps towards the bedroom door, then pauses and turns back to Kathy's lying figure now curled on the floor in a foetal position.

"Are you going to clean up the mess?" Jackie asks.

"Hm?"

"The–the cat. Garfield. His body."

"I dunno," Kathy slurs.

Jackie leans her purse forward in Kathy's direction. "You're the one who killed him, aren't you? You smashed his head in with the computer?"

"Yeah," Kathy mutters. "I *told* you that part, stupid."

Then Kathy snores drunkenly, and Jackie turns and exits.

She waits until she gets to the elevator before she looks inside the purse.

Yes!

The Olympus is still running. It has not run out of data storage yet. They were not talking for nearly as long as it felt. Jackie was not sure if she had turned it on before Kathy had admitted to braining Garfield, so she asked her about it to make sure.

What a strange gift of fate that she forgot to take the recorder out of her purse. *And what delicious irony,* Jackie thinks as she remembers her last visit to that apartment. *I certainly remembered to turn it on this time.*

When she gets outside the building, she wonders what to do with the recording. She could take it to the police; maybe they would charge Kathy with abetting a suicide. But what Jackie *really* wants to do is post it online. She may have to do it anonymously or under a fake name; nobody will take anything Jackie Roberts says or does seriously anymore. Maybe start a new website. F**kKathyMcDougal.com? *Little Jack's Corner*? Or comment with a link to a recording on another well-read site. Or blackmail Kathy with it somehow...

But what if it does not work? What if it backfires? If Kathy's friends and readers are anywhere near as rabid as she is, they may love the nutbar things she says in the recording, and all Jackie will have done is to widen the reach of this toxic culture.

Then again, Kathy *did* confess to murdering one of her cats, and the Internet sure loves cats. There is no way she could come out completely unscathed.

As always, though, Jackie cannot escape her nagging doubts.

Maybe I'm just as bad? I'm just as bad as the rest of them when they get into their mobs and try to destroy someone. Maybe I'm just doing the same thing. It feels like the simplest, basest, lowest-common-denominator vengeance. Jackie knows she watches way too many movies when she considers engaging in this kind of hack-written revenge, convinced that she is doing the right thing.

Is this justice? Poetic justice, maybe. But is it fair? I really don't know.

But I'm still going to do it.

The sky is dark–a pleasing, welcoming dark. She walks quickly to the bus stop, almost marching, with a sense of determination and purpose that she has not felt for a long time.

INFINITY

She hears it once again: "The Song that Never Ends".

This time, it comes from a boy on the nearby playground, which is busy with kids on the wooden climber as parents sit and watch them, some half-checking their phones. It is an unusually warm and bright day for Ottawa in early March; everybody is wearing light spring jackets rather than winter coats. She hears the song, hears the boy laughing, and then another kid–probably the boy's friend–takes up the next verse and continues it. She hears it, leans back on the bench, takes a long inhale through her nostrils and closes her eyes. But the song does not go away.

She opens her eyes and gazes across Andrew Haydon Park. *Of course, it never ends. The world keeps turning, the sun keeps rising and falling, the seasons keep changing, and human beings just keep on fucking each other over for infinity. As long as we have a human race...*

Jackie has been coming to this park by herself every other day for a few weeks, strolling down the path, sitting on a bench and staring, depressed, wondering what her purpose is or if she has one.

Today is different; she sits closer to the playground at a specific spot waiting to meet some guy named Kenny Singh, who responded to her post on the classifieds website Kajagoogoo. Her parents' DVD player is on the brink of death, and they have never gotten the hang of streaming. So she set out to find a new one in better condition. Kenny replied, offering a small, grey Zenith unit for free. He said the player was nearly twenty years old.

Still works perfectly, though, he wrote. ***If you watch a lot of movies, it should serve you well.***

Until recently, she has been a hermit, and not just a physical one. She has avoided leaving her folks' house since she moved back in. And she has rarely been on the Internet in more than three months–only when necessary–in part because of all the threats and abuse from Kathy McDougal's readers, but also because she is sick of the whole thing.

Her self-imposed isolation may not stop anytime soon for reasons that she cannot control. The news is full of the growing pandemic. Lockdown seems to be on everybody's lips these days. Public events are being cancelled, people are working from home when they can, and she has seen the odd passerby wearing a cheap, homemade mask. For all she knows, they might close down this park. Are things about to change for good? Will we be better people when this is over, or worse, or exactly the same? Or food for worms? Will she have to go back online all the time to connect to the outside? She hopes not.

Being locked down will be hard for many people to adjust to–the extroverted, the social butterflies. For Jackie? A cinch. Few, if any, adjustments required. Her last few months have consisted of mooching off her parents while reading books or watching movies, sometimes her own DVDs, sometimes her parents' old VHS tapes from the 1980s and '90s. She has not bothered about getting a new job since Sam fired her back in T.O. Her mother, patient yet concerned, has questioned Jackie, asking if she is all right, if she has any plans to find a job or another apartment, and Jackie has shrugged it off every time. "I'm fine, mom. I don't want to talk about it."

She does not want to talk to anybody again.

Except maybe Paul Shoreditch.

Time-travel movies are not Jackie's favourite genre, but right now, sitting in the park and listening to the kids screaming among the playground equipment, she wishes she were in one of those films. Forget historical events or a glimpse of the future world, she would go back to Mississauga in 1978, or 1985, and find the boy and take him away from the madness that warped and perverted his life. If she could not be a mother, maybe she could be a friend. Or a teacher, or anyone who could make something out of his life, make it worth living in some way.

If nothing else, she would kick Lydia Shoreditch right in the snatch.

Then she would take another trip to beat the shit out of Russ Fullerton and Bobby Skatz while finding a moment to smack Beef McMahon in the face and call him a coward… and then leap ahead to break Morty Bozzer's heart, and then find some other way to fuck up Kathy McDougal…

No. That is not the way, she realizes. Fun in a movie, fun in fantasy, and it seems fun when you are anonymous in a digital network, but wrong when you deal with real people.

If only there had been somebody back then. One person to truly understand him. Just one. Maybe he could have become the great singer he always wanted to be? At least a good one. Or maybe not a singer, but something. One person to give him a purpose. To give him love. Not tough love, not pity, not grudging tolerance, but real, honest love. The way you can change a life just with one word, one gesture, for good or for bad. Kathy McDougal was right about one thing–we can have power. We already have a little, all of us, privileged or not. How do we use it right?

By chance, she remembers an old online video that Kathy e-mailed to her last fall, just before the bus incident. Only a month later did Jackie dig up the e-mail and click on the link. The video title was **"WORST SINGGER EVER!!!!!!! OMG YOU GOTTA SEE THIS =O"** and the summary described a guy killing a karaoke room's vibe with his horrible voice. Jackie did not need the confirmation in Kathy's e-mail to know who it was, although the frozen image on the video screen was too blurry to identify him. Jackie remembers having the arrow on the screen right over the start button, her index finger on the mouse ready to click away, just a fraction of a second from playing it. *How bad could he be?* she remembers thinking. *How bad could anyone be? Has it been hyped too much? Maybe he wasn't that bad. Or maybe they're right. Or maybe he was really amazing, and all these people are too stupid and lacking in taste to recognize how good he was?* The arrow wavered over the play button, seemingly for a handful of eternities. And Jackie decided she did not want to know. She closed the video tab and deleted the e-mail permanently.

Jackie is staring at the grass and thinking about the ignored video, wondering if she should have watched it, when a muffled voice in front of her exclaims, "Holy shit. It *is* you!"

She looks up. A short, stocky, thirty-something, brown-skinned man looks at her with an unwanted air of familiarity. He holds a small cardboard box in his hands, which are housed in disposable latex gloves. A white N95 mask covers his nose and mouth.

"When I saw your name on the site, I was sure it had to be, like, a total coincidence," says the stranger, who has messy, unkempt hair under a fading black Trilby hat. He also wears thick spectacles and a grey denim jacket over a black T-shirt showing a picture of a Dalek from *Doctor Who*. EXTERMINATE! the shirt reads under the image. "But no, it really is you."

"Kenny, I presume."

"Yeah."

Jackie blinks. "And who exactly do you think I am?"

"Jackie Roberts—the movie writer."

She nods, uncomfortable.

"What are you doing in Ottawa?"

"Running away," she mutters after a brief hesitation.

He squints. "Running away?"

"From life." A pause. "Have we met?"

"You could say that. I recognize you from your Internet photos."

She sighs, unsure whether she is about to be attacked verbally or physically, or both.

"I know what you're gonna say," she snaps, "and I'll stop you right there. You're another friend of Kathy McDougal or another *Kat's Korner* reader, and you're pissed that I exposed your heroine as a lying, cat-killing sociopath. Or you saw that stupid bus video, and you're about to lecture me on the evils of yelling at a kid's mom. Or maybe you've read my movie essays and you're about to yell at me about how stupid and wrong and pretentious my opinions are. Or you've found some other lovely reason to tell me I'm an asshole. Well, no need. I've heard it all, buddy. I've heard it from a thousand people who are better and smarter than you, so don't waste your fucking breath. Leave me alone and let me wallow in my self-pity. Just do me that one small favour. All right?"

The man holds up one hand in a conciliatory gesture long before Jackie finishes.

"Whoa," he says. "Slow down. I don't even know about half that stuff."

"Well then, what?"

He puts the box on the ground then pulls the mask down to his chin, revealing a thin goatee around full lips. "It's just that we know each other from Spitter."

"I don't remember following any Kenny Singh."

His mouth twists into a cynical half-grin.

"I think you know me from my handle," he says.

"Which is...?"

"Nagging Conscience 42."

She gasps.

Her jaw falls.

"The beagle?"

"I'd offer to shake hands," he says, "but under the circumstances..."

Jackie does not offer to shake hands either.

Instead, she leaps from the bench and throws her arms around him, and, before she can stop herself, buries her head in his shoulder and cries.

Kenny stiffens. "What are you doing?" he snaps.

"Oh my God!" she wails into his jacket, which is wet from her tears. "Oh my God oh my God oh my God. I... if you only knew what a fucking relief this is!"

"What the hell? Don't you know there's a virus going around?"

She lets go of him. Then she takes a few moments to catch her breath as he stares at her with a look of bottomless confusion. A few passersby stare at them.

"I'm sorry," she says. "I'm so sorry. I forgot about the Corona thing." She pauses to control her breathing again. "And I didn't mean to hug you without your consent! Believe me, I never do that. But this means so much to me. Honest. I thought you were dead."

"What!?"

"Seriously! I was so scared that you... killed yourself. And that it was my fault. It was literally keeping me awake for nights and nights." She almost starts crying again but holds it back. "Jesus. It's such a fucking relief to see that you're alive." Pause. "And that you're a real person, too–not just some puppy pic on a social media site."

He squints at her, his baffled look only deepening. "What in the hell gave you the impression that I—"

"Didn't you read my last Spitter reply to you? That awful, horrible thing I wrote? About your Hamlet quote?"

Kenny shrugs.

"And... all that other stuff you wrote, about depression and being kept from doing bad things to yourself? And then I posted that, and you never responded or posted again."

His expression is blank for a few seconds but widens into a state of realization.

"Oh," he says. "I remember. You mean, 'If you're so pompous that you quote Shakespeare in your Spitter posts—'"

"Something like that."

"No, I just got busy with work and stuff."

"I see." Jackie exhales a deep, relieved sigh.

"And I was bored with Spitter, anyway. Too many stupid

arguments." He sniffs. "Maybe I'll go back to it, though."

Jackie smiles. Suddenly, everything seems so much better.

"I saw the post, but it was such a cheap shot I didn't think it was worth a response." He sniffs. "You don't really think one nasty little comment like that would send me over the edge, do you?" he adds, holding back a laugh. "Especially from an obsessed trolling hobbyist like you?"

She chuckles. *Obsessed trolling hobbyist. I'll have to steal that. Put it in my resume.*

"I may suffer from depression and all, but I've heard worse."

"You never know, Kenny. I didn't know anything about you, and you never know how people will react–what your comments will make people do."

He gives a resigned shrug. "Fair enough."

"So I'm not a murderer then."

Kenny shakes his head. "Not even an accidental one."

"Thank fuck."

"But," he adds, "if it's any consolation..."

"Hm?"

"You *are* an asshole."

He grins and winks at Jackie, then slips his mask back on, nods a farewell, turns, and walks away down the path.

She watches him go, still sniffling from her outburst. Then she thinks.

"Well," she says aloud to herself. "Maybe I am."

The singing has died down from the playground, although the air rings with the children's laughs and cries as they play in the sunny spring day. Jackie picks up the box and looks in the other direction, thinking about starting back home. Paul Shoreditch pops into her mind again, and she thinks about him walking home from the softball game through the Mississauga park that night thirty-five years ago, singing to himself, doing the only thing that he ever loved doing in his life and not caring who heard him or how good or bad it sounded. *If only we all allowed each other that right. If only we could do what we wanted without hurting anybody, without anybody trying to make us feel bad about it. That's all we can ask of this stupid, ridiculous little world. Isn't it?*

Jackie starts walking home, and before she knows it, she is singing. She sings "Moon River" because... why not? Others can probably hear her, but it does not matter. Off-key and careless and unashamed, she sings about a pair of drifters heading away to see the world.

And she no longer feels alone. The dream makers, the heart breakers, the Huckleberry friends, they are with her now.

Acknowledgements

Thank you to my friends and fellow writers Heather Babcock, Timothy Carter, Mike Bryant, Skylar J. Wynter, Una Verdandi, Lizzie Violet, Neil Traynor and David Jaggard for their encouragement and/or feedback during the writing and revision of this novel-especially to Heather, who was the first person to read the early drafts and pressed me not only to keep on writing it, but to write it the way I wanted.

Additional thanks to Skylar for passing on this novel to Lisa Wolstenholme at Dragonfly Publishing. Lisa's enthusiasm for *Hate Story* and her creativity in promoting the book are definitely a lucky find, and it's a rare pleasure to work with her. (And a bonus shout-out to Tim for letting me steal the Blacks Photography joke.)

Sincere thanks also must go to Giles Blunt at the Humber School for Writers for eight months of valuable advice on this book, as well as Giles' group at the 2019 Humber Summer Workshop. The Moosemeat writers' group also contributed a few good suggestions. More thanks to Kathy Vatcher and to the Writers Collective of Canada for their classes and workshops, which helped to give me the confidence to start writing fiction seriously again.

Suicide Hotlines

Canada:

Canada Suicide Prevention Service – (833) 456-4566

United States:

National Suicide Prevention Hotline – (800) 273-8255

United Kingdom:

National Suicide Prevention Helpline U.K.– 0800 689 5652

Australia:

Lifeline – 13 11 14

Worldwide:

en.wikipedia.org/wiki/List_of_suicide_crisis_lines

About the Author

Jeff Cottrill is a fiction writer, poet, journalist and spoken-word artist based in Toronto, Canada. He has headlined in countless literary series throughout Canada, the U.K., the U.S., France and Ireland over the last twenty years. His performance style is influenced by slam conventions, but subverts them with wit, ironic humour and a satirical tone.

Throughout the COVID-19 pandemic, Jeff has continued his spoken-word career via Zoom, which has allowed him to attend literary events in Australia, New Zealand, India, Singapore, Lebanon and other new places. In 2021, he had poetry and flash fiction published in several international anthologies, including *Paper Teller Diorama* (New York), *Sinew: Ten Years of Poetry in the Brew* (Nashville), *Globalisation: The Sphere Keeps Spinning* (Sydney, Australia), and *Things Fall Apart: Mischievous Machines* (Leeds, U.K.).

Other short fiction and poems by him have appeared in *The South Shore Review* and *The Dreaming Machine*. Jeff was also featured in the poetry podcasts *Wordsmith* (Australia) and *Poets and Muses* (U.S.) last year. His poem "This Is Not Real Poetry" (published in the most recent Brownstone Poets anthology) is currently nominated for a Pushcart Prize.

Jeff's journalistic credits include *OHS Canada*, Toronto.com, *NOW*, *EYE WEEKLY*, *Exclaim!*, *Post City Magazines*, YellowPages.ca, *Divorce Magazine*, *JobPostings* and *Digital Journal*. In 2015, he was nominated for a Kenneth R. Wilson Memorial Award for his *OHS Canada* article "Off the Rails." He holds a Master of Arts degree in English from the University of Toronto, as well as a certificate in creative writing from Humber College. Jeff is the former Literary Editor of Burning Effigy Press.

Hate Story is Jeff's seventh or eighth attempt at a first novel.

Jeff likes writing, movies, travel and puppies.

Previous works by the same author

Chapbooks (Burning Effigy Press):

Cruelty and Kindness (2002)

Karaoke Dogs (2003)

Guilt Pasta (2007)

Grouch on a Couch (2011)

CDs (Moody Loner Records):

Cracktastic! (2005)

Clown with a Coat Hanger (2009)

This Album Is NIT FENNY! (2015)*

***copies still available! Contact Jeff at info@jeffcottrill.com**

Hate Story

Jeff Cottrill

Bonus Extra
Simpatica Books Inc.

Dear Mr. Orwell,

Thank you very much for your interest in Simpatica Books Inc. We have reviewed your submitted manuscript, *The Animal Farm*, and we have decided, regrettably, that it is not the right fit for our lineup. Although your novella is well written and has a few interesting ideas, we feel that it also has some serious issues and needs a lot of work.

Our main problem with your manuscript is the characters–specifically, that none of them is very likeable. There isn't a single one a reader can root for. We feel strongly that main characters in fiction must always be likeable and never have any flaws or do anything the reader might disagree with. Most of the pigs in *Animals' Farm* are so nasty and power-obsessed, and they do many cruel things to the other animals–they kill them, they lie to them and manipulate them, they betray them. How is a person supposed to relate to that kind of behaviour? Nobody's like that in real life. And even the animals who are victims of the abuse–you don't feel much for them either, Mr. Orwells. They don't fight back or try to win the day. They just take all the oppression passively. That's so depressing. A reader needs to cheer somebody on to be a hero, but your book doesn't deliver that.

Our other big issue with your manuscript is the story itself–that it's just so unbelievable and unrealistic. A group of farm animals drive the owner away and take over the farm? Don't you find that a little far-fetched, Mr. Welles? A little hard to imagine? Animals can get a little rambunctious now and then, but they could never take over a whole farm like that. And even if they did, it's hard to believe they would run the farm so poorly. There's so much corruption among the pigs that the whole thing turns into a virtual dictatorship. I don't think that could happen even with human beings, let alone with animals. You're not giving the reader much credit.

Our team at Simpatica Books Inc. is confused about your goals for *Animal Farms*. It's too violent and intense for a children's book, and it's too dark and pessimistic for a fantasy. We can't imagine what kind of demographic you're aiming for or why anyone would want to spend their free time with these characters. But I have some good news: our focus group of beta readers has come up with some constructive suggestions that may help you improve your book.

First–instead of all those mean pigs, why not have one really nice pig? And give the nice pig a friend or two. I think it's sad that you never gave the animals any good friendships, but I bet the reader would love to see one. Maybe the nice pig has a cute little spider friend who weaves nice messages about the pig in her web, and that sends the pig on some fun adventures. Don't you think that would make a good kids' book? I think so. And maybe the nice pig learns how to herd sheep, and he goes on to win a sheep-herding competition. That would send an uplifting message about believing in yourself. Another issue: our beta readers don't like the catchphrase you gave to Boxer the horse. "I Will Work Harder"–nobody's ever going to quote that. We came up with a better catchphrase: "A horse is a horse, of course, of course!" See? Now, that's catchy and fun. That's what a reader wants.

The point I'm trying to make: after the years pass and we're all rotting in the ground, the generations after us will remember only one thing about our literature: its marketability. Please keep working hard at your writing, and maybe someday, you'll get a lot better at it and write something worth publishing, Mr. Orson. Something with a fun plot and a likeable hero. Like that nice Nancy Drew! Now *she's* a plucky little one. Why don't you give us a character like that? That would be swell.

Sincerely,

Simpatica Books Inc.
Books for people who don't want a challenge!

CPSIA information can be obtained
at www.ICGtesting.com
Printed in the USA
BVHW071941220722
642813BV00002B/4